# Bertolt Brecht's Me-ti

*Also by Bertolt Brecht*

PLAYS

**Brecht Collected Plays: One**
(Baal, Drums in the Night, In the Jungle of Cities, The Life of Edward II of England, A Respectable Wedding, The Beggar or the Dead Dog, Driving Out a Devil, Lux in Tenebris, The Catch)

**Brecht Collected Plays: Two**
(Man Equals Man, The Elephant Calf, The Threepenny Opera, The Rise and Fall of the City of Mahagonny, The Seven Deadly Sins)

**Brecht Collected Plays: Three**
(Lindbergh's Flight, The Baden-Baden Lesson on Consent, He Said Yes/He Said No, The Decision, The Mother, The Exception and the Rule, The Horatians and the Curiatians, St Joan of the Stockyards)

**Brecht Collected Plays: Four**
(Round Heads and Pointed Heads, Fear and Misery of the Third Reich, Señora Carrar's Rifles, Dansen, How Much Is Your Iron?, The Trial of Lucullus)

**Brecht Collected Plays: Five**
(Life of Galileo, Mother Courage and Her Children)

**Brecht Collected Plays: Six**
(The Good Person of Szechwan, The Resistible Rise of Arturo Ui, Mr Puntila and His Man Matti)

**Brecht Collected Plays: Seven**
(The Visions of Simone Machard, Schweyk in the Second World War, The Caucasian Chalk Circle, The Duchess of Malfi)

**Brecht Collected Plays: Eight**
(The Days of the Commune, The Antigone of Sophocles, Turandot or the Whitewashers' Congress)

**Berliner Ensemble Adaptations**
(The Tutor, Coriolanus, The Trial of Joan of Arc at Rouen, 1431, Trumpets and Drums, Don Juan)

PROSE

Brecht on Art and Politics
Brecht on Film and Radio
Brecht on Theatre
Brecht on Performance
Collected Short Stories of Bertolt Brecht
Bertolt Brecht Journals 1934–1955
The Business Affairs of Mr Julius Caesar

# Bertolt Brecht's Me-ti

## *Book of Interventions in the Flow of Things*

Bertolt Brecht

Edited and translated by Antony Tatlow

Series Editor: Tom Kuhn

Bloomsbury Methuen Drama
An imprint of Bloomsbury Publishing Plc
B L O O M S B U R Y
LONDON • OXFORD • NEW YORK • NEW DELHI • SYDNEY

**Bloomsbury Methuen Drama**
An imprint of Bloomsbury Publishing Plc

Imprint previously known as Methuen Drama

50 Bedford Square
London
WC1B 3DP
UK

1385 Broadway
New York
NY 10018
USA

**www.bloomsbury.com**

**BLOOMSBURY, METHUEN DRAMA and the Diana logo are trademarks of Bloomsbury Publishing Plc**

Original work entitled *Me-ti. Buch der Wendungen*
Suhrkamp Verlag, Frankfurt am Main 1988-2000



First published 2016

Bloomsbury Methuen Drama Series Editor for Bertolt Brecht: Tom Kuhn



**British Library Cataloguing-in-Publication Data**
A catalogue record for this book is available from the British Library.

ISBN: HB: 978-1-4725-7917-1
PB: 978-1-4725-7916-4
ePDF: 978-1-4725-7919-5
ePub: 978-1-4725-7918-8

**Library of Congress Cataloging-in-Publication Data**
A catalog record for this book is available from the Library of Congress.

Cover design: Louise Dugdale

Typeset by Fakenham Prepress Solutions, Fakenham, Norfolk NR21 8NN

# Contents

# Introduction

During his visit to Moscow in March 1935 Brecht wrote to his wife, Helene Weigel, that he had seen the 'really splendid' Chinese actor Mei Lanfang. In a postscript, he asked: 'Have you already picked up Me-Ti? Does it look good now?' His copy of this remarkable book, published in 1922 – the first full translation into any European language, by Alfred Forke, of an ancient Chinese text – was being rebound in Svendborg. Forke entitled it *Mê Ti – the philosophical works of the social moralist and his followers.*[1]

Even given Brecht's shrewd but sporadic responses to Chinese culture, this 638-page example of detailed forensic sinological scholarship, otherwise of interest only to specialists, was an unusual acquisition, and it had surprising consequences. The text is a unique combination of tersely formulated, often witty aphorisms on human behaviour, of advice offered in the course of conversations on how best to conduct human affairs, of systematic, critical descriptions of cultural values and related social dangers, and of obscure, sometimes incomprehensible arguments over logical problems formulated over two millennia ago.

Brecht found it a stimulating treasure trove. This is not to say that his own *Me-ti* is an interpretative engagement with the Chinese work. Brecht's is primarily occupied with the unfolding European crises, with the political theory and practice of Communism in the Soviet Union, as well as with personal affairs. But he could not have shaped his own text without this stimulus, and there are passages in the Chinese work, some of which he

1 *Mê Ti, des Sozialethikers und seiner Schüler philosophische Werke* zum ersten Mal vollständig übersetzt, mit ausführlicher Einleitung, erläuternden und textkritischen Erklärungen versehen von Professor Alfred Forke (Berlin: Kommissionsverlag der Vereinigung wissenschaftlicher Verleger, 1922) in the series *Mitteilungen des Seminars für orientalische Sprachen an der Friedrich-Wilhlems-Universität zu Berlin.*

Given the many systems of transliteration and different European orthographic conventions, the transcription of Chinese names, which may themselves vary, can prove confusing. In order to distinguish between Brecht's *Me-ti*, as text and fictional person or persona, and Forke's translation of the Chinese text, I refer to the latter and its 'author' as Mo Di, which is another version of the author's name. In his text, Forke also uses the common honorific for Chinese philosophical teachers, Mê-*tse*, meaning Master Mê (墨子, in the pinyin transcription, Mozi), which explains why Brecht refers to 'Master Me-ti' and to 'Master Ka-meh' for Karl Marx. Quotations are my own translations. The *Letters* are quoted, where possible, from the English edition, London: Methuen, 1990 (here, with slight emendations, pp. 201–2). Other Brecht quotations are either from the Methuen/Bloomsbury edition or else, if not available, my own translations from the thirty-volume *Berliner und Frankfurter Ausgabe* (BFA).

noted but did not directly use, that seem to echo his own thoughts. To cite one example: 'Generosity does not exclude the self.' Elisabeth Hauptmann, his close collaborator over many years, told me he was reading this Chinese 'philosophical' work from 1929.

*****

Hitler came to power on 30 January 1933. Two weeks later the police started proceedings for high treason against those involved in a production of Brecht's 'learning play', *The Measures Taken*. After another two weeks, the Reichstag burnt down. That night Brecht slept at his publisher Peter Suhrkamp's house, and the next morning fled Germany for Prague and Vienna. In May, his books were burnt in Berlin, with about half a million kilograms of other 'un-German' works. He came to Paris in early June, for the première of *The Seven Deadly Sins*, his last collaboration with Kurt Weill, and on the morning of a performance on 20 June of *The Little Mahagonny* by Lotte Lenya he left to join Helene Weigel, who was already in Denmark with their children. In August they bought a house in Svendborg on the island of Fyn, about thirty kilometres from German territorial waters, from where he would later hear the firing practice of the German navy just over the horizon. Ruth Berlau, another key collaborator, first visited them at the end of the month.

Though Brecht was continuously engaged in projects and plans, and travelled to London, Paris, Moscow and New York, in rural Denmark the character and pace of life changed drastically after the intensity of Berlin, the dramatic flight from Germany, and the recent success of performances before discerning audiences in Paris. Contact with collaborators and publishers became much more difficult. Weigel lost all chance of performing fully for fifteen years, until *Antigone* in Switzerland, and Brecht, with very occasional exceptions, also lost his audiences. With his works largely untranslated, he lost most of his readers as well.

He continued to work on theatre scripts, but with no chance of performances in Germany and little real access to theatres elsewhere, let alone much influence over what they would do. The prospect of Danish and English productions appeared and receded, or, if actually realized, often disappointed, like *The Mother* in New York in 1935, where he and Eisler were ejected from rehearsals, and the uneven *Round Heads and Pointed Heads* in Copenhagen in 1936, taken off due to poor audiences.

Brecht, therefore, turned to other projects: *The Threepenny Novel*, finished in August 1934, favourably reviewed in Prague and Paris but criticized in

Moscow as insufficiently realistic; critical essays, such as *Five Difficulties in Writing the Truth* (December 1934), or the programmatic but often misunderstood *Verfremdung Effects in Chinese Acting* (1935), which appeared first as an English translation in 1936 with an unfortunate title – *The Fourth Wall of China; An essay on the effect of disillusion in the Chinese theatre*. He was also occupied with less structured or unfinished prose writings, many of which were anecdotal in character. The *Stories of Mr Keuner* were the only ones, though then not all of them, to appear during his lifetime; others, unpublished at the time, were the so-called *Tui Novel*, the *Conversations of Refugees* and *Me-ti*. The material and style of these texts sometimes overlapped, the same names occasionally appearing in different contexts.

The Keuner stories, first published in 1930 and 1932, continued sporadically up to 1956. Some could well have appeared in *Me-ti*, like *Apparatus and Party* (from 1954), given its characteristically ambiguous formulation of a social and political problem:

> When the Party, after Stalin's death, began to develop a new productivity, many cried out: 'We haven't got a Party, only an apparatus!' G. Keuner said: 'The apparatus is the bones of the administration and exercises power. For too long you have only seen a skeleton. Don't now pull everything to bits. When you have furnished it with muscles, nerves and organs, the skeleton will no longer be visible.' (BFA 18/42)

Sketches for the Tui 'novel', a satire on intellectuals started around 1931 and continued until 1943, never found a satisfactory form and remain archival material. It is situated in a poetic fiction, 'Chima, the Middle Country, found on no map', where the Taschi Lama, alias the living Buddha, or the Tibetan pope or, among other soubriquets, Pander Lobsam Rhei (a pun on the saying associated with Heraclitus, panta rhei, that everything flows, and on Brecht's central image of the flow of things), accompanied by 70,000 intellectuals, lives off the land while travelling from Tibet to Peking and simultaneously moving from northwest to southeast. Some of this elaborate Chimoiserie later fed into his *Turandot* play, or *The Whitewashers' Congress*, with the 1930s satire transferring to more local 1950s Stalinism.

In *Conversations of Refugees*, which did find a credible form, and is prefaced by an English quotation from P. G. Wodehouse ('He knew that he was still alive. More he could not say'), a worker and a physicist discuss topical events and problems over beers in the Helsinki station restaurant. Some of this varies topics that surface in *Me-ti*. There is even a concluding section proposing a new kind of writing in images 'following the Chinese example', intended to overcome the 'stupendous inexactness of certain words' (BFA 18/296), a problem Brecht knew also troubled Chinese thinkers.

Though not seriously pursued and, apart from one sign for a person, not remotely like Chinese ideograms, what all this shows is, first, that there are some common themes in these prose writings; secondly, that Brecht was casting about for a satisfactory form to convey his response to topical problems; thirdly, that some kind of 'Chinese' disguise occasionally came to mind; finally, that any such disguise was best employed when understated or, occasionally, stimulated by analogy, as happens in some of the *Me-ti* texts, most of which have nothing whatever to do with anything Chinese.

And yet there are connecting threads here, subtle in the original metaphorical sense of lying beneath the surface weave of a text, which form a suggestive counter-discourse throughout Brecht's writing. That Me-ti 'was against constructing too complete images of the world' (in *Against constructing world images*) is the philosophical or political equivalent of the aesthetic counter-discourse evident in his admiration for Chinese painting, whose empty spaces remind us of nature's irreducibility, and which does not, Brecht said, submit everything to a single perspective or point of view, thereby accomplishing what he called 'the thorough subjugation of the viewer', which led him to conclude of Chinese art, in this 1935 text, that its 'order requires no force' (BFA 22/133f.). A similar attitude guided his response, in 1955, to an ideologically strict reading of his early plays, whose author was told: 'You might omit a few value judgements and leave a few questions open. That always helps. Why put everything under one head, even if it's the best of headings?' (*Letters*, 539).

Responsive to Chinese ideas from the early 1920s, Brecht drew on images and formulations from the three main streams of thought that shaped Chinese culture: Daoism, Confucianism and Buddhism.[2] We do not need here to delve deeply into this or to explain how these schools of thought were interpreted according to historical needs or filtered through different Western readings; we merely need to point out two general aspects: the presence of a more pervasive sense of flow and transience than can be found in predominantly essentialist Western philosophy and religion, and in consequence what, especially from a Western perspective, may seem paradoxical, namely a different sense of the interconnectedness of all things, including social phenomena, evident in Mo Di, and which also distinguishes a Daoist from the Heraclitean concept of flow.

2 A short general account of Brecht's response to East Asia can be found in my article 'Brecht's East Asia: a conspectus', *Brecht in/and Asia, The Brecht Yearbook 36* (2011): 353–68, and earlier in greater detail in Antony Tatlow, *The Mask of Evil: Brecht's response to the Poetry, Theatre and Thought of China and Japan. A Comparative and Critical Evaluation* (Berne: Peter Lang, 1977).

In September 1920, Brecht's diary records: 'swimming + Lao-tse'. Daoist metaphors appear in *In the Jungle of Cities* (1923) and, memorably, in his 1938 *Legend of the origin of the book Tao Te Ching*, which was included in the *Svendborg Poems*. The Daoist critique of Confucian virtues is integrated into *Mother Courage* and his *Me-ti* texts, where praise of egoism, common to Daoism and Mo Di, is also developed.

In his poem 'The Buddha's parable of the burning house' Buddha refuses to answer theoretical questions about the nature of nirvana, when what matters most is to get out of the burning house, an attitude that both accords with Buddhist social philosophy and is reflected in popular Buddhist stories.

Brecht quoted Confucian texts and hung the splendid classic portrait of the great educator, who also went into exile at the age of thirty-five, in his study, as a warning that even the best teaching, a skill to which he aspired, can be frustrated and lose its focus. He commented wryly on passages in the Confucian Analects. He planned a play, *The Life of Confucius*, but completed only the first scene, The Jar of Ginger, in which the boy Confucius attempts to teach two young friends the virtues of self-restraint when eating ginger. This delightful scene ends when the jar finally reaches him and there is no more ginger left in it. Brecht made sketches for later scenes, and envisaged a Confucius sharply different from the traditional view. Though initially well-meaning, his advice was followed by the rulers because it suited them, although it was 'wrong'. Significantly, he would have illustrated the temptations facing the intellectual: accommodation with power. Brecht asked himself, in a note among the archive papers, if this view was historically justified (BBA 191/11).[3]

On one page of the *Me-ti* typescripts (BBA 136/49) is written only and in capital letters 'Rectification of names', and in brackets underneath also the phonetically correct German transcription of the Chinese 'Dschong Ming'. This term, a succinct expression of Confucian ethics, reminded of the need to adhere to the correct understanding of the behaviour required of your social and familial position: let a prince be a prince, a father be a father, a son be a son, and so on down the social scale, thereby sustaining the necessary authority structure. Here in Brecht's *Me-ti*, however, what is at stake is a realignment of the meaning of concepts that organize social life.

Confucius, aka Kung, appears in *Me-ti*, and Brecht had found in Forke's Mo Di an extensive and often funny critique of Confucian formalism and trickle-down morality, as in this passage:

> Through his pompous appearance and affected manner Confucius ruins the world, with zither music, singing, bells and pantomime he tries to

[3] An account of Brecht's views on Confucius and of this projected play can be found in Tatlow, *The Mask of Evil*, pp. 382–409.

> educate pupils. Countless rules how to go up and down the steps are supposed to express ceremony and regulations concerning the gliding walk to impress the crowd. The teaching of the Confucians cannot serve as a norm and their ponderings are of no advantage to the people. (Forke, 407)

In the vivid parables of Chinese philosophers Brecht found a welcome practical counterweight to the abstractions of Western, including Marxist, thinkers. Like many people, the empathetic left-eyed Shen Te turns into an unsympathetic right-handed Shui Ta, because the gods have failed her. The Confucian philosopher Mencius (Mengzi), whose writings in Richard Wilhelm's translation (*Mong Dsi. Die Lehrgespräche des Meisters Meng K'o.* Jena: Eugen Dietrichs Verlag, 1916) were in Brecht's library, argued the task of the ruler was to create the conditions that enabled people to be 'good'. That the individual and the common good should coincide is something Hegel also advocated, but he did not speak with the memorable clarity of the Chinese. The *Communist Manifesto* addressed this problem by asserting that in the form of association that would replace that of class in class society, the free development of each would be the condition for the free development of all. But that did not happen, and it is ironic how common memory reversed this sequence and assumed, together with actual policy, that 'all', defined by whoever determined it, should naturally take precedence over 'each'.

Based on their awareness of the *philosophical* acceptance of change throughout Chinese culture, Brecht and others entertained hopes that Mao Tsetung, who accused Stalin of a neglect of dialectics and of losing touch with the people, might indeed enable the 'wisdom of the masses' to prevail over the bureaucratic party, whose primary concern was preserving its own power and privileges. This same expectation resurfaced twenty years later among the French so-called 'Maoists' with their minimal knowledge of China. It was akin to the belief, expressed in then contemporary Brecht criticism, that Mao's 'Hundred Flowers Campaign' of 1956 constituted objective evidence for a liberation of these masses, hence his significance for Brecht, instead of the trick it really was to entice his opponents in the party to reveal their opposition to him.[4] This they did with crushing consequences for themselves. The 'masses' had nothing to do with it.

The so-called Great Proletarian Cultural Revolution, another inner-party struggle, over which Mao presided as an Emperor–Dictator, brought chaos and disaster to the whole country. During this period only the eight model revolutionary operas propagated by the Gang of Four could be performed.

[4] Peter Bormans: 'Brecht und der Stalinismus', *Brecht Jahrbuch* (1974): 53–76.

They created an ideological fairyland, pitting idealized extremes, monsters and gods, against each other, as reality outside the theatre descended into increasing paranoia and misery.

The artists in China who had been associated with Brecht's work spent years in prison. The only happy outcome was that Ding Yangzhong used the paper on which he was supposed to write his confessions to translate *Life of Galileo*. When produced in 1979, the first Western play after the downfall of the Gang of Four, it ran continuously for ten weeks in Beijing in a theatre seating 2,000, the longest performance of any Western play in China. When the churchmen waved their little black book, everybody understood the allusion. The emotional response to Brecht's play was so intense because it enabled the audience to deal with their own repressions.

In the context of such continuing struggles and expectations, we might juxtapose the famous body/state analogy in *Coriolanus*, advanced by Menenius as the commonsense expression of a *conservative* organicism, with the *radical* organicism of this Daoist counterpart in Chuang Tzu (Zhuangzi). The latter was probably only ever realized as a critique of real political control and as the expression of a powerful desire for what might, one day, come to pass:

> The hundred parts of the human body … are all complete in their places. Which should one prefer? Do you like them all equally? Or do you like some more than others? Are they all servants? Are these servants unable to control each other, but need another as ruler? Or do they become rulers and servants in turn? Is there any true ruler other than themselves?[5]

## Mo Di

Many passages in Mo Di criticize contemporary social values and practices, for example:

> Master Mê-tse said: if someone wants to employ a noble person of our day to slaughter pigs and he does not know how to do this, he will refuse. But if someone confers on him the post of minister of state, he accepts, even if he is not able for it. Is that not nonsensical? (Forke, 555)

> If the superiors are only engaged to govern the state and to function as leaders of the people, they may well say: 'If somebody deserves

[5] This translation is by Joseph Needham, *Science and Civilization in China*, vol. 2 (Cambridge: Cambridge University Press, 1956), p. 52.

> punishment, then we will punish them.' But if superiors and inferiors are not in agreement, those punished by the superiors will be praised by the common people. The common people live close together; whoever wins their admiration will not be hindered in his behaviour in spite of any punishment by his superiors. (Forke, 227)

Mo Di, whose traditional dates Forke assumes as 480–400 BCE, making him an exact contemporary of Socrates (469–399), also offers systematic argument untypical of Chinese philosophy. Brecht sought, above all, to employ a way of speaking about contemporary problems, rather than developing any specific content, though there are parallels here too, as with his observation about generosity and the self, cited above, which resonates in *Me-ti* with much the same implications as in the Chinese text. Another passage in Mo Di shows why this is so:

> Love of people does not exclude the self, for it is among those, who are loved, and since this is the case, love also extends to your own person. What is normally called egoism is love of people. (Forke, 507)

There are, of course, less useful views in Mo Di, such as a condemnation of music as an unnecessary extravagance, and the general preference, in spite of concern for the common people, for a form of social organization that Forke described as social aristocratism.

In China, Mo Di has been associated with both left and right politics. His advocacy of universal love was seen as analogous to Christian thinking, and Chinese Christians naturally took pleasure in the fact that he lived long before Christ. It was claimed in the 1940s that the nationalist New Life Movement in the 1930s, an anti-Communist YMCA-inspired attempt at moral rearmament associated with Chiang Kai Shek's Guomintang, was 'virtually a total adaptation of the philosophy of life preached by Mo Di' (A. Tseu: *The Moral Philosophy of Mo Tse*. Taipei: China Printing, 1965, p. 399). Another view, expressed by Guo Morou, held that he preserved social hierarchy and also asked people to love one another, thus requiring the majority to love the minority. His ideas were also said to represent the rising class of freemen opposed to the clan aristocracy.[6]

Forke divided the work into four sections: Systematics, Dialectics, Conversations and Techniques of Warfare. The systematic section, developed in sequences of three parallel chapters, discusses specific topics, such as Preferring the Able, Instituting Similarity (of thought), Unifying Love, Condemnation of Fatalism, Condemnation of Offensive Warfare. Brecht

[6] For further discussion of Mo Di's work, see Tatlow, *The Mask of Evil*, pp. 410–39.

did not attempt to develop a systematic exposition of topics in *Me-ti*, as in these chapters, though one German edition sought to derive a comparably systematic structure for the whole of *Me-ti*.

Brecht was more attracted to the *Dialectics* and *Conversations* sections. In *Dialectics*, logical and ethical questions are approached in the form of aphorisms, while *Conversations*, judged the most authentic section by Forke, presents often lively, short conversational narratives with sometimes paradoxical refutations of topical views and common practices. The term 'dialectics' obviously interested Brecht, who copied in his *Me-ti* papers both the correct phonetic transcription of the Chinese character ming, and even the ideogram itself, 名 (BBA 133/01), which is usually taken to refer to the 'school of logic'. Forke uses it as a heading for passages that state logical problems and explanations by later Moists, some of which Brecht marked in his copy and which certainly gave food for thought, since analogous ideas are formulated in his own *Me-ti*.

Forke interpreted 'dialectics' in Mo Di as skill in argument rather than as insight into a systematic structure of developing relations. Though these dialectics are not Hegelian, let alone Marxist, there are, nevertheless, unexpected compatibilities, and Brecht noted some passages that do link the perception of opposites and draw surprising conclusions from these observations.

Mo Di argued, among other things, against the nepotism of feudal families and social inequalities, which then lead to war, which he also condemned. He held that a belief in fatalism benefitted superiors but damaged their inferiors and observed that, while their superiors profit from it, in warfare two peasant armies attack one other, thereby neglecting to work the land. He believed that the people should be unified by 'love', and that social antagonisms should be prevented, if necessary by imposing unification. Brecht's differentiation, also in his poetry, between two social groups, 'die Oberen' and 'die Unteren' – meaning, literally, the upper and the lower ones – probably comes from Forke's translation, which uses these words to make this basic distinction.

In Mo Di, there are also passages like the following intriguing list of differently conceived opposites:

> white and black, the middle and the sides, talking and acting, studying and reality, justice and injustice, difficult and comfortable … lasting and disappearing

but this particular text begins with the following striking comparison:

> Equal and unequal are interconnected: if you eat in a rich house, you can recognize having and not having. (Forke, 460)

Whatever the original writers, or their translator, may have thought of these enumerations, they certainly seem like a shorthand for a dialectical philosophy and to imply a programme for acting, rather than merely thinking, which, if not definitively read out of them, can certainly be read into them.

## *Me-ti*

Brecht wrote the *Me-ti* texts from 1934 to 1955, mostly between 1934 and 1937. Occasionalist in character, they deal with recurring topics, though these are not systematically structured. Indeed, one of the 'subtle' themes that runs through the texts is the inherent danger of believing in systems. When no longer challenged by experience, practice ceases to innovate. Then, as one text suggests, experience is replaced by pre-established 'judgements'. Such judgements are determined by ideological belief. Professional administrators construct bureaucracies of thought, whose primary interest lies in preserving their own position to the detriment of individual and innovative producers.

This fundamental attitude, while recognizing the need for flexibility, explains why Brecht was so frustrated by the behaviour of what he called the 'camarilla' of opponents in Moscow who, when later installed as the government of the German Democratic Republic, were determined to mitigate as far as possible his influence on public life and, above all, to deny it any effect on policy. What was criticized from outside, especially by conservative political voices in the Federal Republic, as his unquestioning support for, even subservience to the Communist 'system', appeared very threatening to its official proponents. Ruth Berlau describes how these texts came about:

> Brecht's *Me-ti* stories are a collection of philosophical, political and ethical thoughts about problems of our day. Whenever he came across such a question, he wrote a little story. He occupied himself with them for quite a long time. I think he wanted to try out a literary form for representing the dialectical method. His model was Lenin's essay *On Climbing High Mountains*, which he also quoted in *Me-ti*. The Chinese practice of allegorical description really suited him. Everything was clothed in a Chinese kind of wisdom. (Berlau, 78)

If we set aside the cliché of 'Chinese wisdom', which often connotes the wisdom of avoiding difficulties by ignoring infelicities, and think instead of the equally 'Chinese' love of paradox and wit that captivated Oscar Wilde and had its effect in *The Soul of Man under Socialism*, then Brecht's *Me-ti* aphorisms and stories do indeed owe something, apart from the relatively few examples of actual Chinese cultural material, to a fundamentally probing and, in its own way, dialectical view of the flow of things. This found a particular expression in China due, there too of course, to its frustration by the controlling forces it sought to oppose.

The Brecht Archive (BBA) holds around 550 unnumbered pages of *Me-ti* material in seven folders, which include copies or sketches for completed passages. There is no plan, or table of contents, or definitive section heading followed by appropriate texts, except for one folder (BBA 130/01–18), which contains a small number of texts under the heading 'condemnation of ethics'. And there is no authorized sequence for the 360 or so pieces that have been printed in the three separately published German editions, or in the volume of the collected works (BFA 18/45–194) that appeared in 1995.

The archive contains seven folders (BBA 129–134 and 136), with dedicated material, none of which is paginated. Another folder contains just over twenty unnumbered pages with copies and sketches found among papers in nine other separate folders. Folder 136/01–88 consists of a fair copy typescript made by his collaborator Margarete Steffin, entitled *Buch der Wendungen*, of a selection of texts from the other six folders. They are preceded by an introduction, which asserts that the book derives from an English translation of the Chinese by Charles Stephen, and by an incomplete list of invented 'Chimese' names and their real-life equivalents (Mi-en-leh for Lenin, Ni-en for Stalin, Ka-osch for Korsch, Kin-jeh for Brecht, Lai-tu for Berlau, and so forth), and followed by some seventeen pages of copies, handwritten sketches and other jottings.

While Steffin's typescript is conventionally capitalized, the texts in folders 129–134 are written in Brecht's characteristic lower-case typescript. Folder 129/01–50 begins with a page across which is only written '*Me-ti*' in Brecht's handwriting. Folders 129–134 also contain copies of texts, some of which have been differently corrected, but the variations are minor handwritten additions or erasures of a word. Brecht made copies in this manner, but did not get round to collating them with their different alterations into one 'final' corrected and hence 'correct' version.

Various headings, and possible allusions to titles, are written on or across some pages: *Buch der Wendungen* (a verbal pun, since 'Wendung' means 'turn' of events, and, in 'Redewendung,' 'turn of phrase' or 'figure of speech'), which led to the commonly used but unsatisfactory (because it is too imprecise and finicky) English title, 'Book of twists and turns'; *Me-ti*; *Büchlein mit Verhaltenslehren* (Booklet with behavioural teachings); *Buch der Eigenschaften* (Book of qualities/attributes); *Lehrbuch des Verhaltens* (Manual on behaviour); *Buch vom Fluß der Dinge* (Book on the flow of things) – but there is no evidence of a preferred title.

Allusions have been made to a connection with the celebrated Chinese *Book of Changes* (I Ching or, in pinyin, Yijing), one of the five classic books, whose standard German translation is *Buch der Wandlungen* (Book of transformations). The BFA notes to *Me-ti*, for example, state that Brecht 'used' Richard Wilhelm's translation (BFA 18/493) without, however, saying how or where. That truly extraordinary Chinese text works through all sixty-four hexagrams constructed by the possible combinations of three undivided and three divided lines, the undivided symbolizing the sky and the divided symbolizing earth. The commentary encompasses Heaven and Earth, interpreting natural forces in accordance with the Chinese Imaginary. Proposing correlations between these natural or metaphysical forces and human events, the cryptic and suggestive poetic texts constitute ancient Chinese culture's prophetic almanac of universal relations. There is, however, absolutely no affinity between *Me-ti* and the *Book of Changes* except in an entirely abstract sense, since both are concerned with observing and understanding change, though that change is very differently conceived.

Nor is there any visual connection between Chinese ideograms and the few 'image signs', which the same editorial BFA notes to *Me-ti* presume to derive from those sixty-four hexagrams. At one stage Brecht thought of these 'signs' as furnishing a possible, but never realized, *Me-ti* chapter, but he finally placed them in *Conversations of Refugees*.[7]

There is, however, a stronger verbal analogy between Brecht's use in *Me-ti* of the terms 'Great Method' for dialectics and 'Great Order' for socialism or Communism (to be replaced, too late, by 'Great Production') and the title of one of Confucianism's revered four books, the instructional 'Great Learning' (Daxue), which had earlier suggested the Great Pedagogy of the didactic plays, as well as with the expression for an old social ideal, 'Great Togetherness' or 'Great Harmony' (Datong), which was subsequently transferred to the idea of Communism.

Not only was *Me-ti* never 'completed', but the individual texts were not definitively 'signed off' for positioning, and the manuscript collection is unstructured.

[7] They are included and explained in his diaries on 1 February 1942: see Bertolt Brecht, *Journals 19341955* (London: Methuen, 1993), p. 196.

## Editions

The first publication of *Me-ti* was prepared by Uwe Johnson and printed in *Prosa V* of the 1965 Suhrkamp Brecht edition. Johnson chose as title:

Me-ti
Buch der Wendungen
Fragment

Since no preference was ever recorded between the title 'Buch der Wendungen', which prefaced Steffin's typescript in Folder 136, and Brecht's handwritten 'Me-ti', prefacing Folder 129, Johnson used both.

His edition begins with the sequence of texts in Steffin's typescript, followed by texts from the other folders, often in the sequence in which they were found. If there was no discernible order among these papers, they have, Johnson argued, at least been presented exactly as they exist in the archive. He justified some rearrangements, now gathered together under 'Condemnation of ethics', as well as choosing among the variations whatever version had altered an earlier one. Furthermore, he included some texts that may seem more appropriately placed in other projects, such as the *Tui Novel*, and he excluded sketches and incomplete passages, as well as some poems, with four exceptions that had been printed under different titles among the poems of the same Suhrkamp edition. He also corrected obvious orthographic mistakes and inconsistencies in some names, for example when the similar but not identical transcriptions for Lenin and Stalin have been confused, with consequences for understanding the text in question.

Erdmut Wizisla, Director of the Brecht Archive since 1994, recounts how Johnson carried out his task while *persona non grata* in the German Democratic Republic and hence without access to the archive.[8] He worked from photocopies, though in 1964 the prohibition was lifted for a period of six days. Although initially suspicious, Wizisla concluded that, under the circumstances, Johnson did exemplary work in presenting Brecht's confusion of texts. Johnson was also responsible for persuading Weigel to permit the publication of the Berlau texts, which she initially wished to withhold.

The second publication of *Me-ti*, presented by Klaus Völker, appeared in volume 12 of the popular 20-volume 1967 paperback *Gesammelte Werke*. Völker argued that just as the title, *Buch der Wendungen*, derived from

[8] Erdmut Wizisla, '"Aus jenem Fach bin ich weggelaufen": Uwe Johnson im Bertolt-Brecht-Archiv – die Edition von *Me-ti, Buch der Wendungen*', in *'Wo ich her bin …' Uwe Johnson in der DDR*, ed. Roland Berbig and Erdmut Wizisla (Berlin: Kontext Verlag, 1993), pp. 301–19, 406–11.

the classic *Buch der Wandlungen*, Brecht's *Me-ti* was to be closely aligned with the teachings of Mo Di. Nonetheless, this version followed Johnson's sequence, arbitrary in as far as it partly reproduced what was sequentialized in the archive folders, with only two exceptions: some texts that belong to the Keuner stories or the *Tui Novel* complex were removed, and all the Lai-tu and other passages connected with Berlau were taken out of Johnson's sequence and placed at the end. Völker also put between brackets headings for texts that had none. Otherwise his version is identical. Presented as *Me-ti / Buch der Wendungen*, and thus as no longer fragmented, it acquired the appearance of an authenticated text.

The philological and critical plot then thickens, due to the 'contradiction' inscribed within the texts themselves. The Suhrkamp Brecht edition was being gradually reprinted in the German Democratic Republic by the Aufbau-Verlag as the volumes appeared in Frankfurt-am-Main. Johnson's version in *Prosa V*, however, triggered alarm bells in East Berlin. Aufbau, in any case opposed to Johnson editing this text, argued that he lacked the philological skills for such forensically delicate work and was not competent to assess it. He had been employed by Aufbau and had fled the German Democratic Republic. They did not like or trust him, and they were also worried by Brecht's text, which could be seen, in spite of his evident support for socialism, as amounting to an inconvenient, insufficiently 'coherent' argument about the state and development of real existing Marxism in the German Democratic Republic.

Not yet published there, this *Me-ti* text began, partly for that reason, to acquire a subversive reputation as knowledge of it percolated by word of mouth and copies of some passages began to emerge. Political objections to any publication increased within the Ministry of Culture and from higher up. To counter possible further consequences, it was decided that a completely rearranged version should be prepared. This was entrusted to Werner Mittenzwei, whose third and new version was published in 1975.[9] His principle was to do justice to what were perceived as Brecht's intentions with a more transparent organization of the whole text. He aimed to reveal its 'inner order' and hence to show the structure of its thought and the cultural context of its arguments. This would justify the radical arrangement.

The fourth version of *Me-ti*, prepared for volume 18 of the BFA, sought to present all the Me-ti material unamended, and thus to enable readers to achieve their 'own' understanding of these unstructured, then differently arranged texts. Johnson already came as close as possible to this in preparing his readable edition, though taking numerous decisions in respect

9 Bertolt Brecht, *Prosa IV: Me-ti Buch der Wendungen* (Berlin and Weimar: Aufbau-Verlag, 1975).

of sequencing individual passages, which were not always exactly in the order they appear within the folders. He had omitted what seemed extraneous passages, corrected obvious typographical errors, and created the declared fragmented effect, somewhere between individual coherence and intrinsic incoherence. Each passage speaks, of course, for itself, though many need glosses or more extensive commentary, especially when read many years later and under completely different circumstances. But the overall impression, which also changes perspective with time, is less certain.

In a separated section, called 'texts and versions', the BFA edition communicates much of the overlaps and cross-referencing of these documents, and in often extensive comments on individual texts it suggests links to other writings, including Brecht's, and to the historical circumstances. It does not print, in the tradition of a historical-critical edition, every passage and connected additions and detractions in the typescripts. What it does, instead, is to present the individual texts as closely as possible in the historical sequence of their actual composition. The problem with this decision to bring some kind of order to the material is that the actual sequence of composition, with the exception of some few passages that can be linked to documentable events, is not reliably known. In consequence, the texts have been printed in bundles of presumed temporal sequence, starting with 'around 1934', followed by 'between 1934 and 1940', with some more closely placed in 1936 to 1937, then from 'around 1941', and finally nine between 1942 and 1955, some appearing for the first time.

This procedure is unquestionably helpful, but within these relatively large and in part arbitrarily assumed sections the texts mostly appear in the alphabetical sequence of their titles, some of which consist of the first words of the passages that lack proper titles. The effect of this is, naturally, to create another and no less arbitrary assembly of unconnected individual texts, which leaves the reader with an even greater sense of discontinuity and fragmentation than do the first two editions. This is underscored by printing, unamended and uncommented, the typographical mistakes in the names as they appear in the typescript. The benefit, of course, is that those typescripts are accurately transcribed, so the reader, especially when aware of this by comparing them with the 'originals' in the archive, can begin to make a different sense of the whole and come to another view of its thematic coherence.

## Korsch versus Lenin

One purpose of Mittenzwei's edition, made plain in the Afterword, was to counteract the thesis advanced by Wolfdietrich Rasch in 1963 in his article on the unpublished correspondence between Brecht and the dissident Marxist Karl Korsch.[10] Rasch's proposition, elaborated by Klaus-Detlef Müller, Heinz Brüggemann and others, and widely accepted in West German criticism, was that a fundamental thrust in Brecht's *Me-ti* resulted from an argument conducted with, in the sense of together or in accordance with, Korsch, whom Brecht respected and admired and had asked for suggestions when writing the *Me-ti* texts.

Rasch had written a balanced account of the relationship between Korsch and Brecht, based on the then available information, quoting, for example, part of a letter from November 1941 (*Letters*, 342) in which Brecht speaks of their disagreement about developments in the Soviet Union. Here Brecht states that it was not only a worker-*state*, but also a *worker*-state, and asks Korsch what, in his opinion, were the historical reasons for the failure of the councils (soviets) under Stalin; whether this was due to the particular need to centralize the economy in order to increase production, though it was to lead to an unwelcome, but dialectically unavoidable, and presumably temporary, form for that state.

Mittenzwei had criticized what he called this 'Korsch legend' in 1969, arguing that Korsch showed Trotskyist tendencies and that Brecht's rejection of Korsch's views was 'very clearly formulated' in *Me-ti*, where his criticism 'could not be more plainly expressed', such that it was intellectually dishonest to assert otherwise. Mittenzwei's views were expanded in a further lengthy appraisal of *Me-ti* written in 1973 and embodied in this Afterword.

Maintaining that 'Brecht had occupied himself with the Chinese philosopher Me-ti throughout his life', and that his *Me-ti* was a difficult but certainly not a secondary literary product, Mittenzwei argued both that it stands at the centre of Brecht's attempt to bring about a new reception of art, and that his contact with the philosophy and art of the Far East decisively affected his development. In this account, Mo Di offered Brecht the example he needed both in teaching practical behaviour and by offering systematic logical thought. His *Me-ti*, however, was conceived as a work of art, not of theory or politics, a qualification and separation Mittenzwei needed to make in order to sanitize some theoretical and practical implications of the potentially inconvenient political criticisms articulated in this work of art. The 'dialectic' suggested by Forke's section heading is understood as presenting the 'laws of thought'.

Seen as continuing the theory and practice of the didactic plays, while

[10] 'Brechts marxistischer Lehrer. Zu einem ungedruckten Briefwechsel zwischen Brecht und Korsch', *Merkur* 88 (1963): 988–1003.

avoiding the problems of theatrical performance, Brecht's *Me-ti*, a further example of material aesthetics in action that saw the reader/viewer as a participant/producer, is intended to stimulate readers to compare the events and descriptions of behaviour in the texts with their own experiences. The purpose of rejuvenating 2,000 years of historical experience, Mittenzwei argues, is not to reinstate ancient ideas but to stimulate thought processes and the capacity of dialectical thinking in order to find new solutions for current problems by recognizing what is practical and realizable under always specific and changing situations, without insisting on infrangible principles in a dogmatic refusal of compromise.

This development, which is seen as based on Marxist–Leninist aesthetics and philosophy, was, therefore, a contribution to social theory. It was opposed as much to any social-democratic 'vulgarization' of revolutionary theory and materialist dialectics, as well as to the left-wing voluntarism and sectarianism Lenin had attacked as the 'Infantile Disorder of Communism', as it was to what is termed the 'subjective activism' represented by Karl Korsch, whose voluntarism, or decisionism, Mittenzwei argued, sought to bring about social change through conscious intervention, which can only mean through knowledge alone without objective transformation of real social practices.

Mittenzwei sees the central technique of Brecht's aesthetic *Verfremdung* or estrangement effect as a one-dimensional process whereby, in estranging what hitherto appeared familiar, though disguised by ideological belief, the real underlying objective and determining economic forces are made visible, thus stimulating the impulse to intervene and change them. *Verfremdung* strips away the illusions that disguise reality. It is an aesthetic or discursive technique, a sort of ideological stain remover that reveals the unrecognized underlying reality. The thought does not occur that this technique of estrangement might equally question the substance of an orthodox theory that had constructed, and then explains or substitutes for, that supposedly objective underlying reality.

The sequence of chapters in Mo Di, which Forke organized into different sections, allegedly justified Mittenzwei's arrangement of his edition into five chapters or sections entitled 'Book of the Great Method', 'Book of Experience', 'Book on Disorder', 'Book of Upheaval' and, finally, 'Book of the Great Order'. Another heading, 'Book of Qualities' ('Buch der Eigenschaften'), with which Brecht had prefaced a text, 'Calm', on one page (BBA 134/3) was intended, Mittenzwei suggests, as another such 'chapter' rather than as a title for the whole work, and he includes it within an appendix, consisting of five short 'thematically related or fragmentary' texts. The real reason for this particular organization lies, however, in the intended demonstration of its successful cumulative effect, as 'theory' is tested by experience and then realized in 'practice'.

The introductory *Book of the Great Method* formed 'the essential part, the real methodological guide to the work', and therefore includes not just discussion of dialectics but evidence for the practices that demonstrate it. The *Book of Experience* addresses ethical and aesthetic problems determined by competing interests within class struggle and shows Brecht to be a behavioural analyst. The *Book of Disorder* describes phenomena within Capitalism and Fascism. The *Book of Upheaval* offers views on revolution for various aspects of society. The *Book of the Great Order*, finally, discusses issues that arise when creating socialism.

Brecht's achievement, for Mittenzwei, was to have faced a fundamental question for Marxists: how could a subjective desire for revolution be inculcated in the mass of people, not just in individuals, when the objective conditions for its success are given? Transforming art into a 'material' practice was to bring this about. Mittenzwei aligns Brecht's embrace of dialectics with his interest in what Mittenzwei calls the physicists' rejection of 'extreme determinism', in political terms the equivalent of fatalism, which was a major criticism found in Mo Di. Any such 'extreme determinism' is replaced at the centre of this arrangement of Brecht's text by what Mittenzwei sees as its guiding doctrine, 'dialectical determinism', which offers the best description of Marxism in action and constitutes the crucial bond between Brecht and Lenin.[11]

## Brecht and Korsch

Brecht had known Korsch (1886–1961) since 1928, when he first attended his lectures on 'scientific socialism'. A group met regularly, also in Brecht's Berlin apartment, to discuss questions about dialectical materialism from

11 The term 'dialectical materialism', not used by either Marx or Engels, was promulgated in the Soviet Union as the official description of the theory of Marxism in the 1930s. The first chapter of the stirring *Communist Manifesto*, after declaring that the history of all societies is the history of class struggle, states that this constant opposition 'each time ended, either in a revolutionary reconstitution of society at large, or in the common ruin of the contending classes'. Substituting 'dialectical determinism' for 'dialectical materialism' was presumably intended to insist on the inevitable victory, not possible ruin, of the contending working-class, if the outcome of that struggle was seen to be teleologically inevitable. Whether 'dialectical materialism' denotes movement within matter or history, or entails the mutual shaping of matter and mind through whatever means, it entails observation of real things. 'Dialectical determinism', however, is inherently contradictory, if not vacuous, since it merely expresses an ideological belief that, while allowing for perhaps even mutual change, something is inevitably and unalterably the case and must, therefore, finally come about.

November 1931 until January 1933. Korsch had also studied in London from 1912–14, where he joined the Fabian Society. He was interested in syndicalism as a democratic movement vis-à-vis orthodox Marxism. Returning to Germany at the outbreak of war in 1914, he joined the army as a lieutenant but was reduced to the ranks for opposing attacks. He refused to carry a weapon, yet was awarded two iron crosses for saving others.[12]

There are parallels between Korsch's views and those of Lukács in *History and Class Consciousness*. Both were considered heretical due to their stress on the importance of developing individual consciousness in the working class as a precondition for a successful Marxist politics. Where Gramsci accepted the need for a Leninist party to overthrow the bourgeois state, Korsch looked to the 'subjective preconditions' and Marxism's failure to develop them. Lukács later accepted Communist Party criticism, while Korsch did not.

His *Marxism and Philosophy* appeared in 1923. He taught at the University of Jena, was a member of the Thuringian parliament from 1921 and its Minister of Justice in 1923. He became a member of the Reichstag from 1924–8. In 1926 he was expelled from the Communist Party due to his rejection of Leninism. In 1929 the by then Nazi-oriented Thuringian government dismissed him from his professorship at the University of Jena.

Korsch had 'form', and it is no wonder that Brecht respected him. He refused to accept the authority of the Russian party and the centralist control of the Communist Party of Germany (KPD), which argued that Capitalism had stabilized. Korsch maintained it had not and argued for revolutionary politics based on workers' councils, rejecting the united front policy. Brecht adopted this position when writing the didactic plays, which was of course potentially disastrous, in terms of counterfactual speculation, since keeping the Communist Party and the Social Democratic Party at loggerheads will not have hindered the National Socialists coming to power. At this particular time, and for this reason alone, Lukács may have been right to argue for a more conventional realist aesthetic, instead of the radical 'left' position taken by Korsch and Brecht.

Brecht not only called Korsch his 'teacher' but said in a letter, as late as 1945, that he would remain so all his life, 'so take it easy' (*Letters*, 387, this last phrase was written in English). No matter how much they may have disagreed on certain topics, there is no question but that Brecht felt greatly indebted to Korsch and to a degree depended on him for knowledge and stimulation about the history and development of Marxism.[13]

[12] I also draw here on the short biographical account in the introduction to his translation by Fred Halliday of *Marxism and Philosophy* (London: Verso, 2012, first published 1970).

[13] To employ that rough and ready guide to importance within Brecht's writing as

Though their relationship did not have the same degree of warmth that developed between Brecht and Walter Benjamin, it was not only characterized by the exchange of information on theoretical questions and their relation to social practices. Korsch also visited Brecht in Svendborg and they spent time together in London. Furthermore, an unascertainable amount of suggestions and even passages formulated by Korsch found their way in one form or another into Brecht's texts. At least, that is what Korsch also said. What brought and bound them together is perhaps best illustrated by the fact that both fled Berlin within hours of each other, Korsch immediately on the evening the Reichstag burnt down.

In another letter to Korsch in 1942, Brecht wrote that while they disagreed in their assessment of the Soviet Union, which Brecht still largely supported and Korsch did not, due to his rejection of Lenin's party, there were other uses to be made of Korsch's theories, adding: 'For a long time I've mentally discussed all controversial points with you before writing anything' (*Letters*, 352). In a letter dated December 1936/January 1937, he had written that he wanted to continue his little book 'in the Chinese style', which Korsch knew about and for which he had supplied a number of 'so useful' sentences. Brecht asked him to continue sending such material (*Letters*, 239). Worried about his permission to stay in Denmark, he said that plenty of friends told him he should choose between reactionary content or reactionary form, but both together was too much. A prominent Communist said: 'If that's Communism, I'm not a Communist.' Brecht added, 'Perhaps he's right.' The BFA edition surmises that they had discussed Brecht's project when he was in London from April to July 1936, and mentions that Korsch wrote on this letter from Brecht: 'Those are my stories; partly discussed together with B. and shaped by me' (BFA 18/489). We do not know which stories are meant. When asking Korsch for his opinion as to why the councils failed, Brecht adds: 'It's terribly important for us, don't you agree? Apart from you, I don't

evidenced in the index of names and texts in the BFA, there are just over three columns listing Lenin, and two columns each for Korsch and Marx. I can however find no evidence that Brecht made use, as has been suggested, of Korsch's pamphlet *Kernpunkte der materialistischen Geschichtsauffassung. Eine quellenmäßige Darstellung* (1922), when formulating his own texts. Brecht neither employs the selected quotations, nor does his own presentation of arguments in any way resemble Korsch's systematic exposition of what he considers the essential points in the development of Marxism's 'materialist' explanation of history. Perhaps Brecht's term 'Umwälzung' (translated as 'upheaval') for revolution may have been suggested by Korsch's use of it and it could be that he was taken by Korsch's description, at the start of the pamphlet, of Marxism as a disruptive and irreverent (a term he does not use) science upsetting the categories of what passed for the discrete organization of knowledge in contemporary bourgeois society. What is otherwise striking is the complete difference in tone and approach in *Me-ti* from any sober academic disquisition on the effect of Marxist thought in everyday life.

know of anyone capable of looking into that' (*Letters*, 343). In 1945, Brecht tells Korsch that his help on a project, the attempt to describe the nature of society in hexameters, in imitation of Lucretius's *De rerum natura*, would be 'absolutely indispensible' (BFA 29/348).

In 1948, in his last letter to Korsch, Brecht writes, in what also sounds like a description of his own *Me-ti*,

> I sometimes wish you kept a journal with many entries in the manner of Bacon on all subjects in which you were currently interested, in general unmethodical, I mean anti-systematic. Such scientific aphorisms could be employed one by one in this or that connection, for one purpose or another, they would always be to hand at any time; instead of reconstructing one of them you could build a new one etc. – This would be, so to speak, epic science! (BFA 29/449f., *Letters*, 445)

Insisting that Brecht disagreed with Korsch's view of Lenin and of the party he had shaped, Mittenzwei maintained, to the contrary, that Brecht's texts were fully in accordance with that 'dialectical determinism' that was still shaping political practice within the German Democratic Republic. This conceptual oxymoron, able to deal with any tricky explanatory situation by emphasizing either of its two parts, perfectly formulated the theoretical and practical contradiction, which had direct consequences for that state as for the whole Communist movement.[14]

That Brecht both respected and disagreed with Korsch is beyond question, as we can see in his *Me-ti*. What can, however, be disputed is the extent of this disagreement and, in addition, whether Brecht's own position was not significantly modified, given the experience of his last years, an effect that becomes evident in the later texts. It is, therefore, possible to argue that Brecht both disputed Korsch's critique of Leninism and that he later came to appreciate its force, without ever directly saying so because, as practised in the German Democratic Republic, it explained the increasingly apparent political and democratic deficit that continued to frustrate Brecht's conviction, expressly stated in *Me-ti*, that 'experience' should take precedence over 'judgements'.

When judgements, as ideology, ignore experience, power determines policy, and an administration then exercises control over individual production and the products of the imagination. What Marx had called the 'dictatorship of the proletariat' as an alternative to the actual but unacknowledged dictatorship of the bourgeoisie, when there was no universal suffrage, became – as many,

[14] The Christian church, according to Joyce, was built on a pun; it seems that in this view Communism depended on an oxymoron.

including Brecht, observed – a dictatorship over the proletariat, with the inhibiting and destructive consequences Korsch had clearly foreseen.

Brecht admired Lenin's flexibility, and deplored its loss under Stalin. He hoped, together with Korsch, that China might develop differently.[15] But it is impossible to ignore the incompatibility, no doubt temporally obscured under the specific conditions of complex and fast-changing circumstances, between the two parts of that oxymoron: dialectical determinism. Korsch deplored the Russian insistence on an entirely 'material', teleologically fixed developmental process as a form of 'metaphysics', which relegated consciousness to a secondary function, at most as insight into the necessity of the one inevitable historical path.

The clearest expression of the entailed, and troubling, so-called reflection theory to which Korsch objected can be found in this statement by Lenin:

> Materialism in general recognises objectively real being (matter) as independent of the consciousness, sensation, experience etc., of humanity. Historical materialism recognises social being as independent of the social consciousness of humanity. In both cases consciousness is only the reflection of being, at best an approximately true (adequate, perfectly exact) reflection of it. From this Marxist philosophy, which is cast from a single piece of steel, you cannot eliminate one basic premise, one essential part, without departing from objective truth, without falling a prey to bourgeois-reactionary falsehood.[16]

This formulation could be, and was, taken to mean that differences within individual consciousness, in any case relatively unimportant compared with consciousness of the mass, were in effect nugatory because the already determined objective course of history could not be deflected. Since somebody, nevertheless, had to take decisions, when choices were unavoidable, Stalin helpfully euphemized this whole process as 'revolution from above', at which point dialectical determinism, whatever it may have been thought to entail, became indistinguishable from absolutism, though now ruling by historical, rather than by divine, right.[17]

[15] In the introduction to his translation of Korsch's *Marxism and Philosophy*, Halliday remarks that Korsch's despair over what had happened to Marxism gave way to more optimistic feelings after 1953 as a result of possible developments in China.

[16] V. I. Lenin, 'Materialism and Empirio-criticism', in *Collected Works*, vol. 14 (Moscow: Progress Publishers, 1968), p. 326.

[17] Stalin expressed this view in 'Marxism and Linguistics', *The Essential Stalin. Major Theoretical Writings* 1905–52, ed. Bruce Franklin (London: Croom Helm, 1973), p. 426. In conversation with Benjamin, Brecht described Stalin's rule as 'monarchical'. Instead of the state withering away, it became all powerful as the pliant, because terrified, agent of its ruler. Had the state actually withered away, as some supposed it should, the inevitable

Korsch's response to such Marxist–Leninist theory is perhaps best gauged by the following passage from *Marxism and Philosophy*:

> Even today most Marxist theoreticians conceive of the efficacy of so-called intellectual phenomena in a purely negative, abstract and undialectical sense, when they should analyse this domain of social reality with the materialist and scientific method moulded by Marx and Engels. Intellectual life should be conceived in union with social and political life, and social being and becoming (in the widest sense, as economics, politics or law) should be studied in union with social consciousness in its many different manifestations, as a real yet also ideal (or 'ideological') component of the historical process in general. Instead, all consciousness is approached with totally abstract and basically metaphysical dualism, and declared to be a reflection of the one really concrete and material developmental process, on which it is completely dependent (even if relatively independent, still dependent in the last instance). (Korsch, 81)

To place Brecht in relation to the competing influences from Lenin and Korsch, to understand why they matter and why Brecht followed Lenin as a tactician with the greatest admiration, defending him against Korsch's criticism while, however, at the same time more indebted to Korsch in respect of the theoretical grounding of his own aesthetic practice, and how this becomes evident in *Me-ti*, we need to know why Korsch defended his position so vigorously against his many detractors among orthodox Marxist–Leninists.

## Korsch and dialectics

Accused, also by Brecht, of ignoring revolutionary practice in favour of a preoccupation with abstract philosophical idealities, and then of turning away from the political realities which did not live up to his expectations, Korsch argued that disregarding the interrelationship between philosophical theory and political practice was to betray the whole Marxist project. For Marx, as for Korsch, philosophy and practice merge into a way of life, such that one is unacceptable without the other.

What may seem a purely abstract concern with philosophy has implications for developing social formations if they are unaware of what is entailed. Just as Hegel 'regarded "a revolution in the form of thought" as an objective component of the total social process of a real revolution' (Korsch,

consequence would have been a restoration of the law of the jungle, or unmitigated Capitalism, but this unhappy turn of events lay in the future.

41), Korsch insists on the connection between 'intellectual movement' and the 'revolutionary movement [...] contemporary with it' (Korsch, 40). Every philosophy, for Hegel, can only be 'its own epoch comprehended in thought' (Korsch, 43) and, unlike the early Hegel, a period of political restoration led mid- to late-nineteenth-century bourgeois philosophy to lose sight of the connection between philosophy and revolution as a social practice. Marx and Engels aimed to abolish the bourgeois state with a scientific socialism that would realize or overcome philosophy as a separate idealist explanatory system. Marxists later treated this matter of 'absorbing' philosophy as irrelevant for class struggle, instead of informing and helping to shape it.

For Korsch, 'a dialectical conception comprehends every form without exception in terms of the flow of this movement' (Korsch, 58). Though there will, therefore, be changes in the theory of social revolution, an 'unbreakable interconnection of theory and practice' (Korsch, 59) must remain, no matter how more differentiated analysis becomes, instead of being fragmented into autonomous areas. The first stage in developing theory, from 1843 to 1848 and the *Communist Manifesto*, was followed by the suppression of the Paris proletariat and a period of restoration lasting to the end of the nineteenth century. Then, a unified theory of social revolution changed into partial criticisms of social phenomena, to be reformed within the bourgeois state, from the Gotha programme up to the SPD (Social Democratic Party of Germany), whose revisionism was a theoretical critique of society. This purely theoretical orthodox Marxism collapsed with the effect of World War I, and the Russian Revolution is seen, in 1923, as restoring Marxism, whose 'scientific socialism is the theoretical expression of a revolutionary process' (Korsch, 69).

Given this opportunity, Marxism must become again, Korsch argues, not a 'simple return' but 'a dialectical development' in which the 'proletariat must accomplish definite revolutionary tasks in the ideological field' (Korsch, 70). Avoiding this, however, 'creates a crisis within Marxism' (Korsch, 71), just as the problem of the relationship between state and revolution created a crisis that destroyed the Second International. Evading this task for the proletariat, by leaving it to an advance guard acting on its behalf, can later only have politically disastrous results.

Marx famously declared 'I am not a Marxist.' For Korsch, the problem became and remained the relationship between Marxist theory and the working-class movement. Lenin brought Marxism as an ideology from outside to the workers, who had, he said, only 'trade-union consciousness'. The dislike, especially within Bolshevik Marxism–Leninism, of Korsch's stress on the philosophical side of Marxism, whose revolutionary capacity must be realized in and by, not on behalf of, the working class, came about because it was seen as opposed to the prevalent 'anti-philosophical, scientific-positivist conception of Marxism'. Lenin's reaction to Ernst Mach's 'empirio-criticism' is clearly an example of undialectical materialism. And Korsch tasks such thinking with recoursing to a 'primitive, pre-dialectical and even pre-transcendental conception of the relation between consciousness and being', which 'formed the basis of the new orthodox theory, so-called Marxism-Leninism' (Korsch, 122).

The idealist/materialist differentiation was, of course, a false distinction, used as a political argument but, nevertheless, containing serious theoretical and social difficulties that, at the time, it seemed to solve. Crudely transferred to politics, such 'materialism' became a doctrine equated with Being, which consciousness simply reflects, but does not shape or question. This is one reason why the Marxist student of Chinese science and civilization, Joseph Needham, preferred to speak of 'dialectical organicism'.[18] The problem of the relationship between theory and matter is then bracketed or 'solved' by pragmatism, which equates 'knowledge' with what works.

Though Korsch distinguishes between Lenin and later Leninists, he argues that Lenin defended materialism 'on practical and political' not on 'theoretical' grounds, in spite of that quotation, because he subordinated 'theoretical issues to party interest'. Engaged in a party argument with Alexander Bogdanov, Lenin saw the discussion of Mach's views in Russia as endangering his 'materialism', and Korsch says that Lenin regarded these philosophical trends as '*ideologies that were incorrect from the standpoint of party work*' (Korsch, 125).[19] Lenin's task, Korsch recognized, was to reach the millions of peasants and other backward masses throughout Russia, Asia and the whole world, and persuade them of what Lenin called the 'basic truths of philosophical materialism' (Korsch, 127). Brecht, who was not primarily a 'theorist', admired and approved of the practical engagement of the tactician, without appreciating until later the formidable difficulties that the expression of Lenin's 'theoretical' views would cause.

Dialectical materialism slid into dialectical determinism, in order to satisfy a perceived political or disciplinary need. This seems to have

[18] Joseph Needham, *Moulds of Understanding* (London: George Allen & Unwin, 1976), p. 278. See also his discussion of the fundamental ideas of Chinese science in comparison to Western thought in *Science and Civilization in China*, vol. 2 (Cambridge: Cambridge University Press, 1956), especially pp. 289–303.

[19] Given his need for certainty, Lenin was not able to recognize the sort of sense that Mach's phenomenalism makes, as in this quote: 'In reality, the law always contains less than the fact itself, because it does not reproduce the fact as a whole but only in that aspect of it which is important for us, the rest being intentionally or from necessity omitted' ('The Economical Nature of Physical Inquiry', in *Popular Scientific Lectures* [Chicago: Open Court, 1895], p. 192).

continued at least into the 1970s in the German Democratic Republic, at the cost of sacrificing the 'philosophical' or theoretical significance of the original term as indicating the mutual dependence of mind and matter or, as sometimes disputed, consciousness and being. Korsch was right to argue that Lenin substituted matter for spirit, as a new absolute, and thus regressed to before Kant and Hegel (Korsch, 131). He maintained that Lenin's 'materialist philosophical domination covers all the sciences, whether of nature or society as well as all other cultural developments in literature, drama, plastic arts and so on [and] this has resulted in a specific kind of ideological dictatorship which oscillates between revolutionary progress and the blackest reaction' (Korsch, 137f.).

## The Soviet Union

Klaus-Detlef Müller sees *Me-ti* as an argument with Korsch, presented in a literary form as a stimulus to thought, and not as a theoretical or autobiographical work. There is a different tone in Brecht's discussions with Benjamin about Stalinism, and though the views in *Me-ti* become increasingly critical, they do not reach the level of condemnation trenchantly expressed elsewhere.

Mittenzwei acknowledges that Brecht criticized Stalin above all for seeking economic at the cost of political development, but understates or misrecognizes the cost of that political neglect as Brecht evaluated it. This derives from his need to maintain that Brecht's continual stress on the importance of individual production must be seen in the context of those objective laws of dialectical determinism, which constituted the official ideology of the German Democratic Republic in the 1970s.

So even though Brecht defended Stalin in the 1930s as the symbol of the need to construct a socialist state under the most difficult conditions, and performed, when viewing events from his isolation in Svendborg, veritable *salti mortali* in support, though often in ironical defence, of the overpraised heroic leader, Mittenzwei objected to Brecht's 'undifferentiated description of Stalin's influence', especially in one of his most critical passages, *Development and Decline under Ni-en*, by misrepresenting Stalin and views voiced by organizations outside the Soviet Union. Mittenzwei asserted that he had been listening too much to uninformed other voices, where Brecht simply records what was being thought and said about the direction of events. This particular passage alludes to Korsch (Ko) and also mentions Trotsky (To-tsi).

Mittenzwei naturally, and correctly, argues that Brecht took Stalin's side against Trotsky, but his position was not as straightforward, as we can see by carefully reading the *Me-ti* texts. Mittenzwei cites the following passage as proof that Brecht supported Stalin:

> *Me-ti for Ni-en*
> Me-ti stayed on Ni-en's side. On the question whether creating *Order* in one country was possible, he took the view that its creation had to begin in one country and then be perfected in other countries. Creating it in one country was just as much a condition for creating it in other countries as that would be a condition for completing it in one country.

This is supported, Mittenzwei argues, by the following quotation from Lenin: 'The irregularity of economic and political development is an infrangible law of Capitalism. It follows that the victory of socialism is at first only possible in few Capitalist countries or even in one single country'. Mittenzwei assumes that the 'victory' of socialism in one country is possible, i.e. that it has indeed been victorious in the German Democratic Republic, but Brecht's observation is, characteristically, more equivocal.

The nuances implied in Brecht's careful formulations are not always recognized, let alone addressed. He assumes that the 'order', which stands for socialism, has not been 'completed' in one country until it has begun to be 'created' in other ones. That political failure became of course the cause of the subsequent collapse of the Communist states, which proved unable to compete with more successful economies. We can speculate that the outcome might have been different, if the undoubted economic achievements of the Soviet Union had been accompanied by comparable political developments, instead of by political regression.

To-tsi is directly mentioned in six texts: *On the flow of things*, *The philosopher Ko's view of constructing order in Su*, *To-tsi's theory*, *Creating order in one country*, *Development and decline under Ni-en* and *Ni-en's trials*. In only one of these, *Creating order*, does the text clearly take Stalin/Ni-en's side in the argument with Trotsky/To-tsi. In two others, *The philosopher Ko's view* and *Ni-en's trials*, neither is preferred, their positions are simply described. *The philosopher Ko's view* represents objectively Korsch's criticisms of developments after Lenin, without taking either side. In *Ni-en's trials* the conflict of opinion, seemingly justifying those trials, is attributed to squabbling intellectuals in the apparatus; elsewhere and later Stalin would be blamed. In the remaining three texts, *On the flow of things, To-tsi's theory* and *Development and decline*, Trotsky's analysis is supported or objectively described, if anything tending toward Trotsky, because Stalin was more responsible for what was happening, and Brecht did not like it, a position that is clear enough in *Development and decline*.

There is no doubt that Brecht greatly admired Lenin's political skills and tactical flexibility. The question, however, is what became of the system he put in place, and at what point did that system become an objective impediment to the realization of Brecht's expectations for socialism. Mittenzwei does not address this question or see the evidence of its existence in the *Me-ti* texts. Out of a political need to insist that Brecht was a Leninist, he has to separate him from the renegade, Korsch, and underplay their relationship. Similarly, he overdoes Brecht's antipathy to Trotsky in order to keep him safely within the bounds of dialectical determinism, a concept delimited by a theory of reflection that is incompatible with his work. What may once have seemed necessary, perhaps even appropriate, in order to publish and discuss these texts within the German Democratic Republic, has not in the long run served them well, because the teleological design in the arrangement of those texts deflects attention from the ambiguities, subtleties and uncertainties they contain.

Brecht's public loyalty to the Soviet Union was determined, in spite of privately expressed reservations and later acknowledged evidence for the criminality of the regime, by his personal experience of Fascism. Apart from a gut revulsion over the spread of this social disease from within his own culture, he accepted the argument that Fascism represented an extreme of predatory imperialist Capitalism, intent on subjugating other nations and economies. Brecht praised Stalin for opposing 'the robbers, my countrymen' (BFA 23/226). For a while there was evidence enough that the Western liberal democracies hoped Hitler would put an end to the socialist experiment in the East. In that context, only the Soviet Union offered an alternative.

If what happened during the Moscow trials is clearly understood today, as they unfolded it did not always seem so straightforward. Brecht was not the only person to wonder about the position of the accused. Lion Feuchtwanger, who wrote an account of attending the trials, was convinced of their guilt. Ernst Bloch and Heinrich Mann also looked for justifications of what was happening. Furthermore, there is a noticeable difference between what Brecht wrote about the Moscow trials, in an attempt to make sense of them, and what is said about them in *Me-ti*.

Writing elsewhere about the Moscow trials, he begins by saying he cannot speak against them because that would aid the attack of 'global Fascism' against the 'Russian proletariat' and its creation of socialism (*Brecht on Art and Politics*, 184f.). This conviction coloured much of what he would say, until it became untenable. He speaks of the 'defeatism' shown by their critics at a time when this was treated as a capital crime in the Soviet Union. He records, however, that sympathizers also find the accusations incredible, implying forced confessions. Brecht says there is no proof either way, but he feels the need to defend and explain what is happening and attributes it to this defeatism, adding 'I am convinced that this is the truth', an opinion he holds while 'sitting in my isolation in Svendborg'. These are notes written for himself, part of an explanation of his position intended for a letter to someone else.

What he writes in *Me-ti* is far more restrained and focused on criticism of the conduct of these trials. Though Brecht at times supported Stalin, he was no Stalinist. In Moscow in 1936, he was counted among the anti-Stalinists and wisely kept his distance from those who so classified him. This antipathy towards him among party loyalists continued into the German Democratic Republic.[20]

## Critical dialectics

Hans Mayer wondered if Brecht's work was finally not that far removed from Adorno's negative dialectics. Brecht had asked, in a preface written in 1956 for an edition to be published in Moscow, whether, 'mostly set in a capitalist society', his work therefore had anything to offer the new developing Communist society (BFA 23/419f.). Adorno, on the other hand, dismissed it as too aligned with the positive dialectics evident in Lenin's statement. He was particularly scornful about Brecht's recourse to invocations of Chinese wisdom, accusing him of infantility and the idyllic rusticity Marx had mocked. Brecht's own rejection, under the conditions of Stalinist positive dialectics, of the pursuit of the 'harmonious' and 'intrinsically beautiful' proves that he preserved a position ceding neither to the positive nor negative varieties and which can perhaps be described as 'critical dialectics'. He rejected the understanding of 'socialist realism' advocated in the German Democratic Republic, and deplored the imposition of an authoritarian administrative system upon the population. Both were challenged by his *Coriolanus* adaptation, which proved unplayable in his lifetime.

Brecht later decided that his term, the Great Order, was a misnomer and should rather have been called, as a significant entry in his *Journals* for 7 March 1941 records, the Great Production, whose intention was to 'free the productivity of all men from all fetters'. This shift is incompatible with the dogma of reflection theory whether asserted by Lenin, or policed by Stalin, or presented in aesthetic terms by Lukács. There was no place in

20 For a balanced account of this relationship, see Klaus-Detlef Müller, 'Brecht und Stalin', *Von Poesie und Politik. Zur Geschichte einer dubiösen Beziehung*, ed. Jürgen Wertheimer (Tübingen: Attempto Verlag, 1994), pp. 106–22.

such a system for Brecht's innovative, interventionary aesthetic thought, which was viewed as exemplifying 'bourgeois-reactionary falsehood' rather than reflection theory's predetermined objective truth, and would be condemned as such in China by the Gang of Four during the Cultural Revolution.

What is indisputable is that Korsch's view of Lenin's reflection theory was ultimately a better predictor of its consequences than Brecht's descriptions of his pragmatic practice. Brecht stressed Lenin's flexibility as necessary under the prevailing circumstances and criticized Korsch for being too concerned with abstractions, without appreciating how the dialectical qualifier would be sacrificed to a determinism, before long to be defined by whoever had the power to determine it.

The evidence of Brecht's support for the tactical practices of the innovative and indefatigable Lenin is unmistakable in *Me-ti*. Yet the chiastic analogy between Korsch's 'mental action' (*geistige Aktion*), however we translate it, to which the soi-disant 'materialists' took such exception, and Brecht's advocacy of 'interventionary thought' (*eingreifendes Denken*) is surely too close to be accidental.

## Ruth Berlau

Brecht wrote many more letters to Ruth Berlau (1906–1974) than to anyone else, and more than to the rest of his female collaborators together. That there was something special in this relationship is apparent from the texts about Lai-tu or Tu or Tu Fu or Kin-jeh's sister, or Shen Te in *Me-ti*. Beginning in the mid-1930s, the last were written at the start of the 1950s.

Their relationship involved mutual assistance and in both cases real emotional dependency, due to compatible and incompatible needs. Though stylized by literary form, the *Me-ti* texts give a sense of those needs, even if reflecting Brecht's perspective more than hers. Noticeably different from the other texts, they cannot be fully understood without some knowledge of what brought them together, as it eventually kept them apart.

Berlau's schooling stopped at the age of thirteen. She had ambitions as an actor and writer. Employed, for a while, by the Royal Theatre of Copenhagen, she was also closely associated with the first Danish workers' theatre, and had played Anna in Brecht's *Drums in the Night*. Married to a successful Copenhagen doctor twenty years her senior, she met Brecht in August 1933 and proved a valuable contact, able to mitigate his Danish isolation after the hectic Berlin years. She furthered his work, while, far more than his other female collaborators, growing ever more dependent on him for sustaining her self-esteem. After their intimacy had faded, her attachment remained undiminished. Deprived of the response she desired, it drove her into self-destructive behaviour.

While accepting that the *Me-ti* texts were intended to 'instruct and educate' her, which she both wanted and needed, Berlau was not always best pleased by them: 'I should always remember how important Me-ti – that is Brecht – is for me and that as his pupil I should take him as my example.'[21] The descriptions in the autobiographical *Brechts Lai-tu* have been factually challenged, as has the extent of her significance in Danish cultural life as told in Hans Bunge's Afterword. Her account has also been taken 'straight' as credible evidence of the typically disadvantaged woman, though in truth this relationship was less that of a put-upon woman and a dominant man. Berlau was in some respects tougher than Brecht, whom she also described as 'cowardly', something he admits in *Me-ti*. Apart from lovers, she also sought out creative older men whom she could admire.

Yet she called herself his 'creature', and the intensity that tied her to him eventually drove them apart. The dependency was not one-sided, though it had a different character for Brecht, who needed other people to stimulate him, and always looked for suggestions and immediate response. This naturally, in turn, elicited an enthusiasm and a willingness to cooperate in something way beyond the ordinary, especially when it also involved some form of emotional or actual cohabitation.

Without tying himself to the same standard, Brecht expected faithfulness from such collaborators, and his letters contain coded references to this. He sought reassurance and became distressed at Berlau's readiness, in the early years of their relationship, to disregard this expectation. She was, nevertheless, caught up in a romantic and intellectual encounter that completely transformed her life, whether for better or, later, also for worse. To mitigate the extremes of her emotional intensity Brecht invoked for her in *Me-ti*, in his letters, surely also in conversation, and no doubt often in self-defence, what he called the 'Third Thing'. It became an important part of what held them together and kept them apart.

To situate the 'Lai-tu' texts, we need to know what some of these letters reveal about their relationship. Brecht's first surviving letter, written after most of the *Me-ti* texts, and under dramatic circumstances in April 1940, from Lidingö in Stockholm to Berlau in Copenhagen, is particularly revealing (BFA 29/163). Justifiably afraid his visa in Sweden might not

[21] Ruth Berlau, *Brechts Lai-tu. Erinnerungen und Notate von Ruth Berlau*. Herausgegeben und mit einem Nachwort von Hans Bunge (Darmstadt: Luchterhand, 1985), p. 79.

be extended, and about to leave for Finland, when travel everywhere was becoming more difficult and dangerous, Brecht writes:

> From now on I will *always* organize your journey as well. Either in advance or on the spot. Should you have to wait, it will not be on account of carelessness on my part, but because some attempt or other has failed and must be repeated.
>
> You must therefore do everything to get in touch quickly. Since from now on I will be waiting for you, wherever I'm going, and will always be counting on you. And I won't be counting on your coming for your sake but for mine, Ruth.
>
> [...]
>
> Dear Ruth, come soon. Everything is unchanged, safe and good.
>
> J. e d.
>
> And it will stay unchanged. As long as our separation may last. Also in ten. Also in twenty years.
>
> And for Lai-tu: she gets the task to take care of herself and to come through the dangers, until *our* thing begins, the real one, for which one must preserve oneself. Dear Ruth.
>
> e p e p bertolt [22]

Berlau could not resist this call and joined him in Finland, later travelling with the family through the Soviet Union to Vladivostok and on to the United States. Staying for a while in Los Angeles, she then left for New York, where Brecht visited her several times. Their son, Michael, born in 1944 and named after the child in *The Caucasian Chalk Circle*, died a few days after birth. When Brecht settled in Berlin, Berlau moved there too and had an on-and-off position with the Berliner Ensemble. The relationship deteriorated further when she became difficult and aggressive, until banned from the theatre. Brecht, however, continued to support and tried to help her.

Though never as crucial as Elisabeth Hauptmann's or as critically alert as Margarete Steffin's contributions, what Berlau/Lai-tu did for Brecht and their third thing is indeed impressive. It includes unspecified degrees of participation in some ten plays including *The Visions of Simone Machard*,

[22] BFA 29/163f. J. e d. stands for Jag elkser dig / I love you, and e p e p for et proper et procul / both near and far. Brecht used this shorthand (as well as J. e. d.) at the end of letters to Berlau. The full quotation, attributed to Horace, appears in *Life of Galileo* (1938/39), where the Little Monk says that Galileo uses it of his sense of beauty that drives him to speak the truth: 'hieme et aestate, et prope et procul, usque dum vivam et ultra' (winter and summer, both near and far, as long as I live and beyond). Telling the truth is part of what binds them together and to this third, 'our' thing.

*Schweyk in the Second World War*, *The Private Tutor*, *The Good Person of Szechwan*, as well as in *The Caucasian Chalk Circle* and *The Days of the Commune*, for which she is acknowledged as sole collaborator. She participated in translating several plays into Danish, in directing some in Denmark, Germany and other countries, and in preparing productions. There was also a degree of cooperation on the *Conversations of Refugees*, and even more on the *War Primer*. She published the *Svendborg Poems* in 1939 in Copenhagen. Her extensive photographic documentation of performances was invaluable, resulting in the *Modelbooks* and forming the basis of the important record of the Berliner Ensemble productions, *Theatre Work* (*Theaterarbeit*. Berlin: Henschelverlag, 1967), which she considered her real 'life's work'.

Brecht wrote telling letters in March 1950 (BFA 30/17–20), after Berlau had been detained in the enclosed neurological section of the Berlin Charité hospital following a supposed suicide attempt, which she denied. On 14 March he wrote:

> Of all the people I know, you are the most generous. I have hardly ever seen you buying something for yourself. The money I was able to give you from time to time you always spent on me – not just for working material but also for small conveniences. You yourself lived extremely modestly, often in poverty, while also doing the work of several people, small and large tasks, tirelessly and almost invisibly. Suddenly there was a meal, and then an enormous work with photos continued overnight, enough for a whole week.
>
> This was often pioneering work, whose significance people did not understand. Thus you did this work in opposition to almost everyone, without fear of being laughed at or of intrigue. The thousands of photos which you made of manuscripts and performances are a mark of Chinese diligence and of an independence of spirit, hardly found anywhere else. You were helped by your sense of what is important, which is also rare.

In an earlier letter, he said he needed her to give him time to put their relationship, which would become increasingly tense and difficult, on a 'new basis'. In a longer letter of 10 March he responded to suggestions she had made about payment for the work she was doing and about access to him personally for private and emotional reasons which, she said, he had earlier promised:

> 1 Again there is the *Third Thing* and again what's personal and private takes a back seat. The *Third Thing* is socialism and what's important is

> what we can do for socialism at this stage and in these years, in real terms.
>
> 2 Whether something is judged 'good' or 'bad' will be changed again into 'useful' or 'not useful' and even this will apply more to actions than to people.
>
> 3 Since we are facing the future and not the past, as far as the past is concerned the good will be remembered, the bad times forgotten – and that means: the good things one did will be forgotten and the good things the other did will be remembered. In the future there are no more tributes (which are owed), rather presents (which are gladly given), no conditions any more, only requests. Nobody owes anyone anything, each owes everything to the *Third Thing*.
>
> 4 So, as if we were meeting each other for the first time, let's try to make ourselves agreeable to each other. (BFA 30/19 and *Letters*, 490f.)

When the adaption of *The Private Tutor* by J. M. R. Lenz (1751–92) was rehearsed in the Berliner Ensemble, Berlau dreamt the author told her that Brecht himself said he had escaped the tigers, and was now feeding fleas and consumed by mediocrity, whereupon she exclaimed: 'That's just it!'

This story and Brecht's letter together say much about the tensions between them and the frustrations in their attempt to live and work for the 'third thing', never mind how much he thought she made personal demands he could no longer satisfy. Though never abandoning his hope, it became apparent that, quite apart from failing health, his third thing would not be realized in the authoritarian system that ruled its real existing socialist society. This is evident in many last poems and in the hope against hope entertained from events in faraway China, which was not well understood in Europe.

The relationship with Berlau was a reminder both of the third thing he had so often invoked for her, as for no one else, and of the impossibility of ever seeing it realized. The letters and the last short passages in *Me-ti* also reflect these realities, never mind her impossible behaviour.

Brecht and Berlau had chosen Cassiopeia as the heavenly constellation where their gaze would meet when separated. Berlau left an extraordinary, undated account of a dream in a collapsing house, where she tries to extinguish the flames through the dampness of her sex whose hair was burning. She sees him standing close by, for whom the life and death of his works means everything, points to him with her burning hand and calls out 'Bertolt'. He quotes the poem he wrote for her, 'Ardens sed virens': 'Wonderful what in the fine fire / Does not turn to ashes! / Sister see, you're dear to me / Burning but not consumed.' She tries to tell him one of the stars is missing, it has fallen and set her on fire. He does not believe her and thinks she is mad again. W [presumably for Weigel] then seizes his arm and says 'fetch the fire brigade … you can't help her'. The constellation's second star falls as the fire brigade arrives, fetches her and covers her up (Berlau, 293f.).

Among her papers is a poem, dated 28 January 1951, which is also included among Brecht's, written either by or for Berlau:

> Weaknesses
>
> You had none
> I had one:
> I loved.

Brecht's last letter to Berlau on 27 July 1956, just over two weeks before he died, signed again, as in these last letters, e. p. e. p., concerned the house he was going to buy for her in Denmark, as security and in the hope their relationship would 'improve', and encouraging her to 'improve your equanimity'. He had first imagined it would be in Vallensbaek (BFA 30/420, 427), where she had bought the small house for them both, mentioned in *Me-ti*, years before.

In a long letter written to Berlau at the beginning of 1956, when she was for a while in Denmark and seemed to be coping better, Brecht addressed the question of their relationship in the context of the times. The last seven years, he wrote, had been bad for both of them. His health could no longer withstand a repetition. She was making excessive demands, he argued, out of all proportion to her contributions and to the expectations others reasonably entertained. They had not been equal partners in writing in spite of all she had genuinely contributed, but she was asking too much as if he was continuously and literally in debt to her. Her return to Denmark had seemed to work, but only for a while. She now wanted to return to Berlin and Brecht wrote she must come as a visitor to a new country, though only as Shen Te, never again as Shui Ta.

He also wrote a poem for her, 'Change', at the beginning of 1956 (BFA 15/298), in which this verse occurs: 'But today I invite Shen Te/ And Shui Ta comes.' The other four verses of that poem are driven by nostalgia for the person she once was and the relationship they had, the friendliness that reminded him how much of her had shaped Shen Te, the Good Person, her spontaneity and joyfulness, evidently what is missing in these last months.

In a letter at the end of April 1956, he came back once more to their third thing:

> We have sadly abandoned the 3rd Thing, haven't we? The work on the Modelbooks must be made political, communist again, that's what's

> most important now – since in our country everything quickly becomes formal, superficial, mechanical. (BFA 30/450)

The single-minded intensity of Berlau's attraction to Brecht and its effect on her own mental and physical health was assuredly one reason why he will have sought to deflect its energy towards the common goal of the third thing. That Brecht returned again to it not only indicates that he hoped to focus her attention on the working relationship, for which he praises her, at times lavishly, and thereby away from her increasingly destructive behaviour, but it also suggests, in the way it is mentioned, that this third thing as they had imagined it is itself failing. Not only had her behaviour become ever more difficult and potentially dangerous, but the thing to which they devoted their whole lives was also coming apart and proving ever more difficult to predict.

The forces impeding what he envisaged as the release of the productive capacities in a democratically organized population were proving too intransigent. This unresolved problem was part of what caused him to write one of his last poems, whose shortness belies the significance of what it says:

> If we lasted forever
> Everything would change.
> But since we don't
> Many things stay the same.

## This edition

There is no approved or 'authorized' sequence for the *Me-ti* texts and this new edition is differently structured from the earlier alternatives, which furnished the basis for various translations into other languages: the virtually identical Johnson and Völker editions published in West and the Mittenzwei edition in East Germany, whose practices have been described. I follow Völker's only significant variation of Johnson's edition by placing the Lai-tu passages, though now rearranged, at the end of the sequence. Johnson interspersed them among the other texts, but they are differently focused, more personal and emotional, even private. The general effect of such interleaving is to loosen the effect of the other intertwining narratives, dispersing them and turning the whole into something like the experience of a few disconnected passages as in bedtime reading. Mittenzwei splits them up, placing most Lai-tu texts at the end of the second of his five sections, *Book of Experience*, and more politically apposite ones at the end of his *Book of Upheaval*.

The challenge, or danger, in proposing an entirely different sequence to anything hitherto presented, no matter with what 'political' effect – for if none is subjectively intended, its consequences will be objectively present – is the possibility of inferring an argument different from, even out of sympathy with, the perspectives that originally shaped them. They may seem inimical or to have been overruled by the passage of time and subsequent events, by the development of what Brecht called 'experience' confronting 'judgements', which amounts to practice trumping ideology. Mittenzwei's radical rearrangement had its own coherence but it underplayed, especially in the light of his accompanying arguments, the anti-systematic, critical or suspicious strain in Brecht's thinking, as if what he had hoped for was finally being realized in the contemporary German Democratic Republic.

While placing the Lai-tu texts at the end of the sequence, I have also taken the 'Chinese' passages toward the beginning, though not bundled together, but in the context of various unfolding themes. The purpose is not to overemphasize them or the extent to which Brecht was beholden to Mo Di, as some critics have done, because that tends to mystify and to detract from the impact of the whole collection, but rather to show from the start what is happening, why there are suggestive analogies, and where they have their place, but also their limits.

The intention is, as it were, to get this out of the way in order to concentrate on the real historical and contemporary substance of these writings, instead of scratching our head when another 'Chinese' allusion crops up, at best constituting a distraction, as we either ignore it or wonder what on earth it really means. While these allusions do broaden the reach of what is said and also have a necessary estranging effect, the figure of Brecht's 'Me-ti' – part persona, part super-ego, confirming and confronting what the more autobiographical Kin-jeh, in his various guises, says and does – is of course a device for engaging with, and keeping a certain distance from, the often overwhelming difficulties of the day and their always changing, ever-conflicted interface between theory and practice.

Some texts first printed in the BFA edition are included, though a couple whose meaning remains incoherent are left out. The archive folders contain two intriguing allusions, which Brecht regrettably did not pursue: a handwritten note, 'dialog me ti + nietze' and 'nietzsche und seine benutzer' ('Nietzsche and his users', BBA 132/24), as well as three small pictures of a grinning Stalin's head, creating the effect of caricature, which take us some steps beyond the then current cliché in England of our one-time ally, the pipe-smoking Uncle Joe, towards something more comical and hence sinister (BBA 133/63).

Translation always raises its own problems. There is a special one with these texts. Brecht estranges many concepts and institutions, thereby inviting us to reconsider what they stand for and what they conceal. What may at first seem odd in English, either poorly or simply *mis*translated, depends on conveying a similar effect. Thus 'Umwälzung' (frequently used for revolution) becomes upheaval or overthrow, party becomes association, smithmasters stand for factory owners, ploughsmiths for factory workers and headworkers for intellectuals, or Great Method for dialectics, Great Disorder for Capitalism, house painter for Hitler, and so forth. Such Chimese names as can be attached to historical individuals are listed below.

Given the nature of the texts with their allusions to events whose significance and arguments whose intensity has faded, and an occasionally elusive quality occasioned by the estranging style, there is an obvious need for explanatory notes and a degree of commentary. In order to avoid visually distracting numbered footnotes, let alone the irritation of page-turning necessitated by endnotes, which interrupts the rhythm of reading, the commentary is placed directly after each relevant passage.

The texts range in style, from anecdote to short narrative, commentary, aphorism, poetry, paraphrase, incorporating versions of other texts (Kipling, Lenin, Marx). They constitute a defensive or critical response to social and political issues of the day, which are nearly always in some degree estranged by the manner of their telling. They neither aspire, like the writings of Korsch, to theoretical, let alone systematic, explanation of events, nor do they seek to inform about such events in a journalistic sense. Rather, they step back towards the events behind the events, in order to question them and their human causes and motivation from a deeper or wider perspective in the hope of showing what their sheer pressure and immediacy frequently obscures. That is ultimately a philosophical pursuit of the kind that Brecht admired, which seeks to shape a practice by understanding what really guides it.

The aim is not to align these texts with a specific contention, whether intrinsic or attributed, for all that time and changing circumstances must affect any reading, but to allow the contradictions they explore to speak for themselves. Rather than explicitly divided into sections, the passages are loosely gathered around unfolding topics. Many address political tactics and policy, especially seeking to explain, through estranging descriptions, for example, how and why Lenin adjusted his practice in the light of specific circumstances, while not losing sight of his ultimate goal. Others step back from such practice and tactics to reflect on this ultimate goal and whether it was being furthered or hindered by policy and concepts of governance, questions basically addressing the relationship between the individual and the state. The problems Stalin had grotesquely exacerbated did not disappear after his death. They were perpetuated in a system that Brecht later described in his letter to Berlau as too 'formal, superficial, mechanical'.

Facing these difficulties, Brecht sought to open up what we might call desire lines to counter the frustrations, and worse, experienced by so many who had turned to Communism, because of deeply held desires, which were repressed in what has been called the social unconscious, as the repository of what is longed for but cannot be realized under prevailing social rules and practices, and reinforced by alarm at the extent of 'homogenization', which allows for nothing 'undefined, fruitful, uncontrollable' (*On the productivity of individuals*).[23]

An insistent, emotionally powerful under- and often enough counter-current flows through Brecht's writing, which is opposed to system and to theory that has hardened into ideology, especially when policed by a class of administrators, privileged within a social culture, running the risk of turning people into what he calls in one passage 'the servants of priests' (*Ka-meh on realizing the Great Order*).

In *Me-ti*, this dislike often takes the form of an apparently provocative condemnation of virtues and of a seemingly contrary insistence on the need for egoism or self-love, for the self-help that, as Mo Di argued, did not damage, but assisted others. Such deviating desire lines invite individual productivity and creativity, appealing to experience rather than 'judgements' or 'opinions', to the wisdom of ordinary people, once referred to as the masses.

The crisis of Capitalism, of how humanity's affairs are organized, which provoked the response of Communism, has changed since Brecht experienced and faced it, but some of these changes have become even more threatening. Far from over, let alone solved, this crisis is probably only just beginning.

[23] It is well known that Brecht rejected Freudian ego-psychology but, intriguingly, he asked himself in 1938 whether he really wanted 'to do away with the space where the unconscious, half conscious, uncontrolled, ambiguous, multipurposed could play itself out' (BFA 22.1/468). The unanswered self-questioning clearly implies: No! Whether or not subjectively envisaged, the concept, social unconscious, undoubtedly has explanatory strength. I discuss this further in 'Brecht's East Asia: A Conspectus', *The Brecht Yearbook* 36, pp. 356f.

# Attributable names

| | |
|---|---|
| An-tse | Anatole France |
| Bi-leh | Berlin |
| Deh | Denmark |
| Eh-fu | Friedrich Engels |
| En-eng | England |
| Fan-tse | Anatole France |
| Fe-hu-wang | Feuchtwanger |
| Fu-en | Friedrich Engels |
| Ga | Germany |
| Ge-el | Germany |
| Ger | Germany |
| He-leh | Hegel |
| Hi-jeh | Hitler |
| Hu-ih | Hitler |
| Hui-jeh | Hitler |
| I-jeh | France |
| Intin | Einstein |
| Ju Seser | Julius Caesar |
| Ka-meh | Karl Marx |
| Ka-osch | Karl Korsch |
| Ken-jeh | Brecht |
| Kien-leh | Brecht |
| Ki-en-leh | Brecht |
| Kin | Brecht |
| Kin-jeh | Brecht |
| Ko | Karl Korsch |
| Lai Tu | Ruth Berlau |
| Lai-tu | Ruth Berlau |
| Lan-kü | Karl Liebknecht |
| Le-peh | Plechanov |
| Lu | Emil Ludwig |
| Mi-en-leh | Lenin |
| Mo-su | Moscow |
| Mu-sin | Weimar |
| Ni | Japan |

| | |
|---|---|
| Ni-en | Stalin |
| No | Norway |
| Sa | Rosa Luxemburg |
| Shen Te | Ruth Berlau |
| Su | Soviet Union |
| Sueh | Sweden |
| Ti-hi | Hitler |
| To-tsi | Trotsky |
| Tsen | Soviet Union |
| Tu Fu | Ruth Berlau |
| Tu | Ruth Berlau |
| Yu | Arnold Ljungdal |

The above equivalents are identifiable. Other names of persons may refer to unidentified individuals. Had Brecht prepared these texts for publication, he might have settled on one version among the two or three that refer to a particular individual, 'himself' included, of which there are five versions, as there also are for Berlau.

Unlike the other editions that correct obvious mistakes, the BFA prints what is found in the typescripts. The mistakes or potential confusions corrected in this edition include changing the names Hü-jeh and Hi-jeh, when they refer to Hegel, to He-leh, which also stands for Hegel. Hi-jeh frequently designates Hitler, as do Hu-ih and Hui-jeh.

# [Prefatory note]

*The Book of Interventions* has been translated into German using an English version of the Chinese by Charles Stephen. It is not one of ancient China's classic books, even if its core comes from *Mo Di*. After being almost entirely displaced by the Confucians, in the last century Mo Di's philosophy attracted attention since elements within it recalled certain trends in Western philosophy and appear almost modern. The chapters *On Music* and *On Behaviour* are genuine Mo Di. Other chapters are not by Mo Di but are equally old. Others again are more recent yet are written, also in the Chinese version, in the old style. From a strictly academic perspective, works like the *Book of Interventions* are not unobjectionable. However, the reader who is less concerned with authenticity than content will read it with pleasure in spite of its eclectic character. The inclusion of modern ways of thinking and the often quite amusing choice of comparisons from modern history with the basic thoughts of an ancient Chinese philosopher will be a source of pleasure for many readers.

[BFA 18/194. Brecht wrote this as a foreword or afterword to his *Me-ti* text in order to cover his tracks, referring to never written chapters as 'genuine' Mo Di, or simply for the fun of pretending, in a parody of learning, that there was a more authentic relationship with the writings of Mo Di. He certainly persuaded a few critics that this text constituted a modern reading or reinterpretation of an ancient Chinese philosopher's exemplary teaching, which had a profound impact on his work. That he may have seriously had concealment in mind, given the critical nature of much that it contains for the unpredictable 1930s, and the following decades, is implied by a note (BBA 1334/145) that states: 'Exiled in a half Fascist country Bertolt Brecht wrote a Book of Experiences in which the following story can be found. In order to conceal its authorship it is written as if it derived from an ancient Chinese historian.' See also the note to *Destroying as a form of learning*. This 'explanatory' text refers to chapters that were not written and to titles not used to organize the material.]

# Me-ti: Book of Interventions in the Flow of Things

## Interrogating tools and interrogating thoughts

Me-ti said: If you find bits of bronze or iron in the debris, you ask: what kind of tools were there long ago? What were they used for? Weapons indicate warfare, decorations point to commerce. You can make out all kinds of predicaments and possibilities.

Why don't we do the same with the thoughts of long ago?

['Long ago' reaches back to Mo Di (Mozi), a contemporary of Socrates, out of whom Brecht furnished a mask and persona for his questioning teacher, Me-ti. Foreshortening this perspective, a young reader today may wonder if 'long ago' might not also include Hegel, Marx, Lenin and even Brecht himself, and how their predicaments and possibilities can illuminate ours. If the past is a present construct, what might their 'then' tell us about our 'now' and the future of our successors?]

## Pointing out what matters most

Master Me-ti was chatting with some children. One boy suddenly left. After a while, when Me-ti also went out, he saw the boy standing behind a bush in the garden and crying. In passing, Me-ti said to him casually: No one can hear you, the wind is too strong.

When he returned, he noticed the boy had stopped crying. The boy had realized that what Master Me-ti told him was the point of his crying – namely, to be heard – was what mattered most.

[The point of many texts often lies beneath their narrative surface. Nearly all were written in exile, when predicaments were acute and intervention at best uncertain, if not impossible. Lines in a contemporary poem, 'On teaching without pupils' (ca. 1934), suggests what is at stake here: 'There speaks one to whom no one listens: / He speaks too loudly / He repeats himself / What he says is wrong / No one corrects him' (BFA14/315).]

## Dependent on good deeds

Mi-en-leh, in exile, fed the birds all winter long from his window. They depend on it, he said; they've nothing to eat and cannot form an association.

[Lenin (Mi-en-leh) was banished in 1897 for three years to Siberia, where some of the Decembrists, protesting authoritarian rule and serfdom, had also been exiled by Czar Nicholas I after the 1825 revolt. They began to transform a backward Siberia and were respected by the population for their good deeds. 'Association' stands for '(political) Party' throughout *Me-ti*, inviting us to ask what such words mean, sometimes in relation to their original intentions. The German word Brecht uses in place of 'Partei' is 'Verein', meaning literally something unified. Another equivalent of 'Verein' in English is 'club', which is too comfortable a word to transmit what such association entailed.]

## It can be harmful to lament wrongs without naming their avoidable causes

On no account should anyone be hindered from expressing sadness about unavoidable wrongs. Often they only appear unavoidable to that person, and vigorously expressed sadness increases the effort and the number of those who know how to eliminate them. Only, it mustn't be the apparent unavoidability that saddens them, otherwise their complaining discourages those who suffer these wrongs and supports those who cause the suffering. If, for example, these sufferings are due to certain property relations, deplored as inevitable and 'eternal in this vale of tears', then those whose ownership causes such suffering attain the, for them, welcome appearance of forces of nature, they become the snow of the freezing, the earthquake of those under whom the ground moves, powerful, natural, inevitable forces, whose actions cannot be stopped.

[This and the following text appear on the same manuscript page (BBA 134/37).]

## The difficulty in recognizing violence

Today many are ready to fight violence done to the defenceless. But can they also recognize violence?

Some acts of violence are easily recognized. If people are mistreated because of the shape of their nose or the colour of their hair, then most people clearly realize that is a violent act.

But we see people everywhere who appear just as disfigured as if they had been beaten with rods of iron, thirty-year-olds who look like old people, even though there is no visible sign of violence. People are living in holes, year after year, which are no more friendly than prison cells, and they have no more chance of escaping them than from prison cells. Of course, there are no jailers standing in front of these doors.

There are immeasurably more of those suffering such violence than those beaten up on a certain day or thrown into a particular prison cell.

## The fate of man

Me-ti said: The fate of man is man.

[Mo Di criticized the Confucians for encouraging fatalism, saying it benefited the rulers but not the common people. For Ludwig Feuerbach, in his thirtieth Heidelberg lecture (1848/49), 'the fate of humanity does not depend on a being beyond or above itself, but on itself'. In *An Essay on Man*, Epistle II, Pope formulated an analogous thought: 'Know then thyself, presume not God to scan; / The proper study of mankind is man.' Brecht probably knew a celebrated passage in Marx, which relates to much of what is said in his *Me-ti*: 'The weapon of criticism cannot, of course, replace criticism by weapons, material force must be overthrown by material force, but theory also becomes a material force as soon as it has gripped the masses. Theory is capable of gripping the masses as soon as it demonstrates *ad hominem*, and it demonstrates *ad hominem* as soon as it becomes radical. To be radical is to grasp the root of the matter. The root for man is man himself' (*Contribution to Critique of Hegel's Philosophy of Law, Introduction*, in Karl Marx, Friedrich Engels, *Collected Works* [London: Lawrence & Wishart, 1975], p. 182). A concern for Brecht was the need for speaking to and of the individual, also as reader. The German word, 'Mensch', is gender neutral.]

## Protection and plundering

In the old days the barons of Wei sucked the peasants dry. But when attacked by neighbouring barons, they protected the peasants with the sword. Plundering was a form of protection, protecting a form of plunder, for the servants of the barons, billeted in the peasants' houses, took whatever was there. There was something contradictory in the behaviour of the barons and the peasants. The barons beat up their charges, the peasants awaited the barons with impatience.

Observing these contradictions can lead to good solutions. Whenever enough peasants recognized that all barons plundered, but for the sake of plundering were divided and fought among each other, those, who might have mistakenly driven off only their own barons, were able to start driving off all the barons by taking advantage of the quarrels over booty. That put an end to plundering.

[Mo Di went as ambassador to the state of Wei. He approved of defensive warfare but condemned inequalities as a cause of war, during which conflicting interests become particularly apparent. Brecht takes the observation of this predicament one step further than Mo Di could ever have done, and imagines a possible solution.]

## The difficulty in writing history

The Prince of Wei built a dam against flooding. Some historians therefore praise his philanthropy. They fail to see that he used violence to compel many people to work on it, who had nothing to fear from flooding since they owned no fields, and that he continued to demand high taxes for his dam, so one can really say that he built it for the sake of the income. Some other historians take this into account and blame the Prince of Wei. They fail to see that the dam was very good against flooding and that it cost the Prince of Wei a lot of trouble to keep people on the job and organize them properly.

Both kind of historians stood in need of the *Great Method*.

Protecting the people of Wei could change into plundering them. As they scraped together money in a pot for the taxes, they could hear the water breaking on the dam. The Prince of Wei could build the dam with one hand and demand money with the other. But the description gives rise to a lack of agreement, an either/or, such that historians come down on one side or the other.

[On one of Brecht's typescript pages (BBA 133/02) this text appears under a general capitalized title, 'On the GREAT METHOD', which may have been intended as a chapter or section heading. The Great Method, opposing either/or with both/and logic, stands for dialectics, tracing change driven by interconnected difference.]

## Wei and Yen's inability to maintain discipline

Winter, the worst time of the year, surprised the enemies in a country almost deprived of food. The laziness of the peasants, caused by the cruelty of the land owners, was the reason there was so little, and the peasants were at least selfish enough to remove all their own provisions and hide them. The enemy army began to feel extremely hungry.

Callous and unscrupulous as were the people of Hao, after being inculcated in military virtues from childhood on, they seized the landowners and slaughtered most of them, because they could not procure anything. But then their army disintegrated in the terrible famine and fled to the border. The greater part of the people of Hao died in the borderlands they themselves had devastated.

In spring the peasants crawled out of their huts again, and as Yen had hoped, their old weakness, selfishness, manifested itself to an astonishing degree. The landowners had been killed by the enemy or were intimidated and helpless, and the peasants, certain they could bring in their own harvest, began to sow like men possessed.

Wei prospered.

When the good ruler Yen died, people could truthfully say that through the cowardice of his subjects he had won a great war, and without a lot of government decrees and exhortations had turned the country of Wei into a garden.

[This story also moves beyond Mo Di in exploring attitudes suggested by other styles of Chinese thought. Preserving the Chinese disguise, with the state of Wei and the good ruler Yen, an allusion to the mythical emperor Yen Ti, and referring to topics in Mo Di, the strife between states and the distinction between lazy peasants and their grasping superiors, the 'solution' is here apparently sought in the Daoist practice of non-contention. The people's pusillanimity preserves them and their natural egoism eventually enables them to prosper, but this 'Daoist' solution is only possible due to the martial Hao. The prosperity of Wei was inhibited by its system of land tenure, which a Daoist morality could not by itself alter.]

## Thought and action

Me-ti said: Thought is something that follows from difficulties and precedes action.

[Where passages in *Me-ti*, like this, have no title, editors have suggested one. Mo Di frequently asks if a particular proposal is practicable. Many passages support what Me-ti here declares. Chinese philosophy was preoccupied by the problem of the connection between thought and action, best expressed by Wang Yangming: 'Knowledge is the beginning of action, and action the completion of knowledge.' This text and the following appear on the same typescript (BBA 133/39).]

## Ro asked: Will you talk about books?

Ro asked: Will you talk about books? Is philosophy the result of thought to be found in books?

Me-ti answered: No, let's leave philosophy aside and talk about philosophizing. That's something you see people doing. And let's start with ordinary people. They say: so and so is a philosopher, he died like a philosopher, he speaks to his wife like a philosopher, he behaves to the state like a philosopher.

Ro said: People sometimes say: this and that person is as batty as a philosopher, doesn't speak clearly, ponders on abstruse things, is incompetent.

Me-ti asked: Do people speak about them respectfully? Ro said: No, with contempt.

Me-ti said: So let's also speak about them without respect. Let's return to the first kind who are talked about with admiration. They differ from the others because their philosophy enables action, useful activity.

[One passage Brecht marked in his copy of Forke's translation of Mo Di reads: 'Master Me-tse said: Words that can lead to actions may be continuously spoken, but if they are not followed by actions, there is no point in talking about it.' (Forke, 554)]

## Bad habits

Going to places that can't be reached that way is a habit you must give up. Talking about matters that can't be decided by talking is a habit you must give up. Thinking about problems that can't be solved by thinking is a habit you must give up, said Me-ti.

## Against constructing world images

Me-ti said: Judgements reached on the basis of experiences are not usually connected as are the events that led to the experiences. The combination of judgements does not amount to an exact image of the events that gave rise to them. If too many judgements are connected with each other, it's often very difficult to reconstruct the events. It takes the whole world to come up with an image but the image does not include the whole world. It is better to connect judgements with experiences than with other judgements, if the point of the judgements is to control things. Me-ti was against constructing too complete images of the world.

[The German title, *Kein Weltbild machen*, literally means 'Don't make a world picture'. A world picture or image infers a coherent or systematic understanding or model of the world. Deriving from Hegel's term, *Weltanschauung*, or way of viewing the world, it connotes a body of linguistically and culturally acquired perceptions, or a mode of apprehension. In this passage, Me-ti implies an anti-teleological position, closer to a pragmatics, contrasting with, and certainly avoiding, prevalent determinisms, dialectical or otherwise. This attention to experience, instead of reaching 'judgements' on the basis of what ought to be rather than what actually is, of what too easily become pre-established theoretical constructs, which then seek to order the world in their own image, also reflects an ingrained Chinese proclivity for induction – as, for example, Deng Xiaopeng's 'seek truth from facts' – with which Brecht/Me-ti sympathized.]

## On thought

Me-ti taught: Thought is a relationship of one person to another. It is much less occupied with the rest of nature, since a person always reaches it in a detour through another person. Hence, all thoughts must seek out the people they go to and come from, only then do we understand their efficacy.

[Suggesting Lenin's 'who whom?' as well as Nietzsche's 'Cui bono?']

## On the realm of thought

Certain thoughts of an organizing character, thoughts that create order between thoughts, can be usefully compared with bureaucrats in terms of their behaviour. Originally employed as servants of the public, they soon become their masters. Their job is to enable production but they devour it. Making use of certain contradictions between thoughts they elevate themselves into masters; in the process they stick with the powerful, not with the useful.

You can compare the realm of thought with the usual realms, said Me-ti contemptuously. It employs the worst kind of suppression. There is no other kind of order except suppression. Certain groups attain power and subject all the rest. Achievement is not decisive, only origin and connections. The useful are forced to serve the powerful. Those who have once seized power suppress all who strive for it. Certain accumulations of rebellious thoughts are mercilessly thwarted. You really can say that the realm of thought is exactly like the realm in which it arises.

A huge group of thoughts exist only by virtue of the services they deliver to others; only in this regard have they any purpose. The system of examinations is totally corrupt. Connections are decisive.

Particular thoughts are only employed for the sole purpose of declaring this realm eternal. They prove day and night that it is a part of nature and unalterable. Occasionally these thoughts, after turning grey and putting on weight in service, are replaced by others, younger and more efficient. They then support the old with new words.

[Habermas describes knowledge as a function of interest, and Foucault deplored its control in the academy. Here thought is seen as subject to social control exercised by an administration to protect a governing elite. That 'there is no other kind of order except suppression', an observation that haunts history, eventually prompted Brecht to say his term in *Me-ti* for socialism, *Great Order*, should be changed to the differently aligned *Great Production*.]

## In the vicinity of large crowds

In the vicinity of large crowds individual thinking changes. The politician Si-jeh noticed that he spoke quite differently in front of listeners when they were gathered in large numbers than he had planned to do at home. The philosopher Min considered this a physical process. He pointed to the nervousness speakers feel before speaking. That's why the accused in court usually has a certain difficulty keeping himself free from the thoughts of his judges. If he doesn't succeed, it's as if he were to sit down among them, only because they are so many (seem to represent many).

[The 'Chimese' names here have not been connected with any individuals. The text (BBA 136/29 in Steffin's copy and, in Brecht's typescript, 132/70 and 134/32) appears under a capitalized general heading: ME-TI: BUCH VOM FLUSS DER DINGE (Me-ti: Book of the flow of things). Johnson, Völker and Mittenzwei all take it as the title for this text (while BFA 18/58 does not). Titles in Steffin's typescript (folder 136) are not otherwise capitalized. All four editions include the sentence separated by a gap beneath this text: 'The danger usually lasts longer than the flight.' I do not believe this sentence is connected with the text above it. Nor do I think that text is related to the capitalized heading on the typescript. This heading is, nevertheless, interesting in that it shows Brecht evidently thought of *Me-ti* in terms of 'the flow of things' and that as a possible title for this work.]

## The basis of thoughts

Ro said: Thoughts speak for themselves. Me-ti replied: Every evening a configuration appears down the waterway where I live with two lights – a high up, golden one and a lower one that is red. What sort of things can I think about this configuration, which I see, if I don't know that it's formed by a ferry, how much and how little can I think about it?

## The treatment of systems

Philosophers usually get very angry if you take their sentences out of context. Me-ti recommended this. He said: Sentences within systems are connected to each other like members of criminal gangs. It is easier to overcome them individually. So you have to separate them. You have to confront them individually with reality, in order to recognize them. Perhaps they've only been seen all together at one crime, but each of them at different ones. Another illustration: the sentence 'the rain falls upwards from below' applies to many sentences (for example, to the sentence 'the fruit comes from the blossom'), but not to the rain.

[One of many passages that question the effect of language on constructing what passes for reality, part of the difference between theory and practice, a significant theme in *Me-ti.*]

## On reading books

I see many people reading books, said Me-ti, a difficult art that nobody has taught them. Their previous knowledge isn't sufficient to spot either the weaknesses or the strengths of books. I don't want to talk about science books that are almost always written in such a way that you need knowledge in order to know more.

But stories are also difficult to read. The author, mostly in no time, gets the reader more interested in the world of his book than his book is interested in the world. He makes the reader forget the world by means of the book that should be describing it. With a few easily learnt but not so easily discernible tricks a tension is created that makes the reader forget what is happening by arousing curiosity about what happens next. In order to experience further lies, the reader swallows those already encountered.

An author who writes in such a way that the reader is able to lay the book aside now and again in order to think about what has been read and to compare the author's thought with their own, is considered lightweight. It is said that such authors can't do what they want with their readers.

According to the conventional aesthetic, the author's thoughts must be concealed, as difficult as possible to deduce. Besides, readers are supposed to ask: to what extent has the writer achieved his intentions? The question to ask is not whether it was right to murder, but whether it was well murdered.

In reality books must be read as the depositions of suspects, which is what they are. How else except with maximum distrust should we tolerate stories about people, who either participate in driving large numbers of helpless people into bloody wars or are themselves helplessly driven into them?

Who let the corn rot and the people die of hunger? Those who kick or who let themselves be kicked?

[Brecht disliked any (artistic) practice without space to question its (aesthetic) intentions. In such a world you either manipulate or are manipulated. To provoke such questions was, of course, the purpose of the so-called *Verfremdung* or estrangement effect.]

## On different kinds of philosophizing

Staying in balance, to adjust without losing yourself: that can be one aim of philosophizing. Just as water stays still to mirror perfectly the sky, clouds and overhanging branches, also moving flocks of birds; as a top that keeps spinning, so it can glide evenly, blending beautifully its colours – that way a person can find how to mirror the world, show themselves to it and get along with it. How well is the cloud reflected in the water? When is it clearest? Where does the branch come from, whose origin is not reflected? What difference does the wind make above and the mud below the water? These are questions that then arise. Where does the top find space, when most of all? Which speed is best? How are the other tops spinning? These are philosophical questions.

Sounding out philosophies – that can be philosophizing. What people were thinking (or allowed to be thought) when they built towns, introduced guilds, established workshops, manned ships, cultivated rice, sold rice, fought wars inside and outside the walls: you don't hear about the towns from them, nor about the guilds, workshops, ships, and yet when thinking this way towns could be built, ships manned, or when building towns and manning ships, you could think like this. That ships and towns don't appear in their thoughts shows that thinking easily detaches itself. That is a characteristic of thought.

[Brecht's central metaphor, the path of flowing water, traces the topography of his imagination, from the early poetry's indifferent natural process, to the utopian image, directly quoted from the Daodejing, of soft water wearing away hard stones in his 1938 poem on Laotse's journey into exile. The comparable image in Heraclitus had no social implications. Here its contemplative opposite, still water, mirror of the emptied, self-reflecting mind, also originates in Chinese writing. Brecht found it in Richard Wilhelm's translation of Chuang Tse (Zhuangzi), where it expresses the quietism with which Daoism was often exclusively, and mistakenly, equated, entailing withdrawal from the troubled world into the self: 'Man does not view his reflection in flowing water, but in still water. Only stillness can still all stillness' (Dschuang Dsi, 38). In the first decades of the twentieth century, some Westerners found here an alternative to their own unpeaceful world. Brecht acknowledges the psychological reality of the contemplative life and questions its use. Mo Di responded to the favoured image of still water by saying: 'The superior man does not mirror himself in water but in people. Water only shows the face – people reflect happiness and misfortune (Forke, 277).]

## On tranquillity

Me-ti said: Passionate people find no peace of mind in tranquillity, only in liveliness. Circumspection is not much use to them. For them, rapid, vigorous decisions are often the most sober and practical of all. If they can't travel in a car, they must at least pull it, otherwise it will drag them along.

## Calm

Me-ti said: Many think that a calm attitude is best of all. That's a mistake. Calm nerves are not always good for thinking. Under some conditions, confusion is good. In any event, you must be able to act when confused. There is such a thing as making good use of your own confused nerves.

## On the flow of things

And I saw that nothing was completely dead, not even the deceased. The dead stones breathe. They change and are the cause of changes. Even the moon, said to be dead, moves. It casts light, although extraneous, on the earth and determines the trajectory of falling bodies and causes the sea water to ebb and flow. And if it only were to frighten one person, who sees it, and even if only one person were to see it, it would still not be dead, but alive. Yet, I saw, it is in a certain way dead; if, namely, you accounted for everything in which it lives, it is too little or is not relevant, and so it has on the whole to be called dead. For if we did not do that, if we did not call it dead, we would lose a designation, the very word dead and the possibility to name something we really can see. But since, as we also saw, it is not dead, we must simply think both things of it and treat it like something that is both dead and not dead, though actually more dead, in a certain sense deceased, in this sense absolutely and irretrievably deceased, but not in every sense.

[This intriguing passage seems to echo thoughts, and problems, formulated by the Daoist Chuang Tse (Zhuangzi), which grapple with a topic central to Chinese thought in ways that, while also present, were less determining in contemporary Greek philosophy. Here it is the nature of change and the relationship between life and death as a continuous, unbroken material process. The totality of that which is, the Dao, is in permanent flux. Since there is no individual soul, no personal survival, no immortality, peace of mind can only be obtained through understanding our place in the totality of nature. Joseph Needham has shown the parallels between this Daoist acceptance of cyclical change, the ultimate flux of things, and the position of the Epicurean Lucretius, the Latin poet whom Brecht so admired (BFA 15/120) and sought to emulate, who looked to mitigate the fear of death and the power of the gods by observing the cycle of life in nature: 'All things depart; / For nature changes all, and forces all / To transmutation; lo, this moulders down, / Aslack with weary eld, and that, again / Prospers with glory, issuing from contempt.' (*De Rerum Natura* [London: Dent, 1916), verses 830f., Needham, 75]. The passage also touches, from its perspective, on a critical topic in Brecht's *Me-ti* and elsewhere in his writings: how fetishized concepts misrepresent the nature of the continually changing natural and human universe, a phenomenon Engels sought to conceptualize as the dialectics of nature, as nineteenth-century science re-described our understanding of reality.]

## Humanity's emergence out of the primeval slime

Gi asked Me-ti if he believed that humanity had developed out of the primeval slime. Me-ti replied, the thought, if supported by science, had nothing unpleasant for him.

Gi said, a little disappointed: I welcome the thought enthusiastically, because it jeopardizes the idea of a personal creator. Does it really, asked Me-ti in astonishment? Have you established that it does this? Is really nobody, among those interested, preoccupied with the creation of the primeval slime?

At least the chances are somewhat reduced, Gi countered in irritation. But doesn't the future of humanity, given this thought, develop undreamt of possibilities. Ah, said Me-ti, understanding, unlike those who wish to place God at the beginning of everything, you lot place God at the end! I'm not wild about this, to be honest, Gods without humans for torturing and making sacrifice aren't up to much. And as for bringing about the changes that would make life on this planet fit for human beings, humans would certainly be enough.

[Unlike those who believed that humans and animals emerged perfectly formed from the earth, the pre-Socratic Greek philosopher Anaximander argued that they were created in a primeval slime caused by the effect of the sun on moisture, an early version of the dispute between evolutionists and creationism. Me-ti uses this dispute about origins to question the uses of teleology.]

## On the fear of death

Me-ti said: Generally speaking, I find that in our times people fear an insufficient life too little and death too much. The reason they fear death so much stems from their constant attempt to hold on to what they have, because otherwise it will be snatched away from them. Only with great difficulty can they free themselves from wrong ideas. What's awful when something is snatched away from you is that, deprived of what's been taken, you are still there. If your life is taken, you are no longer there. It would certainly be awful to be deprived of life; but you are not there, if you're not alive any more.

[Versions of this reflection occur in two poems, 'Song against a bad life' in 1930 ('Don't fear death so much! Fear more a bad life.' BFA 14/106) and in 'Resolution', written in 1934 and also known as 'In Consideration', referring to a formula used by the 1870 Paris communards, and set to stirring music by Eisler in 1935, with the refrain 'We shall fear death less / Than we fear living wretchedly (BFA 12/27).]

## Bad times

Me-ti read the following story: A revolutionary undertook a task that was bound to lead to his death. When he went off, he couldn't stand upright. Are you afraid? asked his companion. He answered: Yes, I am afraid.

But why don't you turn back, if you're afraid? He said: My fear is my own weakness, but my death is a public matter.

Me-ti said: These are bad times when a person can't give in to his fear. But let's hope many go for the sake of a community in which whoever takes care of themselves also takes care of the community.

## The dangers of the idea of the flow of things

The proponents of development often have too low an opinion of what currently exists. The thought that it will disappear makes it unimportant to them. They consider all periods as phases and imagine they last for a shorter time. Because they see them in movement, they forget that they exist. They know that the house painter rules, but since they say 'he's *still* ruling', his rule seems to them less awful, already doomed to die. The temporary seems to them less awful, since it is only temporary, but even what is temporary can be deadly. And what disappears on its own unless it is forced to disappear?

[Brecht called Hitler the house painter ('der Anstreicher') because, unlike the artist he once wished to be, he was only redecorating the old house instead of building a new one.]

## On egoism

Yang Chu taught: If people say: egoism is bad, they are thinking of the condition of a state in which it has bad effects. For me, the condition of such a state is bad.

If merchants sell inferior goods and can charge high prices; if the have-nots can be forced to work hard for little pay; if inventions can be withheld from people for the sake of profit; if family members can be kept in a state of dependency; if you can get what you want through violence; if fraud is useful; if craftiness is advantageous; if justice is detrimental – then people are egoistic. If you want to do away with egoism, then just don't talk about it, but create the conditions that make it unnecessary.

Criticizing egoism often means wanting to preserve the conditions that make egoism possible or even necessary. (If there are too many people and too little to eat, then either they all die of hunger or some stay alive by behaving egoistically.)

There's nothing wrong with self love if it's not at the expense of others. But you can certainly object to the lack of self love. Bad conditions result both from self love on the part of some as well as the lack of self love on the part of others. Whoever doesn't love themselves enough; whoever doesn't obtain the means to make themselves lovable; whichever woman doesn't obtain the soap to wash herself; whichever man doesn't obtain the knowledge to educate himself; whoever doesn't fight for the care he needs to stop being treated like a leper, infects the community with his misery.

Whoever is content with living in a damp hole, with having their back bent early in life through drudgery, is content with knowing little, makes the community look barbaric just like whoever ordered them to live in a damp hole, or bends their backs, and prevents them educating themselves.

If you want to have self-love that isn't opposed to others, you must look for the conditions that create the right kind of self-love.

[Yang Chu is not another invented but the authentic name of a philosopher whose praise of egoism, naturally disparaged by the Confucians for its potential to disrupt hierarchical social order and the necessary inculcation of 'proper' virtues, is strongly aligned with the Daoist concern for self-preservation as a more reliable guide in life. Such views are also expressed by Mo Di, not only in the chapters on 'Unifying Love', which wonder if it could be actually practised, but also in single observations. Brecht noticed this, marking in Forke's translation the tersely, and memorably, formulated opinion 'Generosity does not exclude the self' (Forke, 510). The account of Yang Chu's teachings is contained in chapter seven of the Daoist work, *Lieh Tse*, which Brecht possessed in Wilhelm's translation: *Liä Dsi. Die Lehren der Philosophen Liä Yu Kou und Yang Dschu* (Jena: Eugen Dietrichs Verlag, 1911).]

## On egoism

How should egoism be resisted? A state must be organized so that there's no difference between what serves an individual and what serves everybody. In badly organized states like Hu-ih's egoism is terrible. In well-organized states egoism serves everybody.

[Hu-ih stands for Hitler. Most of *Me-ti* was written in 1934–5, and much of it is energized by the political struggle in Central Europe between Hitler's Fascism and Stalin's Communism, whose final outcome was then uncertain. In any conflict between 'Hitler' and 'Stalin', Brecht unequivocally supported the Soviet Union. Brecht hoped, and initially believed, that the Soviet Union would eventually overcome its huge and unprecedented organizational problems and serve all its people equally. For a while the Soviet Union, due to the massive industrialization, appeared to offer a better alternative for growth and prosperity than Western Europe, when still affected by the Depression.]

## Order and disorder

Me-ti said: Hu-ih's saying, *Help the Community before Yourself*, sounds like a recipe for order. But it betokens the greatest disorder. A state in which whatever helps the state does not help the individual, and whatever helps the individual does not help the state, is no help to anybody. Hu-ih thinks he embodies the state. Hence his saying simply means: whatever helps Hu-ih precedes what helps every single citizen.

## Mental exercises

To those who think the house painter is personally an honourable man with the best intentions and only his patrons and subordinates are rogues.

Many who see him decorating are greatly moved by the trouble he takes to paint over all the rifts and cracks in the old, collapsing and infested ramshackle building. Isn't he dripping with sweat, does he take a moment's rest? Does he cheat when buying the whitewash? Is the whitewash poor quality? Does he just say everything will look great again after it's painted, and does he not believe it?

But he doesn't touch alcohol, he lives in a farmhouse, he doesn't waste time with women.

Now, there are people who do stupid things when drunk; unfortunately there are also people who do them when they're completely sober. It's not only after downing ten glasses of beer that crazy things are done – that can also happen after a glass of water. So it's possible when living in a simple farmhouse to ruin the economy of a great people; sitting on a cheap wooden bench you can approve the plans for a temple you are building and still add a few kilometres of walls around it. You can lose a lot of time with women, but if a man who's planning to attack me oversleeps the chance of meeting me because of a woman, is that so terrible? When the concentration camp guards are lying with women, the inmates are not beaten up.

It would be much better if the house painter drank, and announced when totally drunk, and as far as I'm concerned slurring his words, that the factories should belong to those who work there and the East Prussian countryside to those who plough it. As far as I care, he could sit in a palace, if he was preparing peace there and not for war.

Others find much of what he does bad, but not everything. That the workers should not have the same rights as the governing classes, is perhaps not good; but that Germany should have the same rights as other people, is that so bad?

That being freed from external enemies in this way means enslaving your own people, that one thing can only be achieved through the other, that the house painter, in order to conquer the French, must first conquer the Germans, and that the defeat of these Germans was completely sealed for a long time by the defeat of the French, is not seen by those, who …

[This uncompleted text, dated 1936/37, in one of the *Me-ti* folders (BBA 134/01,02) is included in the three other editions, though without the last two paragraphs and marked as fragmentary. The BFA edition places it, as not belonging to *Me-ti,* in BFA 22, 183f., even though its topic, attitudes towards the house painter, Hitler, is discussed elsewhere in *Me-ti*.]

## The house painter's slogans

When the house painter proclaimed *Help the Community before Yourself*, many people thought a new age had dawned. You could also say: Above all most people thought a new age had dawned, because they interpreted the slogan as meaning the common good referred to the good of the many, and it would now precede that of the few. That's why this slogan made a terrific impression.

Most expected the house painter would not find it that easy to persuade people to accept it. But it soon became apparent this was not so difficult for him. He didn't ask the few well-to-do, specially or individually, to help the many before themselves; on the contrary, he asked the many – each one of them – to help the community before themselves. The worker was to forego adequate wages and build roads for the common good. The small farmer was to forego good prices for his animals and deliver them to the public on the cheap, and so on. As a result, the slogan began to seem a little less terrific.

It turned out that the nation was in such a state that what really helped could only be obtained from somebody if he harmed someone else, and such help was greater, the more he harmed others. The larger the factories, the more earnings they provided. All of this remained; the terrific slogan changed none of it. What the many needed was not this terrific slogan, but such a transformation of property relations that would have made it impossible for one person to help themselves at the expense of others.

This would have happened if the house painter had taken away all the businesses and factories and rental properties and fields that helped individuals and given them to the many. In a country that does such a thing, helping one person no longer opposes helping others. Then, the more you help one person, the greater the help for others.

But in the house painter's country, it both is and remains the other way round, in spite of all the warnings and terrific slogans.

## When do vices acquire notoriety?

It can happen that real vices acquire notoriety in a country. Brutality, fanaticism, unreasonable impositions, extortion, belligerent attitudes, national egoism, a lack of critical spirit and so forth achieve a certain popularity even among ordinary people. They sigh but admit that these vices are necessary. If you ask 'why are they necessary?' you discover that a number of vices were practised for too long, for example, the laziness of superiors, the egoism of superiors, the stupidity of superiors and so forth. Without doubt, something special is then needed in so discontented a country. But it would be better to put a stop to the old vices – as well as the conditions that enabled them – than putting the new vices to work.

## Committing injustice and tolerating injustice

Me-ti said: More important than stressing how wrong it is to commit injustice is to stress how wrong it is to tolerate injustice. Only a few have the opportunity to commit injustice, many have the opportunity to tolerate it. Pity for others that isn't pity for yourself must be thought less reliable than pity for yourself that is also pity for others.

## The decisive point

The student Rho said: That poor and rich exist is an injustice. Me-ti added: of the rich. The student Rho said: Love of justice is greater among the poor. Me-ti said: I'm not sure of that. But the poor depend on justice, the rich depend on injustice, that's the decisive point.

[This and the following text appear on the same typescript page (BBA 134/08).]

## On a poor attitude

The poet Kin-jeh was chased out of his native land because he was accused of having a poor attitude. He himself said he was accused of having the attitude of the poor. That was the best one.

## How do we learn?

Seeing the dismay at our actions in the eyes of those we esteem, we also learn.

## On leadership

Breaking off discussions when the situation is urgent, looking for obedience instead of enthusiasm, confusing urgency with haste, stealing responsibility: that is a mark of bad leadership.

## Undependability

An ounce of understanding, said Me-ti, and a person will be as undependable as drifting sand. Two ounces of understanding and they will be as dependable as a rock.

## No country should need to be specially moral

If a campaign is badly planned, its aim too great for the available armies, its execution inadequate, then the soldiers need to be specially brave. By virtue of their special bravery the soldiers are expected to achieve what the stupidity of the generals could not.

It's also the same with morality. Bread and milk are dear and work is not well paid or not available. The poor are then expected to be specially moral and not steal. Under such conditions we hear that the better off are all for morality and don't steal and even pursue their own kind, who obviously have stolen. Aren't they therefore in favour of morality, if they do pursue those who have stolen? We shouldn't say they're in favour of morality, because every situation has its special moral precepts, which must above all be respected and may supplant all otherwise valid precepts that would stand in their way. And in a situation such as we have described only he can say he's for morality who ensures that there's no need to be specially moral – since food is affordable.

As a general rule, every country that needs to be specially moral is badly administered.

[This argument extends the critique of virtues trenchantly expressed in Lao Tse and Chuang Tse and that surfaces in many of Brecht's writings in the 1930s, in the *Conversations of Refugees* and in these examples from *Mother Courage*: 'if there are such great virtues anywhere, that proves something has gone wrong' and 'A good country has no need of virtues, everyone can be just ordinary, not specially clever and cowardly, as far as I care.' Oscar Wilde, who shared Brecht's delight in 'paradox', was also impressed by Chuang Tse, and states in *The Soul of Man under Socialism* that, given prevalent conditions, moral teaching was an insult: 'Sometimes the poor are praised for being thrifty. But to recommend thrift to the poor is both grotesque and insulting. It is like advising a man who is starving to eat less.']

## On countries which produce particular virtues

Me-ti said: Lots of people praise certain countries because they produce particular virtues like bravery, self-sacrifice, love of justice and so forth. I myself mistrust such countries. If I hear that a ship needs heroes as sailors, I ask whether it's ramshackle and old. If every man must do the work of two men, the shipping line is either bankrupt or wants to get rich too quickly. If the captain has to be a genius, his instruments are probably unreliable.

## Kin-jeh's Song of the abstemious Chancellor

I have heard the Chancellor does not drink
He eats no meat and he does not smoke
And he lives in a small apartment.
But I have also heard the poor
Are hungry and prostrated in misery.
How much better would be a state of which you could say:
The Chancellor sits drunk in the cabinet
Watching their pipe smoke rising, the unlearned
Change the laws
Nobody is poor.

## The farmer and his ox

Hu-ih demands, said Me-ti, that the people should be heroic. The weaker the farmer's brain, the stronger must be the muscles of his ox.

## Conditions which necessitate particular virtues

Should we also go on strike when special virtues are demanded, asked Me-ti's students when he spoke against countries that demanded special virtues? People in general, he replied quickly, can't refuse to practise special virtues. They will have to practise them as long as those in power can use it, and they will have to practise them in order to overthrow those in power. Love of freedom, a sense of justice, bravery, incorruptibility, sacrifice, discipline, all of that is necessary so to transform a country that special virtues are no longer necessary in order to live in it. You can say that it's precisely the miserable conditions that require such a special effort.

## Goodness

Some people appear kind-hearted as a result of helping others without thereby advancing their own interests, so without a reason, out of sheer goodness. It's relatively easy for someone to earn this reputation for goodness if their interests are unclear (more subtle) or are unclearly, carelessly asserted. If, for example, someone gives someone else money and only wants flattery in return, they can earn a reputation for goodness, since you usually part with flattery more easily than money. In social structures with great variations in income it is not difficult to earn a reputation for goodness. After looking more closely, from a social point of view this sort of goodness seems meaningless, after looking very closely, it rather seems on the whole to be harmful.

This sort of goodness also seems to include taking lightly harm done to you, a certain readiness to praise the motives that caused the other person to harm you. So good a person says something like this: What I myself would do to somebody, I also allow somebody to do to me. In the process you can earn a reputation for particular goodness, if someone gives the impression of allowing themselves to be harmed worse than they, for their part, would be prepared to harm someone else.

Thus a reputation for goodness is earned both by whoever gives a hungry person a piece of bread as well as by whoever excuses a burglary. Looking more closely, it's a meaningless, and, very closely, a harmful reputation.

Like practising this sort of goodness, the extension of such goodness among others is not that significant. Forgiving people for being barbarians, putting them off being barbarians, is also not significant and even harmful. Certain circumstances of a social nature, for example, make wars necessary. In these times many earn a reputation for goodness by preaching against wars.

## Defence of honour

Me-ti said: I hear that Ki-kau is defending his honour. He doesn't seem to have any. He seems namely to have no friends. They alone could defend his honour, which only exists with them, not with him. Honour is reputation, my honour is not what I proclaim to you about myself but what you proclaim to me.

[BBA 129/03 contains under this title two further separately spaced short paragraphs, about a reported supposed attempt at infidelity by Shen-te, which Kin-jeh does not want talked about, and another unrelated passage about Mr Keuner.]

## Lovers make images of each other

Me-ti said: For many people the image their friends have of them can't be high enough. Their vanity makes them forget that a lover creates something new. You should associate with people who have a good image of you, then you can become better by trying to justify it. But it's bad to put up with one that isn't justified. For the lover takes revenge if the original image fails, not on the image but on the original.

## On the behaviour of homosexuals

Homosexuals are often accused of deliberately acting in too sweet a manner and of appearing ridiculous to the sober minded when talking with their friends. But do men behave differently to women? We ought either to combat this sweet style and acting as if intoxicated, wherever it happens, or to excuse it, wherever it happens.

## Two kinds of cleverness

To earn your dinner, you need to be clever; that can mean obeying your superiors. Another kind of cleverness may cause you to do away with the system of superiors and inferiors. However, to carry out this undertaking you still need the first kind of cleverness, since you also have to eat your dinner.

[This and the following text appear on the same typescript page (BBA 132/73).]

## Clever, kind, brave

The clever create cleverness, the kind create kindness, the brave create bravery.

## On success

Me-ti said: Only fools are bitter if, when successful, they see the mood changing to their advantage, when unsuccessful to their disadvantage. Success breeds success; failure debilitates. Not only others have seen the sure steps that brought the successful person to the difficult mountain top, he saw them too; not only the others, he too noticed the stumble that resulted in failure. Success makes you look good, generous and confident, at least it gives you face. In failure you lose face. That form of society is best that guarantees most people the greatest success.

## On respect

### *Getting rid of social snobbery*

The petit bourgeois want to get rid of social snobbery. But class distinctions are supposed to remain. The house painter demanded that nobody who owned more, or through his position could cause more harm or be more useful, should demand greater attention from his fellow citizens. Isn't it obvious that such a person, whether or not he demanded it, would in any case receive such attention.

### *The need for respect*

It is good to respect those who are useful to us. And you can be more useful, if you are respected. The room should be quiet when someone is speaking who has wide experience. Whoever assumes that their proposals will be carried out will think about them more carefully.

### *Quotation*

The poet Kin said:

> How can I write immortal works, if I am not famous?
> How can I answer, if I am not asked?
> Why should I waste time on verses if they will be lost?
> I write my proposals in language that will last
> Because I fear it will be long before they are realized.

To achieve great things, there must be great changes.
Small changes are the enemies of great changes.
I have enemies. So I must be famous.

### *Incorruptibility*

To the question, how someone could be taught to be incorruptible, Mr Keuner replied: By filling his stomach. To the question, how someone can be induced to make good proposals, Mr Keuner replied: By ensuring he participates in the benefits of his proposals and cannot achieve these benefits in any other way, that is, on his own.

[Keuner belongs in the *Stories of Mr Keuner* and has strayed into this Me-ti text, a reminder that Brecht never returned to the manuscripts to edit them.]

## Me-ti on canniness

Ken-jeh's son was pretty clever for his age and read a lot. He admired nothing so much as canniness. Being canny soon gave him great pleasure. Me-ti heard tell of his canniness and said:

One of the canniest people I ever met was my school friend Fen. He learnt nothing and still got good marks. He tricked his friends effortlessly playing games and none of them became more than mildly suspicious. There was never any proof. When he had grown up, he hired out his canniness to others for payment. Of course he lost many of his clients again because he was also canny with them, but he always found new ones. He looked for stupid ones and there are great numbers of them. He considered all those stupid who were not on to his canniness, also those who only trusted him or didn't check up on him because they had greater things in mind. A client of his once got angry, because he couldn't find any proof for an obvious deception, and beat his spine crooked. Fen cannily exaggerated the injury, won considerable damages and dodged military service. Thus he stayed at home during the war, profited from the general misery and afterwards even received a decoration, because he suddenly maintained he had been injured in the war. Unfortunately, the revolution then broke out, and since all sorts of valuables were found in his fine house, which were only due to his canniness, he was arrested. Before he could explain that he was only taking care of the valuables and they were not legally his – the exigencies of the time forced him to take refuge in truthfulness – someone he had once outsmarted made use of the temporary condition of lawlessness and shot him to bits. I am, however, certain, that also in his last hour his canniness did not leave him in the lurch: even in the face of death he surely swallowed a valuable ring or something similar.

Thus he owed a lot to his exceptional canniness: that he didn't learn anything, that his friends mistrusted him, that he made money out of those with greater things in mind, that he was able to keep the ring and so on.

## On accountability

Me-ti heard: In our country you can't be held accountable for everything you do. We can't judge a person according to his actions. It can happen that someone must do something bad and we still can't call that person a criminal. We conceal thieves from the police because they often steal out of hunger. Of some who commit crimes you have to say: They don't know any better. We take the view: You can't ask more of someone than they have.

Me-ti said: The person you view with such forbearance doesn't seem to have much. Less than you, or perhaps you and he have less than others? You must be living in a lousy country. What are you doing to improve it?

But after thinking for a while he added: Your course of action seems to me more and more unsatisfactory. You pretend to talk about the destitute. Given such circumstances you would be kind enough to concede them the right to violence if they suffer from want. But perhaps you're also talking about those who are the cause of their misery? You are probably thinking, they don't know any better. You have to let the tigers roam where they will, since they only kill because they can't eat grass. I realize that in your eyes even the judges are guiltless if they would otherwise have to convict those you conceal from them, because they only stole out of need or called for violence to get rid of misery that isn't caused by heaven but by people, since the law demands it, which they have to administer to keep themselves from starving. There are people who live from factories, which are a heap of tools without which others cannot work. These people live by lending their tools at a huge charge so that others can work, but because they live like this at their fathers' behest, they are supposed to be guiltless? And although they are guiltless and cannot be held accountable, the others go hungry on their account. They have a clear conscience and should have a bad one, but you treat them like people who have a clear conscience, because they do good. In short: with such views nothing is solved.

It isn't the tiger's fault that it eats meat, but nor is it mine, said Me-ti.

## Me-ti talks about sharp practices

Me-ti heard: Most of all Me-ti likes talking about sharp practices and you can see how he's amused by gangsters' cunning and strength. Is that okay?

Me-ti defended himself like this: I'm amused by strength and cunning. If you have a country where the cunning and strong can do crooked things, then I must take my pleasure in cunning and strength where they are employed in crooked deeds. It's entirely up to you to make me behave properly without having to sacrifice my pleasure.

## On criminals

Kin-jeh had a certain weakness for the simpler sort of criminals like thieves, murderers, forgers and perpetrators of violence. He said: They do not misbehave with the same justification the masters suggested for misbehaving, but for the same reason: because people are hungry and you can benefit from violence. You can say: They violate self-interest out of self-interest. At least it's the bad laws that they break. That's why people love them. Countless books glorify them. These criminals have no solution for the difficult task, but they demand one. They are on their own yet still only apparently opposed to the general public, that is to everyone else. They are really only opposed to a few who however manage to appear to represent the general public. Far more dangerous are those they pursue and who pursue them, for they act like a horde when they commit their crimes, calling them moral deeds. The minor criminals have lost any belief that people can behave selflessly, and in view of our circumstances, which turn selfless behaviour into acts of self -destruction and use force to compel the mass of people to neglect their own interests, that is really only a realistic assessment. In any event they are much smarter than those who even among their pursuers believe they act out of altruism. Our age has no right to condemn egoistical people as long as it won't create the conditions that turn selflessness into a good deed, that is into one that's good for the selfless. The minor criminals only break the egoists' rules of the game. But these rules are the most detestable of all.

## On inventions

Me-ti said: Much is invented for and much against people. Inventions for people are suppressed, inventions against them are supported. If a lamp is invented that will not burn out for decades, the invention will be bought up by the lamp makers, not in order to produce such lamps, but so that they cannot be produced. If an invention increases the price of fuel, thereby darkening the rooms of the poor, the invention will be bought in order to make it work.

## The country that needs no special virtues

A country in which the people can govern themselves has no need of specially brilliant leadership. A country where oppression is not possible has no need of a special love of freedom. Without experiencing injustice you won't develop a special sense of justice. If war is unnecessary, bravery is too. If the institutions are good, a person doesn't have to be specially good. Of course, given this possibility, a person *can* then be good. A person can be free, just and brave without themselves or others having to suffer for it.

## The occupation with morality

There are few occupations, said Me-ti, which so damage a person's morals than the occupation with morality. I hear it said: You must love the truth, you must keep your promises, you must fight for the good. But the trees don't say: You must be green, you must let the fruit fall vertically to the ground, you must rustle the leaves when the wind passes through them.

[One reason, apart from its expressive clarity, why Brecht found Chinese thinking attractive was its awareness of practical situational necessity. Iring Fetscher once spoke of 'a certain Rousseauism' in Brecht, meaning a residual belief in 'natural' human qualities, which he described as a 'theoretical weakness'. But it is not a question of 'belief', either one way or another. What matters is the context in which such statements are made. Too much administration, whether moral or political, is counterproductive. In *The Soul of Man under Socialism*, Oscar Wilde refers to Zhuangzi (Chuang tse): 'As a wise man once said many centuries before Christ, there is such a thing as leaving mankind alone; there is no such thing as governing mankind.' The Daoists disliked the Confucian proclivity for moral teaching. Invoking virtues was a means of organizing and disciplining populations. Left to themselves, people were more likely to achieve contentment.]

## The virtue of justice

There are states in which justice is too highly praised. We may assume that in such states, it is specially hard to practise justice. Many people are excluded because they are either too poor or too disadvantaged to behave justly, or to understand justice as anything other than help for yourself. The sort of justice demanded for yourself doesn't rate very highly. These oppressed people are seldom praised as friends of justice; they are lacking in selflessness. They don't show it because they are deprived and oppressed. Other people's idea of justice, yet again, awakens mistrust that they're only temporarily satisfied and are now also thinking of the next weeks or years.

Others are worried about the circumstances that guarantee them continuous satisfaction, the outrage of the unjustly treated. Yet again others defend the right of those whom they themselves wish to exploit.

In well-administered countries there's no need for any special justice. There the just person lacks injustice like an afflicted person misses pain. In such countries justice is seen as something inventive, a fruitful activity that adjusts the interests of different people.

An act of justice attracts attention. It is expensive. It costs the perpetrator a lot, or the family.

## On laws

Me-ti said about laws: In earlier times laws were thought to be the fundamental factors in a plan for people's behaviour devised by higher beings. Now they are considered pointers given by human beings to other people, very imperfect guidelines. Their usefulness is determined solely by whether they are useful to the case to which they are applied. They serve no other purpose than to make life together agreeable. Basically, it's the job of those who apply the law to improve the laws by their treatment of specific cases. Society as a whole is no less in need of improvement than the individual.

[This text is perhaps more telling in a culture that uses statutory Roman law rather than case law derived from consulting earlier judgements.]

## On the smallest unit*

Kung pointed to the family. Me-ti said: That may have been the case in the old days. Families defended their property against each other. But who has such property today? The father had all the experience, for only he took decisions. Today he has only got wounds, he only has scars and the younger ones have them too. They are beaten just like the father, but in different places, since they work outside the family house. In former times, the father knew how to find help. Today he has no idea how to.

Me-ti taught about the smallest unit: it exists where there is work or where there is a demand for work. It gathers all experience with the world around it under one roof. It is smarter than all its members. The association does not consist of single people but of the smallest units. If the association decides, the smallest units can split, but then the single parts of the smallest units immediately seek to form new smallest units. A single person is strong as part of the smallest unit.

Kung said: The family doesn't exist by chance. Other groups exist by chance. Me-ti said: That may have been true long ago. Is it not fortuitous today which woman chooses which man in order to have children? If it isn't fortuitous, then that's because there are groups within which men and women can associate. Kung's students said: People work for certain other people, not for all other people. I see people working everywhere for certain other people, but I'm not happy about it. I would like them to work for themselves. The smallest units don't need to put individual earnings into one pot. They are fighting for the chance to earn money and against one pot. Kung says, children should love their parents. But love can't be commanded and why should their parents in particular be loved? The members of the smallest units don't need to love each other; they just need to love the common goal. The families stay put, but the smallest units are full of movement; they facilitate contact, the families facilitate separation.

*Tau ming, indivisible smallest unit, translated into English as cellule, cell. The federations had such Tau ming as their smallest units.

[On the typescript Brecht wrote: 'they can consist of always different people + come together in a myriad of ways' (BBA 133/60). This 'footnote' is part of Brecht's contemplated Chinese disguise. 'Tao Ming', standing here for 'party cell', is mock Chinese, while 'the association', in the main text, signifies the Communist Party. Kung is the Chinese name for the Latinized Confucius. Brecht takes a central argument between the Maoists and the Confucians as a paradigm for contemporary problems. Beside this un-Confucian sentence in Forke's translation, 'One loves the parents of those next to you as your own', Brecht wrote 'against the family'. The Confucian system, which Mo Di roundly criticized, depended on a hierarchical order, where the individual deferred to his superior. The Chinese family was the model for this structure. Mo Di saw that this concept of hierarchical order created unbearable divisions and, ultimately, justified warfare. He, therefore, wished not to abolish the family, an unthinkable proposal, but to subjugate its interests to the whole of society. His doctrine of 'universal or unifying love' was revolutionary and rejected by the Confucians. Where Me-ti argues that the families facilitate separation, Mo Di found that such separation caused great harm to the kingdom. The conditions under which such proposals are made were naturally completely different, but there is a basis for the analogy suggested in this text.]

## On transforming the relations of production

Me-ti said about Su: After the relations of production, that is to say the order through which everything necessary to life is socially produced, had greatly developed those forces that create everything, so that from then on more goods could be produced, this order as is well known was toppled by the workers because it left the workers in misery and no longer further developed all the forces of production. The new order, in which from now on everything necessary to life was socially produced, began to develop further the forces of production. However, you must not imagine this new order as something imposed in just one day, as complete in all its parts, all different from the old order. For a long time and in many ways it depended on the state of the forces of production, a state that was constantly changing. Thus for a long time the wage differentials were very large, and even for a while increased considerably. Society had to pay a lot for particular skills. Learning such skills was open to everyone. However, since this was troublesome and required particular effort, it had to be specially rewarded. The old kind of family too, characterized by many unreasonable ties, was preserved for a long time, and even supported again for a while by all kinds of laws, since wages could not be arbitrarily raised, so that small units were needed that pooled their earnings. For a long while there were also many kinds of social distinctions, among them even new kinds, and they were maintained or encouraged as long as they were able to increase the country's forces of production. Many observers complained forcefully about such phenomena. They had seen that in the old countries the police sustained something like the family. Now they saw that the police could not do away with it. Without knowledge of the *Great Method* they could not work out what to do.

## Condemnation of ethics

Me-ti said: Ka-meh and Mi-en-leh did not establish a moral philosophy.

Me-ti said: To me, moral behaviour can only mean productive behaviour. The relations of production are the source of all morality and immorality.

Freedom, kindness, justice, taste and generosity are questions of production, said Me-ti confidently.

About the famous sentence 'Thou shalt love thy neighbour as thyself' Me-ti once said: If the workers do that, they will never get rid of the conditions under which you can only love your neighbour, if you do not love yourself.

Their bloodsuckers preach continuously to the workers about morality. Due to circumstances the preachers of morality urge them to be immoral. But fighting against their oppressors they sweat morality out of every pore in their body.

Me-ti said: Our morality is determined by what's needed in our struggle against the oppressors and exploiters.

## *On Justice*

Ka-meh proved it wasn't justice that created law, but that whatever regulations, courts and prohibitions existed at any time gave rise to vague and general ideas, as if there were a divine being that had invented something like justice or an innate sense of justice in people. The law must take account of many contradictory social needs, so it is full of contradictions and often appears imperfect. Justice, however, which the law pretends to embody while only being its abstraction, eliminates all contradictions and can do so because it never has to engage with individual human cases. That's why it seems more perfect than the law.

The oppressed and abused are in favour of justice, but for them pressure and abuse shouldn't stop so that justice can rule, rather justice should rule so that pressure and abuse might stop. The oppressed and abused are therefore not just people.

Particular grievances call for particular virtues. If these virtues are not conditional upon overcoming the grievances and flourish for too long after they have been removed, they often become the source of new grievances. That's often been experienced with bravery, tenacity, love of truth and willingness to make sacrifices.

Some people, who have studied the classical writers inexactly, say the workers have a mission on behalf of humanity. That's very damaging nonsense. The workers are the most progressive part of humanity, when they have realized that it's worst for them if they stand still, but they don't owe humanity anything, humanity owes them. Mission means a calling, those with a mission are those who have been called. I can't say, for example: I have a mission to fetch myself a piece of bread. The workers should specially mistrust all those who send them on a mission for something.

The old teachers of morality insisted that only those virtues should count that were practised for their own sake. Ka-meh warns the workers about such virtues and advises them only to practise virtues that are useful to them.

Me-ti said: Hunger is a bad cook.

Me-ti said: The poor are generous spenders. The hungry are good hosts. Those we economize on are not economical.

Me-ti said of a worker whom some called good: Harmlessness is not goodness.

Me-ti said: If the little people are small minded, they are lost. They must be generous to themselves and those like them. That's what their struggle teaches the workers.

Me-ti said: Whoever doesn't enjoy liveliness will have no joy in life.

Me-ti said: Those who demand no other life beside their own, lead a poor life. Little people must take from others, big people give them presents. The workers I met who fight were big people.

Me-ti said: You must fear a bad life more than death. Sometimes you must risk your bad life in order to gain a better one. But you should never seek certain death.

[These eighteen texts are all contained by themselves in this sequence in a separate folder (BBA 130/1–18). The second and sixth relate to Lenin's remark that morality is determined by what serves the interests of the working class. In the tenth text, the 'classical writers' stand for Marx and Engels.]

## Me-ti and ethics

Me-ti said: I haven't found many Thou-shalt-principles I'd like to proclaim. I mean by this principles of a general nature, principles that can be addressed to people in general. But such a principle is: *Thou shalt produce.*

[When not equated with economic productivity, production, perhaps *the* critical value in *Me-ti*, involves self-realization, energized by the self-love that also benefits others, hence entailing social watchfulness and stimulating the interventionary thought, which questions authority.]

## Ka-meh and Fu-en as philosophers

Ma-te asked: Can Ka-meh and Fu-en be considered philosophers?

Me-ti replied: Ka-meh and Fu-en demanded that philosophers should not merely aim to explain the world, but also aim to change it. If you agree with that, you can consider them philosophers.

Ma-te asked: Is the world not already changed by explaining it?

Me-ti replied: No. Most explanations consist of justifications.

[This invokes the celebrated eleventh and last of Marx's Feuerbach theses, as a summation of the others, that philosophers have hitherto only interpreted the world differently. The point now is to change it.]

## Should you confront philosophers as a philosopher?

Me-ti said: Master Ka-meh confronted philosophers differently at different times of his life. At first he approached them as a philosopher and demolished their assertions from their own perspective. Then he treated them as a non-philosopher and merely used them as an example to show what absurdities result if you live in order to philosophize instead of philosophizing in order to live. Finally, he no longer concerned himself with philosophers but only occupied himself with practical research, occasionally swatting away philosophers like tiresome flies.

## On Ka-meh's principle of the dependency of thought

Me-ti taught: Master Ka-meh says that consciousness depends on the various ways people make what they need to live. He denies that people can achieve greater freedom from economic life through their heads than in the economy. At first that sounds depressing. But the simple realization that all great works were nevertheless created in this dependency and that conceding this dependency doesn't make them any less great, settles the matter. By the way, at some time this principle is destined to lose, not its fame but certainly its importance. It was formulated to remind people that the ruling thoughts of the age are the thoughts of the rulers. That ought to limit their value. When there are no longer any rulers and when dependency on the economy is everywhere no longer felt so oppressive by most people, then Ka-meh's principle can no longer depress anyone.

[Marx's observation that consciousness is shaped by being or 'life', rather than the other way round, and that the ruling ideas are the ideas of rulers, formed to stress the material pressure of circumstances and events, refers more to social character and social attitudes and not, of course, to any innate capacity for thought. Brecht relativizes it, since it has not affected literature and will lose its importance.]

## The origin of philosophy

Me-ti said: We must let philosophy escape again. It's imprisoned.

His student Ro asked: By whom? Me-ti replied: By those who take prisoners everywhere.

Ro asked: Why should they be freed? Me-ti replied: Mi-en-leh, who freed the people of Su, asserted he did this with the help of philosophy.

Ro asked: Can we also learn what kind of philosophy that was? Me-ti replied: I told you that they were imprisoned. Prisoners are preoccupied with liberation.

Ro said: Your answers move in a circle, we're not getting anywhere. Me-ti replied: Running in a circle we move ahead. We assert this and that; this and that is passed down to us. We construct lots of sentences about how to choose allies for the struggle. Not all are equally reliable; they don't all have the same interests. We'll find out their interests during the struggle. Perhaps we'll then have to turn against some of them. One step after another.

Ro said: Our opponents know a lot. Me-ti said: It isn't enough to say that about our opponents. That they oppose us tells against their knowledge.

Ro said: People will say our opponents have thought a lot about this and found out a great deal. They are very advanced. How can we counter this? Me-ti replied: They haven't caused us to reconsider, why not? They haven't found out anything for us; if so, what? They have advanced? Away from us perhaps?

Me-ti quoted the poem by the poet Kin:

Interrogation of the good man

Step forward: we hear
You are a good man.

You are not corrupt, but the lightning
Which strikes the house, is also
Not corrupt.
When you've said something, you stick with it.
What did you say?
You are honest, you say what you think.
What do you think?
You are brave.
Facing whom?
You are wise.
On whose behalf?
You don't think of your own advantage.

Whose do you think of?
You are a good friend.
Also of good people?

So listen: we know
You are our enemy. That's why we now want
To stand you against a wall. But considering your services
And good qualities
Against a good wall and shoot you with
Good bullets from good rifles and bury you with
A good shovel in good earth.

[Philosophy is equated with the search for what has been withheld from life's prisoners: liberation. For those who feel imprisoned, it is equated, like Lenin's definition of morality, with what serves the interests of the deprived. Kin stands for Brecht, and the 'shocking' poem forces awareness of the difference between an abstract and a focused moral philosophy.]

## Ken-jeh, the negative one

Many considered Ken-jeh someone who denies and destroys. Even in the association some called him a mere rejectionist. They admitted he rejected evil things and approved of this, but they still regretted a certain one-sidedness in him. According to him, they said, moral means whatever helps the exploited classes do away with social class, but is that all there is to morality? What happens when classes are done away with? Whenever he sees a forest, he moans straightaway about the newspapers printed from its wood that fool the people, or asks around who hasn't got any firewood. At most he complains that the poor don't …

[This story is incomplete. The BFA editors suggest it may refer to Lenin. Ken-jeh, however, elsewhere stands for Brecht. It clearly refers to a Leninist argument. The passage reminds us that Brecht's *Me-ti* voices more than one point of view and is more 'dialectical' than 'determinist'.]

## Dangerous thoughts

When the Chinese philosopher Me-ti came from an audience with a very high official, he reported to his students, the leading personality spoke to him mainly about so-called dangerous thoughts. The gentleman, Me-ti reported, expressed himself imprecisely, if very vigorously, but I wouldn't be surprised if he treated such thoughts as 'Whoever works, has to eat' or 'If you want to build a bridge, you need bridge builders' or 'The rain falls down from above' as dangerous thoughts. You can believe me, I had the impression that it must be very dangerous to be in this gentleman's shoes.

## The end of Ro-pi-jeh

Ro-pi-jeh's opponents became a danger for him when it was too dangerous for them to appear dangerous.

[Ro-pi-jeh is not identified. His problem, however, is a familiar one.]

## Investigating the limits of knowledge

Me-ti was against too intensive an investigation of the limits of knowledge. He said: It is very useful to establish what are felt to be the inhibiting limits of knowledge in various fields in order to extend them. It's good to know how far the eye can see into the large and small and to invent instruments to improve such insight. But philosophers when talking about knowledge go both further and not so far. They are not interested in knowing more or less but in knowing everything or nothing.

Master Eh-fu said that you can certainly speak of possible knowledge of the things you can handle. If you can plant wheat and predict eclipses then it's also permissible to speak of the possibility that nature is knowable. Those who want to know more really want to know less, because they don't want to know what's just been said. They want to reach a decision with words alone without the use of experiments, and this has consequences for behaviour. They really only try to line up a lot of words in such a way that it can be asserted with a kind of inevitability since, namely, the words they use don't change their meaning and obey certain rules of sequence, that everything is knowable or nothing is knowable. Their main interest is that the result is 'nothing' (where 'everything', by the way, would have no special meaning), and when they have so arranged the words that things are left over, which are not knowable, they don't concede these things are of no further interest to people but rather that they have a particular influence on what people do. In all of this they seem extremely doubtful, like people who can't be deceived and are under no illusions, but only with the result that for them there is a God or a spirit in which they can absolutely believe. With all their doubts and scientific character they only refute, bathed in sweat, the objection of the real doubters that there is no divine influence coming from elsewhere because it isn't perceivable. They say: If humans cannot know, how can one ask of the gods that they should be knowable? They maintain that these reflections do not cripple human activities; they demand that people act even if they don't really know, and they point out with contempt that people do indeed continuously so behave. For such activities, in short for all human activity, they say, turning up their noses, knowledge, this half-blind, insufficient knowledge, is completely adequate. They don't say, of course, what it isn't adequate for.

[Eh-fu also stands for Engels, and Me-ti probably here follows his argument with Hegel's claim to establish absolute knowledge, because it is based only on a certain form of words without further evidence. Knowledge does not extend to what we cannot engage and change; beyond that lies the unknown.]

## Fan-tse's parable

The author Fan-tse and a colleague went to a funeral. Overcome with sadness that he could no longer speak with the dead person and disgusted by the gloom of the grave, the colleague indulged in the following reflection: I believe as little as you do, he said, that there are gods. But why shouldn't there somewhere be a spiritual power at work in the universe? I wouldn't find anything absurd in such an assumption.

Fan-tse said straight away not without amusement: Why shouldn't there be in the town Pin Chau, in the fourth house of Vixen Lane, a man by the name of Lu? I wouldn't find anything absurd in such an assumption.

[Fan-tse and An-tse stand for the prolific and socially conscious novelist Anatole France, Nobel Prize for Literature winner in 1921. This other Lu is not connected with the author Emil Ludwig.]

## On death

Me-ti admired the way our friend An-tse had died. As he was dying he had tackled some easy algebra problems. Engaged with their solutions he passed away. 'He had either already finished contemplating death or had at least decided the question was not among the soluble', said Me-ti. And when I asked him if it couldn't be called a shallow way, he replied: 'If you have to cross the river, it's best to find a shallow spot.'

## The helplessness of old people

The helplessness of old people, which needs to be indulged, depends on the fact that they can no longer rely on their power to convince and hence must assert their authority. Their experiences justify their many suggestions but they have often forgotten their experiences. They are no longer strong enough to attract love, so they have to rely on love earned earlier. They can only speak softly therefore you should be silent in their presence. They talk a lot because they lose the thread. They are tyrannical because they are no longer loved. They are impatient because they will soon die. They are mistrustful because they can no longer check anything. They remind you of experiences you had with them before because you cannot have them any longer. It is hard to benefit from what they can give and hard to prevent the harm. They must be treated with particular friendliness.

## About the Great Method

Master Hegel taught: Everything that exists only exists because it also does not exist, that is to say because it comes into being and disappears. Becoming entails being and not being, as does disappearing. Becoming changes into disappearing and disappearing into becoming. The disappearing thing becomes another thing, in the becoming thing another disappears. So there is no tranquillity in things, nor in their observers. Even when speaking, you, the speaker, are changing, and what you speak about is also changing. But if there is also something old in every new thing, we can still speak well enough about new and old things. Those who apply the *Great Method* properly do not speak unclearly but more clearly.

Master Hegel said: Things are occurrences. Conditions are processes. Events are transitions.

[The *Great Method* stands for dialectics as the hypothesized 'law' of change.]

## On humour

Me-ti said: There are people who cannot laugh about serious things. You shouldn't hold it against them, but there's no need to be stopped from laughing at serious things.

You can talk humorously and seriously about serious things and humorously and seriously about humorous things.

Generally speaking, people without a sense of humour find it more difficult to understand the *Great Method*.

[All previous editions include this cheerful piece except the BFA, which argues that on one carbon copy of the typescript Brecht bracketed everything except the last sentence. That seems to go against the spirit of the text (BBA 132/35).]

## The Great Method

Master He-leh's sentence that one is not equal to one, is not only equal to one, not always equal to one, is a starting point of the *Great Method*. He means that you can say this or a similarly constructed sentence for too long, meaning that at a certain time and under certain circumstances you can be right about it but after a while and under changed circumstances you can be wrong. If you investigate this assertion, you must be prepared for fairly complex thought processes but must never forget that what is meant is basically simple.

Thought has difficulty holding onto the concept of a flower bud, since the designated thing is in the throes of so impetuous a transformation, is showing such an urge, while you are busy with thinking, not to be a bud but to be a blossom. For the thinker, therefore, the concept of a bud is already the concept of something trying not to be what it is. And yet these are simple things and there are no difficulties with this designation and its application.

At first many people do not understand the *Great Method*, because of the two parties, observer and observed, they only take one seriously, namely the observed, and ascribe to our thinking an imprecision and superficiality that is lacking in the observed object. But this imprecision and superficiality is not lacking in the observed object and our thinking is not so faulty, if it is superficial and imprecise, rather it is right and for this reason has a chance of commanding nature by obeying it. If we say 'science is science', this sentence is apparently correct because the same word is used twice. But the same word signifies different things and not just at different times. Nowadays the physicists deny that historians have a science, to them only their own methods seem scientific and Master Eh-fu agreed, and still he disputed the scientific character of the physicists, since they understood too little of the new science of history. It is simple and greatly advantageous to think of science as an attempt to discover and prove the unscientific character of scientific claims and methods.

The great revolution in Su demonstrates the advantages that can accrue from repeating for too long sentences like, 'the peasant is a peasant'. Mi-en-leh discovered that in Su, as elsewhere, the figure of 'the peasant' appeared in so many guises, that this figure responded in exactly the opposite way to certain events. He defined this difference, which characterized the different behaviour, as different ownership and derived thereby powerful advantages for the great revolution. But he could only do this because at the same time he also noticed that at first, in spite of the differences he observed, the peasant behaved in a similar way: unlike the workers, who wanted to do away with individual property, the peasants wanted to keep it. The poor peasants wanted to get hold of some. Here and to this extent the sentence 'a peasant is a peasant' was correct. It was correct and had to be the basis for action at the same time that the opposition among the peasants was so great that some peasants couldn't remain peasants, if the others became peasants.

For a good while the workers under the leadership of Mi-en-leh and Ni-en fought for the acceptance of the sentence 'a peasant is a peasant' by declaring the rich peasants and the poor peasants as equal in respect of ownership. And then within the same generation opposition arose in the association of workers that, based on the sentence 'a peasant is a peasant', predicted (or recognized) struggles between peasants and workers, which could only be brought to a halt by the victory of the peasants or the workers, and they demanded for the workers that action be taken for such a struggle. The association got into difficulties over these quarrels, but at this time the sentence 'a peasant is a peasant' began to demonstrate its fragility again, because the peasants changed into workers, such that the sentence 'a peasant is a worker' seemed in many respects more appropriate. The opposition was overtaken by events and was defeated. But those who could no longer recognize the peasant character in the new worker, which arose through the removal of the individual ownership of land, and considered the sentence 'a peasant is a peasant' completely redundant, made great mistakes. So, in a changed form, it still remained correct.

[He-leh stands for Hegel, Ni-en for Stalin and Su for Soviet Union. Brecht returns here to a problem inherent in the nature of language: that it can have the effect of isolating things and arresting or masking processes in the minds of those trying to understand them. This is also a critical topic in Buddhist philosophy and the reason why the Chan or Zen Buddhists distrusted language. Brecht takes an observation of Hegel's from the preface to his *Phenomenology of Spirit* about the transformation of a bud into a blossom and pursues the implications of such natural change, which Hegel of course saw as an organic unity, for political change and social transformation. That, in turn, runs up against the problem of believing, with Engels, but also with Lenin and lesser Marxists, that such change is part of a natural process and hence inevitable or unstoppable, even as Hegel's 'bud disappears into the unfolding blossom, and one could say that it has been contradicted by it' to be followed by the fruit that has the same effect on the blossom. Hegel argues that thought which, in naming it, hangs on to a particular stage of change can never see the whole unfolding process.]

## The Great Method: Philosophy of Nature

Some people contended that the classical writers had established a philosophy of nature. That is not the case. They gave some hints how we might think about this or that, but in the main they were occupied with human nature. Still,

Master Eh-fu has written instructively about nature. He showed the workers, namely, there were also revolutions in nature, so they could understand that revolutions were quite natural. Actually, he finds illustrations everywhere for the workers' struggle and their view of society in the observation of nature. He points out how much easier it is to understand natural appearances if you investigate them in a larger context, how each thing changes in order to continue its existence, and how it continues to play a role for a while, although it changes. He shows that natural associations are comprised of contradictory qualities and tendencies and that it is precisely these that give them life. Thus he teaches them that peace and order, which they are so often enjoined to preserve, arise from division and disorder and are full of potential division and disorder. You can say that when Master Eh-fu explained nature, the oppressors and exploiters had nothing to laugh about.

Master Eh-fu passed on the principles that the citizens had derived for the study of nature and logic from their revolution to the workers for their one.

[When Engels speaks of the dialectics of nature he means, not that there is any established teleology, but that nature proceeds through change and constant interaction. He wished to counteract prevalent, truly metaphysical views of absolute determinations and fixed species, which appeared as shaped by divine intervention, thus he was following the changes that accrued in early nineteenth-century understanding of species development and environmental interactions.]

## The principle of inequality in the Great Method

Me-ti said: There are certainly people who understand He-leh better if you present them with his assertions in a paradoxical form. To others you must carefully present his bold and at the same time circumspect ideas as intending circumspection. The sentence 'one is not equal to one' points to certain difficulties but is in itself tricky. It ought really to be 'one is not only equal to one but is also not equal to one'. It expresses the thought that you can't find one thing that you can induce to be true to itself over a long period of time; nor can you find a concept that proves ready to stick to the point at least for as long as you're speaking if you're saying more than one sentence. The sentence 'wood is wood' can prove useful, but only as long as it is carefully employed. If I order a wooden house I can use it against any builder who delivers a house of stone. I'll then say '*wood* is wood, iron is not wood'. But the wood can be made of wood and be lousy, and the builder can say 'wood is wood'; in other words, lousy wood is also wood, and thus my contract would have been badly formulated.

## The flow of things

Mi-en-leh said: Sentences like 'rain is good' or 'rain is bad' are far too short. If the rain the young corn needs so as not to die of thirst falls too long, then it will drown.

Another example: If you expose a photographic plate too long, it first turns grey, then black. If you expose it even longer, it turns grey again.

Sentences like 'exposing a photographic plate turns it black' are wrong.

['The flow of things' is the original title of this text (BBA 129/27 and 134/09). Unlike the other editions, the BFA prints only the first paragraph. In the 1950s Brecht placed it among some other texts and changed the title to 'Inexact assertions' (BBA 233/17). This and the following text appear on the same typescript page (BBA 133/09).]

## On the turn of events

Mi-en-leh taught: Introducing democracy can lead to dictatorship; introducing dictatorship can lead to democracy.

[The BFA refers here to remarks by Lenin in *State and Revolution* that, following Marx, in the existing class society, democracy was in effect a dictatorship of the bourgeoisie. Replacing this with a dictatorship of the proletariat should then lead to a real democracy in a classless and stateless Communist society.]

## The Great Method

The *Great Method* is a practical science of alliances and dissolving alliances, of making use of changes and of dependence on changes, of bringing about change and changing those who bring it about, of the separation and formation of unities, of contraries' lack of independence without each other, of the reconcilability of mutually exclusive contraries. The *Great Method* enables us to recognize and make use of processes in things. It teaches how to ask questions that make action possible.

## Breaking the rules

The mathematician Ta drew a very irregular figure for his students and set them a test to measure its surface area. They split the figure up into triangles, squares, circles and other figures, whose surfaces were measurable, but nobody could calculate exactly the surface of the irregular figure. Then master Ta took a scissors, cut out the figure, placed it on a pair of scales, weighed it and placed an easily calculable rectangle on the other scale and cut off sections of it until the scales were in balance.

Me-ti called him a dialectician because, unlike his students who only compared one figure with another, he had treated the figure to be calculated as a piece of paper with a weight (and thus solved the test as a real test without bothering about rules).

[This is the most suggestive of three variations of this story, with the best title, as in Johnson's 1965 edition, p. 56. The other titles are 'A good fighter' and 'Finding a new angle' (BBA 136/72), as communicated in BFA 18/54 and 498f. BFA 18/54 prints an early version with a typographical muddle, 'Ni-en-leh', which confuses Stalin (Ni-en) and Lenin (Mi-en-leh), in place of Me-ti in this version.]

## Changing the means

Me-ti recounted: Three people from Su were seen fighting with three people from Ga. After a long battle, two of the people from Su were killed; of the people from Ga one was severely and another lightly wounded. Then the sole survivor from Su fled. Su seemed completely defeated. But then it suddenly seemed that the flight of the man from Su had changed everything. His opponent from Ga pursued him, alone, since his compatriots were wounded. He, alone, was killed by the man from Su. And without delaying the man from Su went back and easily killed both the wounded opponents. He had understood that flight was not only a sign of defeat but can also be a means to victory.

Me-ti added something to this: For this reason too you must call the man from Su a dialectician since he recognized that the enemy, from one particular perspective, was a disunited enemy. All three of them could still fight, but only one could still run. Perhaps it's better to say: The enemy could fight together, but only a third of them could run. Realizing this made it possible to separate them.

[Brecht uses this story of the apparently disadvantaged side winning, a contest recounted by Livy, as the basis for his play *The Horatians and the Curiatians*. How the apparently weaker can overcome a stronger force is a mytheme from Brecht's early writing onwards, drawing on Daoist thought, which is analogous to what Claude Lévi-Strauss described as *pensée sauvage*. This later develops political associations. In his *Theses on the Philosophy of History*, Benjamin described as a weak Messianic power that which can interrupt and 'brush history against the grain', thereby changing the course of events otherwise seen as inevitable. On one typescript Brecht notes: 'the enemy was still unified when fighting but no longer when running. Then it dissolved into three parts' (BBA 133/09). Here the story is imagined as an encounter between the Soviet Union and Germany.]

## On dialectics: When did the Great Method begin?

Me-ti says: When people saw that two classes decided about satisfying all needs, but neither worked to satisfy the needs; that these two classes did not represent the interests of the other classes but that both had opposed interests; that the conditions for the wealth of one was the misery of the other; that what in a certain sense could be called progress in another sense appeared regressive; that the precondition for a unified state was disunity among the classes that constituted it; that large groups of people formed to assert particular interests immediately split up in the face of other interests and began to fight each other; that every day ownership could turn into indebtedness; that everything through which you could not exploit someone was valueless; that predictions about the behaviour of large groups were uncertain, if you did not understand their composition and know about their contradictory interests; that you could not determine anything over long periods of time; that many concepts like military, state, worker, money, force and so on could not be applied when left without further determination of the time and place and the relative social structure; that similar situations were less frequent in which the same action is the right one, as you may have assumed or as was previously the case:

When people saw such and similar things, the *Great Method* came into being.

## The Great Method

At the start of the great war, many in the association expected that at least in a few states the workers would prevent the authorities from conducting warfare. They did not believe that the rulers would be able to convince the working population of the need for war. Two things happened. First of all, it emerged that it was not all that necessary to convince the workers of the need for war in order to conduct it; there were powerful means of bringing them into the war without convincing them. Secondly, great numbers of workers were convinced of the need for war. Within the whole economic system the war was indeed necessary, it was part of this economy, and whoever among the workers doubted that this whole system must or could be done away with, was of course persuadable that war was necessary. When the workers showed little of no inclination to resist the war, many of the association were convinced that nothing could be done. Mi-en-leh fought against this conviction. The nature of production has created a contradiction, he said, between the different sections that sustain it. The argument has ceased. But the nature of production has remained. Therefore, the contradiction must still be present. The people seem very united, the government very strong. But oppression has grown enormously. The strength of the government is the strength with which it oppresses the workers. The ruling economic system that cost the workers so much now receives support that also costs the workers a great deal.

[The approval of the war by the Social Democrats in Germany in 1914 astonished Lenin for whom this was a betrayal of socialism.]

## The Great Method: On concepts

How many experiences do we unify into a single one, if we use the concept *freedom*. The room stinks and is full of smoke, the tyrant commands, the mother begs, the shoe is hurting. Then something always has to be done about it. You must step outside, you must organize an uprising, you must get money, you must take off your shoe. You must do a lot of things when freedom calls! Perhaps you must submit to the stink and smoke if you want to depose the tyrant, but you must perhaps escape from the mother's begging if you want to get rid of the uncomfortable shoe. When dealing with so constructed and general a concept as *freedom*, you must be careful and in a certain sense small-minded.

To hunt something down, you have to kill it. To consume it, you have to heat it up again. If I determine that one equals one, I have determined something – now it equals itself, only equals itself, does nothing else – yet it's now no longer unconstrained in my consciousness. But it's certainly unconstrained in reality, namely occupied, allied, caught up in dangerous undertakings, engaging in compromises, treacherous, exposed, threatened, self-centred and so on. When I go on to consider what characterizes it, I observe a characteristic consisting in the fact that what is characteristic changes, decreasing or increasing until it's unrecognizable.

The *Great Method* is best understood, if you think of it as a theory of mass events. It never considers things on their own; rather, it sees them in a mass of what are both similar or related but also dissimilar things and, besides, it itself dissolves them into masses.

In the *Great Method* rest is only an exception within conflict.

[Like other passages, this warns that concepts, as abstractions, unlike their referents, do not change. The recognition that rest is the exception between conflicts has also been a fundamental belief in Chinese culture, where nothing is absolute or isolate. This is one reason why Brecht hoped for a possible effect from China, due to Mao's stress on a continuing contradiction of interests within Communist society, something denied by Stalin.]

## Catalogue of concepts

### *The people*

Me-ti recommended extreme caution when using the concept 'the people'. He considered it permissible to speak of the people as distinct from other peoples or in the form of the people themselves (in contrast to the government). Usually, however, he suggested the term population, since it does not imply that artificial sense of unification that the word *people* falsely suggests. It is, namely, often used where really only nation is meant or may be meant, which refers to a population with a particular form of government. But the interests of such a nation are not always the interests of the people.

### *Discipline*

You should not speak of *discipline*, Me-ti said, if you could also use the term *obedience*. Every worker knows that a factory cannot produce without discipline among the workers. Because of this he uses the word discipline with respect. But this discipline also contains the concept of mere *obedience* without which the products of the factory could not be taken from the workers. Just in respect of production, referring solely to it, you could achieve a more perfect discipline, that is to say, a more productive discipline as a result of powerful disobedience. In many matters of government the concept of discipline, which can be required for a well-functioning administration, is only required for certain administrative purposes that are completely unproductive, even parasitical: there the administrators are highly undisciplined and compel obedience.

### *Lebensraum*

For his nation Hu-ih demanded space for living, that is to say, districts made available to the nation for exploitation. Me-ti called that space for killing.

[The National Socialist term for people, *Volk*, was ideologically overloaded, implying exclusion (often with extreme prejudice) of whoever was not counted among it. Me-ti's distinction between discipline and obedience will not have suited what he calls parasitical administrations.]

## Catalogue of concepts 2

### *Nature*

By *nature* we mean everything not made by man, and since all of it produces, in order to exist, we also mean the creator of everything not created by man.

Were a spider to use the same concept of *nature*, its net would not be part of nature but a garden chair would. The obsession with *nature* occurs because towns are uninhabitable. But *nature* on its own is equally uninhabitable. The love of country people or sailors for *nature* is first of all love for their place of work or being accustomed to it. Sailors are right to say that they love life at sea, it's a particular activity and a particular society. Me-ti, an urban dweller, said: Nature *itself* leaves me cold, but here and there (and he mentioned one or two landscapes) I love nature.

### *Soil*

Hu-ih constantly used the concept *soil* in a mystical sense. He spoke about *blood* and *soil* and alluded to secret powers that people supposedly drew from it. Me-ti recommended saying property for soil or furnishing the word with such adjectives as fruitful, infertile, arid, humus rich etc. He pointed out that farmers no longer mostly need *soil*, but rather still more or at the same time, fertilizer, machinery and capital.

### *Popular*

Me-ti warned against uncritical use of the concept *popular*. It comes, he said, from on high and has a degree of condescension. This or that is *popular* is supposed to mean that people understand it, it's simple enough for them. And if you use *popular* instead of simply *clear* speech, you often appeal to the laziness of certain sections of the population. Progressive people are engaged in a struggle with long established customs in which suppression and lack of independence become apparent. As far as literature is concerned, certain people often consider the previous epoch's way of speaking to be still *popular*. They think that the people have now probably reached that level of understanding. Better terms would be *easily intelligible* or *easily followed*. The most that can be usefully said is that this or that should be made *popular*.

## The curvature of space

Following Me-ti's wish, Master Yu explained the mathematicians' picture of the world.

Previously, he said, space was seen as a kind of box without walls, as that which contains everything. The newer mathematicians just consider space the extension of matter. So matter is no longer suspended in nothing, but is itself everything. Only matter is something, but apart from it there is nothing, not even empty space. The void of the old metaphysicians is really nothing and in nothing there can be nothing. Space has, therefore, become a space for possible movements that matter can perform, so to say its path. Now, this path is curved, for matter cannot perform straight movements, as we know from experience.

[Master Yu stands for the Swedish author Arnold Ljungdal, who worked in the Stockholm Town Library and explained Einstein's Theory of Relativity to Brecht's son, Stefan. Brecht also turns the definition of curved space as a relation of matter into a joke, since matter is not straightforward.]

## The weight of light

Light too, Master Yu continued, is matter and has weight and can only travel in curved lines. Based on his theories Master Intin predicted that a certain star known to be in a particular place in the sky would be seen in another place during an eclipse of the sun. Namely in the extension of the ray of light it projects on to the earth; it doesn't, however, lie in this extension. It only appears to lie there, if you search for it during an eclipse, because its light ray is in reality attracted and thereby curved by the sun that it must pass. And in fact during the eclipse the astronomers found the star in the predicted place, where it wasn't to be found.

[Meister Intin stands for Einstein. This and the following text appear on the same typescript page (BBA 132/580).]

## Space

Me-ti recommended that space be considered as matter's form of existence.

## Peace and war

We saw that the nation, which lived in peace with other nations, fostered a war between its own classes. But the war against other nations, which was caused by the war between its own classes, brought about a truce among the classes. And yet at the same time it worsened the war of the classes; so the truce collapsed and the war of the classes ended the war between nations.

[This refers to two kinds of war: national and class. The truce in the class war occurred in Germany on 4 August 1914, when the Social Democratic Party with a parliamentary majority voted for war credits – 'We will not desert our Fatherland in its hour of need' – excoriated by Rosa Luxemburg as a betrayal of socialism. One consequence was the later outbreak of revolution in Russia, and subsequently in Germany, thus hastening the end of the war of nations.]

## Asking too little can be asking too much

Me-ti said: For some years the country of Ga had a democracy. It did two things for the people. Externally it pursued a policy of peace and internally it raised the incomes of the working population. But it did not change business practices or how manufacturing took place. The prevailing method of manufacturing did not unleash all the forces but rather reigned them in. Thus no more was produced than before but more was distributed. And war was just as necessary as it had been, but preparations for it were not undertaken. The country went into decline and democracy was chased away.

[Ga for Germany refers to the Weimar Republic and why it failed.]

## Bread and work

The people of Ga had demanded bread and work. For many there was namely no work and so no bread. The demand meant they didn't want bread for nothing but to earn it by working. When Ti-hi came to power, he had proclaimed that he first wanted to give the people work and then sufficient bread, and in fact he instigated large public works as preparations for war. Since there wasn't any proper work, scarcity increased. At that point Ti-hi devised the slogan: Bread or Work.

[This otherwise puzzling slogan implied that work (or preparation for war) was more important than bread (or an easy life).]

## The oppressor Hu-ih

The oppressor Hu-ih was not able to satisfy himself by giving his people high-minded guarantees. His best protection was their crimes. By participating in oppression they exposed themselves to punishment by the oppressed. That ensured Hu-ih of their loyalty best of all.

## The nationalism of the poor

Since Hui-jeh had suppressed many nations, some people thought that their nationalism ought to result in something useful, namely the fall of Hui-jeh.

Me-ti said disapprovingly: If these nations throw off Hui-jeh's yoke in a nationalist manner, they will accept the yoke of their own masters. The nationalism of the great masters serves the great masters. The nationalism of the poor also serves the great masters. Nationalism is no better because it exists in the poor; it just becomes absolutely senseless.

## Appeal to nationalism

As a refugee Me-ti also came to the country of Su. There he met other refugees from Ge-el, supporters of the *Great Order*, and they bored him with their self-accusations that they failed to make use of the inherent nationalism of the Ge-els that Hu-jeh had so cunningly exploited.

Me-ti said indignantly: There was no nationalism in the workers and poor farmers in Ge-el; history hadn't created any in them; this was done by Hu-jeh, if any is to be found there, and it can't go that deep. And how could we have made use of it, even if it was there? For what? By what means? There were 1,000 unsolved problems, but none could be solved on a national level, if we had the *Great Order* in mind. The affairs of the great masters require wars with other nations, ours don't and would even be interrupted by them.

['Great masters' refers to the nationalist rulers of imperial states.]

## The advantage of renaming

When the officers in Ni killed a whole lot of statesmen who opposed a war of conquest, the newspapers called them activists, not culprits. Activists, meaning those who love action. As a result, people didn't judge the deed, rather whether it was better just to talk or also to act.

[Ni stands for Nippon (Japan). Extreme nationalist officers murdered many Japanese politicians in 1936 after a putsch. The Second World War began in Asia when the Japanese army invaded and annexed Manchuria in 1931, setting up a puppet state. The Japanese newspapers and population mostly supported this imperialist move.]

## Hi-jeh's teaching and the young

Hi-jeh has the young in his hands; he says, the young are our future, in twenty or thirty years the people will have absorbed his teaching, a person in despair reported to Mei-ti, who was living in banishment.

What teaching, asked Me-ti? That there are no classes and the existing order is a just one, replied the person in despair.

Me-ti said: In twenty or thirty years these young people will doubtless notice that classes exist, since they'll have to bear the burden for everyone, and will find this unjust. When the young people are no longer young, Hi-jeh won't have them in his hands any more. The young represent a people's future but only after they've grown up.

## What Me-ti did not like

Me-ti did not like celebrating New Year, saying good-bye, giving birthday presents, seeing unhappy people, making plans for the future, enjoying successes, complaining about defeats, savouring brief moments, improvising speeches, talking about nothing in particular and having his attention drawn to natural beauty. He said: It's difficult enough to apprehend the real turning points.

## On drinking

Kin-jeh refused an intoxicating drink he was offered with the following words: We see twice as many chances of surviving the next years as the war preparations of our governments allow us to; we don't see our duties clearly; we follow the path of reason only hesitantly; what the other person earns we confuse with what we are earning; if someone asks us what we want to do for the common good, we mumble incoherently; what's the point of drinking as well, unless you know of drinks that sober you up.

[This and the following text appear on the same typescript (BBA 134/24).]

## Describing cities

Kin-jeh recounted: In the city of Ni Ji I drank. In the city of Ko I talked. In the city of Bi-leh I worked. In the city of Len I wasted my time. In the city of Mo-su I learnt. So now I've given you my description of these cities.

[Presumably Mo-su stands for Moscow and Bi-leh for Berlin. Maybe Len stands for London, and perhaps Ko for Copenhagen, but Ni Ji is up for grabs, and, anyway, Brecht was not a drinker.]

## Me-ti's scepticism

Somebody accused Me-ti of being mistrustful and sceptical. He defended himself like this: Only one thing justifies my saying that I really am a supporter of the *Great Order*: I have doubted it often enough.

## On doubt

Me-ti's student Do took the view you should doubt everything you don't see with your own eyes. He was insulted for taking this negative position and left the house dissatisfied. After a short while he returned and said on the doorstep: I must correct myself. You must also doubt what you have seen with your own eyes.

Asked, what then sets a limit to doubting, Do said: The wish to act.

## How to help yourself

Tu-su complained to Me-ti about emotional disturbances and told of his intention to go on a long journey. Me-ti told him the following story.

Mi-ir didn't feel comfortable with himself. One after another he changed his girlfriend, his profession and his religion. After this, when he felt a great deal more ill, he went on a long journey that took him across the whole world. He came back home from this journey more ill than ever. He lay in bed and waited for the end, when his house caught fire through a bomb slung by soldiers, since there was a civil war, in order to kill a few workers who were hiding behind the house. Mi-ir got up angrily, put out the fire together with the workers, pursued the soldiers and in the following years took part in the civil war, which brought an end to the troublesome state of affairs. If you never heard him say at this time that he felt well emotionally that can only have been because nobody had asked him how he felt.

## On seeing yourself historically

Me-ti found only a few hints about the behaviour of individuals in the classical writings. They mostly spoke about classes or other large groups of people. On the other hand, he found that the historical point of view was praised as very useful. Hence he recommended, after thinking about it carefully, that the individual should consider himself just like the classes and large groups of people in historical terms, and behave historically. Life lived as material for a biography acquires a certain importance and can make history. When the military commander, Ju Seser, wrote his memoirs, he wrote about himself in the third person. Me-ti said: You can also live in the third person.

[The classical writings refer to the works of Marx and Engels. Ju Seser stands for Julius Caesar. This and the following two texts appear on the same typescript page (BBA 132/64).]

## Workers and the working class

Me-ti said: From the classical writings you can learn more easily to make predictions how the working class will behave under such and such circumstances, than how the worker will behave. The *Great Method* is a theory about the movement of masses. The units are treated as particles within masses or as masses themselves by also identifying non uniform processes, mass processes in them.

## Hints for the single person

The classical writers hardly ever give the single worker a hint how to behave, which isn't connected with his behaviour in relation to the working class. They show all the time that he can only have an effect if he acts as a loyal part of the mass.

## Living in the third person

Me-ti recommended his students note down their activities in such a form as if for a biography, prepared for the class for which they intended to fight.

## Me-ti's students no longer recognize their teacher

For his students, Me-ti was the best teacher and the best friend. One day he came to their classroom for an hour, on another for six hours, perhaps only for five minutes, but they always knew he would have something to say to them. He often laughed at the many false sayings, which are called folk wisdom, so also at this one – that a healthy mind only exists in a healthy body. But they recognized his great friendliness in that no student's infirmity was too small for him to enquire about it and offer advice, and no worry too trivial for him quickly to find out its cause.

Thus it came about that his students were appreciated everywhere, because he helped them to reach the highest level of their capabilities. Also when he wasn't among them, they knew they could reach him any time they needed him.

But one morning a strange man arrived in their midst, still like their old teacher's in voice and appearance, but his movements were different and he used different words. When they said that to him, quickly and in a friendly manner, as he had taught them, he turned away in irritation. On that day they didn't see him again.

He still came to their classroom every day, but as if wishing to perform a recognizably necessary but still tiresome task, and they observed that he used every excuse in order to leave quickly.

At first some still believed he had work that completely occupied him. But after weeks had passed in this fashion, Me-ti said: We can no longer talk to each other.

The students were appalled.

Me-ti didn't see this and also didn't see that one of his students wore his arm in a sling, on which a rafter had fallen that morning. He went away again quickly.

He still had them read aloud and discuss his old sayings but if they suggested changing this or that, he called it carping at finished work and declared bad-temperedly he now had nothing more to say to his students.

And they weren't there for him any more. What they were doing didn't interest him and what they had to say he didn't want to hear. Their worries were a matter of indifference to him. But he still ordered them to spend a few hours in the old classroom every day. Only, the teacher no longer came.

Towards the end of the year, the people of Ma requested that Me-ti send them one of his students. He looked for them in the classroom. They were there but they talked about things to which he was indifferent with unfamiliar words. After a few minutes, before he had been able to explain to them his reason for coming, he shouted angrily that he had no use for any of them.

One of them then read aloud the following parable from an old book:

> A delegate from Sun came at harvest time to the Province of Kwan. Beside waving fields of corn he saw a large piece of fallow land which he knew was fertile. He went to the farmer, called him to the door and said: Go and mow your wheat, the ears are bent under the heavy grain and the workers in the town of Sun have no bread.
>
> But the neighbours said: How could there be ripe corn in his fields? He didn't plant them in the spring.

For a short time there was silence. Then the teacher said disparagingly to a stranger with whom he was now mostly to be seen: They have changed.

And the stranger looked at the students a little more disparagingly than he had seen Me-ti do it.

The students still hadn't given up hope. But Me-ti snatched the book out of one of their hands, threw it on the ground and went away quickly.

Some of them began to cry.

But then they all left the classroom and locked it behind them.

## The art of ceasing to teach

Me-ti said: Every teacher must learn how to stop teaching, when the time comes. That is a difficult art. Only a few are able, when the time is right, to allow reality to take their place. Only a few know when they have taught enough. Naturally, it's difficult to watch how the student, whom you've tried to save from making your own mistakes, now makes such mistakes. Difficult as it is, not to get advice, it's just as difficult, not to be allowed to give any.

## Concealing failings

Me-ti said: The worst is not having failings, not even not resisting them is bad. What's bad is concealing them. Not to seem what you are, that's unfortunate for yourself. To seem what you are not is unfortunate for others. How should anyone go into battle at your side, if you haven't shown them your failings? The effort of appearing to be what you are not already exhausts all your energy for the fight. You're afraid, for example, that your friend might reject you, if he knew you're a coward. But what he needs to fear are only the consequences of your cowardice. He can avoid them better than you can – provided he knows about your cowardice. Even someone who tells lies must at least make his best friends aware of it; he's not allowed to lie about that.

[This develops Lenin's confident and self-defensive remark that a clever person is not someone who makes no mistakes, which everyone does, but who is able to correct them 'quickly and easily'.]

## The classical authors and their age

The classical authors lived in the darkest and bloodiest of times. They were the most cheerful and most confident people.

## On oppression

The classical writers did not say: Oppression and exploitation always existed and always will. They also did not say: They have always existed and won't last much longer. What they said was more precise. They said: They existed at one time or another in one form or another for such and such people and for this and that reason. They even considered they weren't always simply superfluous and unproductive. Because they were so precise, they achieved the certainty with which they said: Now they have become dispensable and disposable.

## Many ways of killing

There are many ways of killing. You can stick a knife in someone's stomach, take someone's bread away, not cure someone's illness, put someone in poor accommodation, work someone to death, drive someone to suicide, take someone to war and so on. In our country some of this is forbidden.

## On killing

The classical writers did not establish any rules that prohibited killing. They were the most compassionate of all people but they were confronted by the enemies of humanity who could not be defeated by arguments. All the thoughts of the classical writers were directed towards creating such conditions where killing would be no use to anybody. They fought against the violence that strikes you and against the violence that hinders movement. They did not hesitate to face violence with violence.

[Marx: 'material force must be overthrown by material force.']

## Me-ti and the wickedness of the Chimese under Hu-jeh

Me-ti said: A good cause can be helped by good people, on behalf of wicked people, killing good people, who are serving a wicked cause.

La-eng said to Me-ti: The Chimese are a wicked people, because they either want or tolerate the suppression of the whole world. Me-ti said:

[The second paragraph is incomplete. Brecht sometimes used Chimese for Germans and Chima for Germany, based on the analogy of the Middle Kingdom.]

## On violence

The raging river is called violent
But nobody calls violent
The river bed constricting it.

The storm which bends the birch trees
Is thought to be violent.
But what about the storm
Which bends the backs of the road workers?

## Me-ti on the principle of peaceful fighting

During the great war of the ten states Me-ti pointed to how the non-combatant state of Su influenced the military operations of all the combatant powers almost as much as if it had itself engaged in military operations. It forced the state of Li into awkward, expensive and unsuccessful operations against the enemy state of Ta by extending protection to certain countries and blocking passage through them. The powerful Ma could only engage half of its chariots for fear of an intervention from Su. Ta, for its part, had to do without help from the state of Tur, since Su also kept this state out of the war. The state of Ni could only engage in battle with the state of Chi with a fraction of its forces for fear of Su and slowly bled to death in this war.

[If, for Clausewitz, war was the continuation of politics by other means, Chinese strategic military thinking sought to avoid war by political means. This reads as if Brecht was projecting a Chinese strategic principle, derived from the experiences of the period of Warring States, into the possibility that the 'non-combatant state of Su' (Soviet Union) could still influence the outcome of the unfolding war. Ni may here also stand for Japan and, as a corollary, Chi for China, expressing the hope that Japan might be restrained by fear of intervention from the Soviet Union. That eventually happened, but far too late to help China. The other state names are arbitrary.]

## One of the classical authors' greatest deeds

One of the greatest deeds of the classical authors was that they abandoned the uprising with no sign of discouragement, when they saw the situation had changed. They predicted another upswing for the oppressors and exploiters and adjusted their activity accordingly. And neither their anger against the rulers diminished nor did their efforts to topple them decrease.

## The ideal of a man in an earlier age

To keep your head when all are losing theirs; to trust yourself when all are doubting you; but to allow them their doubt; to be able to wait and not grow tired of waiting; to hear lies about it but not take part in lying; or to be hated without giving cause, and still not look too good and speak too wisely; to be able to dream and not be ruled by dreams; to be able to think and not make thoughts your goal; to meet triumph and disaster and treat both these imposters equally; to be able to hear the truth you have spoken distorted by rogues, who turn it into a trap for the credulous; to see the things broken to which you gave your life, and to bend down and piece them together again with worn-out tools; to make a heap of all your winnings and risk it in a single throw; and lose and start from scratch again and never say a word about your loss …

[Not for the first time, Brecht found something useful in Kipling. What's interesting is also where he stops, without completing this paraphrase of Kipling's poem, 'If'.]

## 'Beautiful as the truth'

Kien-leh sometimes used the image 'beautiful as the truth'. Somebody said to him in irritation: If we always knew the truth, we'd know a lot of ugly things.

Kien-leh seriously contradicted him.

## Be careful how you retain experiences

Me-ti said: Our experiences usually change very quickly into judgements. We remember these judgements but we think they are the experiences. Naturally, judgements are not so reliable as experiences. A certain technique is needed to keep experiences fresh so that you can always reach new judgements based on them.

Me-ti called that kind of knowledge the best which is like snowballs. They can be good weapons, but you can't keep them that long. They also don't survive, for example, in the pocket.

Many said of Mi-en-leh that he was a great practitioner, but Le-peh was a great philosopher. Me-ti said: Le-peh's practice proved that he wasn't a great philosopher; Mi-en-leh's practice proved that he was a great philosopher. Mi-en-leh's philosophy was practical and his practice philosophical.

Before Mi-en-leh founded the association he took part in general discussions. When opinions were sufficiently in agreement and preparations sufficiently advanced, he laughed at those who continued the general discussions, and turned his attention completely to building up the association. But there were always times when problems were not clear, and opinions still distant from daily work (even if themselves daily work), and little was agreed, and Mi-en-leh participated again in general discussions. That was simply practical. While others looked at life as a source of opinions, Mi-en-leh was concerned with opinions for the sake of life. Only if you assume a philosopher lives for the sake of philosophy, Mi-en-leh wasn't a philosopher; but to assume that didn't seem to him philosophical.

Me-ti said: You can aspire to generalities like a bird fleeing the ground because it has grown too hot, and like the sparrow-hawk that seeks the heights in order to spot the rabbit it wants to swoop on.

[The distinction drawn here between judgements and experience is another way of expressing the critical relationship between theory and practice, which proves insoluble for an opinionated authoritarian government and eventually leads to its collapse. Le-peh stands for Georgi Plechanov (1856–1918), the theorist of Marxism, highly regarded also by Lenin, but who disagreed with Lenin about participation in the war against Germany, believing it would hasten the revolution in Russia. That particular issue does not affect the general point, here attributed to Mi-en-leh or Lenin, that the precedence of what is called 'life' (or experience) over 'opinions' (or ideological principle) is what really counts.]

## The apolitical doctor

The philosopher Me-ti was discussing conditions in the state with some doctors and exhorted them to participate in their removal. They refused with the justification that they were not politicians. Whereupon he told them the following story.

Doctor Schin-fu took part in Emperor Ming's war to conquer the province of Chensi. He worked as a doctor in different field hospitals and his conduct was exemplary, in as much as for a long time afterwards the medical schools still taught that his conduct as a doctor must be called exemplary. His construction of an artificial hand for soldiers who had lost one was much discussed. As a doctor he was able to consider the problem of replacing limbs with prostheses as solved. He used to say that this perfection of the art of medicine was due solely to his dismissal of all other interests except medical ones. Asked about the purpose of the war in which he participated, he said: As a doctor I can't judge it, as a doctor I only see damaged people, not profitable colonies. This was not held against him at court because of his service as a doctor. The court could turn a blind eye since, when asked his opinion on the writings of the rebel, Ki-en, who condemned the war, the conquest, the obedience of the soldiers, the empire and the low wages of the farmers and coolies, he only replied: As a philosopher I might have an opinion about this, as a politician I might oppose the empire, as a soldier I might refuse orders or to kill the enemy, as a coolie I might find my wages too low, but as a doctor I can't do any of that, and can only do what none of them are able to, namely heal wounds.

However, on a particular occasion, Schin-fu is once said to have given up this elevated and consistent position. When the enemy conquered a town where his hospital was, he is said to have flown head over heels, so as not to be killed as a supporter of the emperor Ming. He is supposed to have slipped through the enemy lines, disguised as a farmer, when attacked he is said to have killed people and as a philosopher to have answered those who criticized his behaviour: How can I continue working as a doctor, if I'm killed as a person?

## The headworkers' interest in the upheaval

Fe-hu-wang asked: Apart from the general one, what interest do the headworkers have in the upheaval?

Me-ti answered: Let's choose the doctors. Everyone knows there are too many doctors for them to earn well but too few for them to heal well. Many doctors are badly employed and they still have to cram their studies into a few years and end them hastily and perfunctorily. Those with the most patients earn least of all, for most patients are poor. The poor have the greatest exposure to illnesses and are cured worst of all. Their doctors have no time for further study. They are so occupied with wrong methods that they have no time to study better ones. The sellers of medicine have the last word on how it is used. The sick are often not prescribed what cures them best but what costs them most. But worst of all is that the doctors can do nothing about preventing illness. They can only influence the state where they can achieve profits for the exploiters; that can sometimes happen through measures that are useful to people but just as often or even more through measures that damage them. The doctors say, in their surgeries everyone is equal. The sick person appears before them as they are not: as a naked, out-of-work body without a particular past or future. The cause of the illness is not removed, at most it's the consequence that is removed, the illness itself.

The position of doctors is easiest to discern in wartime. They cannot do anything to stop warfare, they can only patch up smashed limbs again. And in our towns there is always warfare.

[Fe-hu-wang stands for Lion Feuchtwanger, one-time mentor and lifelong friend of Brecht. Beneath this text, Brecht wrote: 'the doctors say, in their surgeries people always seem the same. Praise + blame for doctors' (BBA 134/14).]

## Kin-jeh's theory of medicine

Me-ti recounted: Kin-jeh once studied medicine. He said, on the basis of the *Great Method* he could imagine the following: It has been shown that certain bodily symptoms can be cured by means which produce similar symptoms in healthy people. It's possible, for example, to cure fevers by means which also induce fever. You can view the sick body as one that cures itself. A contradiction is said to occur in the body that then tries, in its illness that constitutes the bad side of the contradiction, to reach a condition that responds to the new demands that are made on it. The means that are said to support this bad side then produce a cure by completely developing the bad side and helping it to establish control.

Me-ti also recounted Kin-jeh's theory because to him it seemed to offer a good image of revolutions.

[This proposes a not completely serious homeopathic theory of revolutionary politics through a cure that makes things worse, either literally or by increasing knowledge of how bad they really are, thereby provoking a revolution that, in taking control, transforms what was 'bad' into something 'good'. Beneath this text Brecht had handwritten: 'body does not wish to stay the same but to change itself'.]

## Contradiction

Part of Mi-en-leh's practice was to seek out the contradiction in appearances that seemed unified. If he saw a group of people that formed a unity when compared with other groups, he expected that in certain matters they held very different views, whereby the interests of some damaged the interests of others to the point of enmity among themselves. And also vis-à-vis the other groups the members of the group did not behave in a unified manner, not completely unified and not only unified. So the group was not completely and uniformly and for all time opposed and hostile to the others and to the other groups; instead, there were changing relationships that, even if in varying degrees, constantly questioned the unity of the group and its difference from other groups.

Ka-meh had already warned the workers from seeing their oppressors as too harmoniously unified. Precisely the task of oppressing, which unified the oppressors, also split them: they were at loggerheads among themselves and behaved differently in many questions. The workers could make use of this. Naturally, they couldn't do that, if at the same time they didn't also keep the unity of their oppressors in mind.

Many people saw Mi-en-leh as a canny swindler, who made friends with enemies in order finally to defeat them, but that was quite wrong, whether or not, according to your point of view, you condemned or welcomed such deceit. There really were questions in which a part of the oppressors, in its struggle with other parts, advocated the interests of the workers, not because these were the workers' interests but because they were their own. The workers could honestly ally themselves with this part as long as it took this position. Ka-meh was not of the view that the workers, who supported the enemies of the merchants and factory owners, had thereby made a mistake, because they were also pursued in the cruellest possible way by the merchants and factory owners, when they helped to overcome the nobility. In a certain sense they did participate in the success of their enemies. Commerce and manufacture now developed more freely, and, if these were the centres of their exploitation, they also became the centres of their liberation.

During Hu-ih's time the association instructed the workers to support the struggle of the pious against Hu-ih. It might appear that Hu-ih, by combating piety among the workers, was carrying out the job of the association. The association should therefore have supported him or at least allowed him to continue. But the association knew that the piety of the workers resulted from their earthly helplessness; piety had long been used to make them forget their earthly interests, but they themselves had used it to forget their sufferings. Hu-ih now wanted them to forget their earthly interests in a different way and to take away the means of enduring their sufferings, which he left them with and even increased. The association knew that the struggle for the means of enduring suffering could easily be changed into the struggle for the elimination of suffering. The means of enduring it were then superfluous. The association recognized the unity of the workers in the struggle against their sufferings and in the process didn't disregard the contrast between the pious and the un-pious workers. There was also, namely, a contrast between the working and the exploiting pious.

Hu-ih was forced to admit that there was a contrast between property and piety. In order to own, you had to break all the commandments of piety, in order to be pious all the commandments of ownership. The association assumed that once this question had occurred, the workers among the pious would give up property, which is to say the property that was incompatible with piety and needed wars and violence against workers. To give up such individual property did not however mean giving up all property, for the workers it meant acquiring property. If piety hindered them in this struggle, they would then have to give it up. So the association did not want to deceive anyone, but only represented the often changing interests of the workers.

[The first part of this passage discusses the compatibility and difference of interests between the bourgeoisie and the working class, and the second part describes the response to changing policies in Fascist Germany towards the Catholic and Protestant churches, which shifted between short-term alliances and oppression.]

## Proof that the crimes of Hi-jeh made sense

Me-ti was trying to prove that even the crimes of Hi-jeh made sense, since he said: Those who follow him don't do so because of his crimes but because there's a certain amount of sense in his actions. As well as the workers' exploitation by the moneymen of Ga there was also their exploitation by the moneymen in foreign states. Hi-jeh's predecessors in the government left the system of exploitation in the country untouched. But they didn't carry it out thoroughly since, for example, they rejected war with other states needed by this economic system, and since they did not establish any clear barriers to the distribution of goods without removing the barriers applied to their production.

In contrast to this Hi-jeh adopted more sensible positions, at least for those who had an interest in the prevailing system; this way he won them over. Showing the petit-bourgeois that war was necessary for their butchers' and clothes shops, and teaching them active service was not nonsensical. Of course, to the workers in the large factories he seemed like an idiot, because they felt that for them wars were unnecessary if only they were allowed to develop their production freely and without barriers. To the petit-bourgeois the workers could only sensibly say they would have to abandon their businesses, since they necessitated war, but not that they would have to abandon war, because it did not require this. And as long as the peasants maintained their practice of small farming, Hi-jeh's speeches were also not unreasonable for them. What was unreasonable was maintaining their practice of small farming. Whoever didn't take all of this into account, was not able to dismiss Hi-jeh's arguments.

## Why the regime was not overthrown

The regime was not overthrown because a way out seemed open to it, which was available for regimes of this kind, namely a war of conquest. The regime was still able to force the people down this way out.

## The people and the regime in the war

When an incapable and rapacious regime in En-eng sent its army overseas without sufficient weapons, where it was defeated, the coastal inhabitants rowed across in small boats and fetched back their sons and fathers under heavy fire. In this way the link between people and regime grew stronger.

When Hu-ih sent his army against Su, without supplying it with warm clothes for the cold winter and had to appeal to the people to send the soldiers woollen clothing, the people sent woollen clothes and in the process forgot for a while the criminal foolishness of the regime. The link between people and regime in this misfortune grew all the stronger.

[En-eng stands for England. This describes the similar response of the British and German people to appeals under very different circumstances to help their own endangered armies, at Dunkirk and in the Soviet Union. The point is to distinguish between the people and their regime. The British regime is judged incapable because its army was badly equipped and thousands of French soldiers, who had covered their retreat, became prisoners of war. That it is called rapacious probably has to do with Brecht's dislike of all imperial powers and his suspicion of the hope once entertained, also by Churchill, that the German army might put paid to the Soviet Union.]

## On the origin of contradictory units

Many did not understand why the people of Ger took part in Hu-ih's war. Me-ti explained it like this: Few believed in the possibility of simply introducing the *Great Order*. But it would have brought relief and people knew or suspected it. Therefore the superiors had to oppress the people through Hu-ih. But when they had to decide whether they should exploit the people more severely or declare war in order to exploit other peoples, they decided on war. Thus, to exclude the third possibility, introducing the *Great Order*, which needed neither exploitation nor oppression, the oppression of the people was indeed increased, but their exploitation was not particularly increased and the nation took the path to war to which the *Great Disorder* inevitably leads. For a while the people did the work they lived from, in the factories preparing for war and in the form of acts of war in the extermination machine.

[The Great Order stands for Communism, and the Great Disorder for Capitalism. Brecht holds to the belief that Fascism is the logical extension of Capitalism.]

## Exploiting the earth and people

Me-ti said: Before Master Ka-meh we thought that riches came from exploiting the earth. Master Ka-meh taught us that riches come from exploiting people. It isn't the forest that brings in money, but the people who are sent to cut it down. It's not the cotton that is profitable, but the pickers, spinners and weavers. The forest and the cotton fields are tools for extracting money from human beings. (This system leads to an ever increasing exploitation of people but to an ever decreasing exploitation of the earth.)

Me-ti said: According to Ka-meh, with the looms it's like this: if they are improved, five weavers can weave a hundred times more cloth on one loom as before. The profit, however, does not come from the increased cloth, but from the workers. The reason is: every piece brings in only as much as the labour time needed to produce it. The person who buys the loom also buys the workers, or rather he buys their labour power for whole days of work. The loom, the cotton, the workspace, the oil and the labour power cost as much as the labour time needed for their production. The cloth also, produced with the loom, the cotton, the workspace, oil and the manpower, only brings in as much as the labour time needed to produce it. So where can the profit come from? If everything costs as much as it brings in? The profit comes from the fact that of all the things needed to manufacture cloth, the labour power is the only flexible one. Everything necessary to produce one day's output (the food, shelter and clothing a worker needs each day in order to work) is cheaper than what can be gained from it. Because the weaver does not need much more whether he works for a day or an hour. That is why his labour is the most profitable commodity

[This basic calculation argues that profit accrues when the price of the product of labour exceeds its cost and that of the processed material, and, if material expenses are constant, the less labour is paid as productivity increases, the greater the profit.]

## Exploiting the earth and people 2

Mi-en-leh said: In the old days a person could only exploit the earth, by making use of other people. Today it is easier to exploit the earth. Now such a person uses the earth to exploit other people.

Mi-en-leh said: Whether you can eliminate the exploitation of people depends on the easiest way of exploiting the earth. If exploiting people had been eliminated when it was very difficult to exploit the earth, hunger and death would have resulted. Today, hunger and death will result if exploiting people is not eliminated. In order to be able to exploit people, the owners of tools and hirers of people have even begun to limit the exploitation of the earth.

Those who say: If the exploitation of people could be eliminated, it would have happened long ago, have got it wrong. It was always oppressive but it couldn't always be eliminated.

[To limit exploitation of the earth in order to exploit people presumably refers to the effect of induced scarcity and price policy assisted by tariff barriers. Neither Lenin nor Brecht could have anticipated the speed with which exploitation has now extended to the whole environment, adding a huge new dimension to the problem. The same title is used twice. To distinguish between them, I have added '2' to this second one.]

## The price of cotton

Me-ti said: A hundred years ago a pound of cotton cost as much as it costs today. During this period it sometimes cost fifteen times and sometimes half as much. Great inventions were made, huge dams were built, wars were conducted. Today three thousand times as much cotton is harvested as a hundred years ago and the price is still the same. It isn't the fall in temperature, it's speculation that makes cotton dearer. Inventions won't make it cheaper, but the *Great Upheaval* will.

[The Great Upheaval stands for the revolution.]

## If the silk worm were to spin

Ka-meh said: If the silk worm span just to eke out a living as a worm, it would be a real wage worker.

[In the typescript (BBA 134/07), above 'wage worker' is also typed 'coolie', without an indication of preference. This passage needs some context. In an essay, *Wage Labour and Capital*, Marx wrote: 'Consequently, labour-power is a commodity which its possessor, the wage-worker, sells to the capitalist. [...] And this life activity he sells to another person in order to secure the necessary means of life. [...] The product of his activity, therefore, is not the aim of his activity. [...] What he produces for himself is wages; [...] Life for him begins where this activity ceases, at the table, at the tavern, in bed. [...] *If the silk-worm's object in spinning were to prolong its existence as caterpillar, it would be a perfect example of a wage-worker*.' Marx writes that John Milton 'produced *Paradise Lost* for the same reason that a silkworm produces silk. It was an activity of *his* nature. Later on he sold the product for £5 and to that extent became a dealer in a commodity.' Karl Marx, *Capital*, vol. 1, trans Ben Fowkes (New York: Random House 1977, p. 1044).]

## Foolish use of clever heads

The author Fe-hu-wang said to Me-ti: Those who work with their heads keep apart from your struggle. The cleverest heads think your views are wrong.

Me-ti answered: Clever heads can be applied very foolishly, by those in power as well as by their owners. Precisely to shore up the silliest or least sustainable assertions or institutions, clever heads are hired. The cleverest heads are not concerned with discovering the truth but with gaining advantages through lying. They are not seeking applause for themselves but from their own stomachs.

## Opposition from the head workers

Why are the headworkers not in favour of radical change? Asked Fe-hu-wang.

Me-ti said: They relate to it not as heads but as stomachs. They're afraid that we could disturb their main occupation, filling their own stomachs, by urging them to fill our larders and stores of knowledge. They believe the one will necessarily interfere with the other. They live within a system that produces scarcity, they produce scarcity themselves and are afraid of scarcity. They see that only a few can live well and don't realize that this good life for a few is only produced in the current bad system through the bad life of many others. They consider this system natural and inevitable. They say: how can the flower bloom differently from the way it does? And they forget that after the blossom come the fruit, something different and just as natural.

## On headworkers

The headworkers take care that they can live by their head. In our time the head can feed them better if it dreams up what harms a lot of people. That's why Me-ti said about them: I worry about their diligence.

## What headworkers mean by freedom

Ka-meh taught that in order to understand people's ideas you have to study the history of how they produce the necessities of life. If, in order to recognize what the headworkers of our day understand by freedom, you study the history of their production of life's necessities, you find that the class with which our headworkers are aligned sought a freedom that was the freedom of competition. That was a particular kind of freedom. Competition was also a particular kind of competition, unlike other forms of competition, which the world had already seen. It was namely competition in the sale of commodities. The commodities the headworkers had for sale were knowledge and opinions.

The freedom they seek is free competition in the sale of knowledge and opinions. That does not sound so good; but that it doesn't sound so good only proves that in our day the production of life's necessities in the form of free competition in the sale of commodities no longer functions so well. At the time when it was promoted in this form, it didn't sound so bad if you paid for knowledge and opinions like fishes and fish nets, cloth and tailoring, and if the headworkers formed their opinions and applied their knowledge in such a way that production was promoted, nobody saw anything wrong in such dependency.

Personalities are developed though competition, and even if inventors demanded payment for the use of their inventions and artists and philosophers decried the adoption by others of their style and manner of thought and prosecuted it as theft, they proved themselves useful inventors, artists and philosophers for production. Since many interests opposed each other, there was room for many opinions that could be openly expressed. In our day the production of life's necessities in the form of free competition in the sale of commodities can no longer be supported, it comes to a halt time and again, and time and again turns into the production of instruments of destruction and there is a new urge for freedom and a new concept of freedom, which does not envisage free competition in the sale of commodities, but rather freedom from competition in the sale of commodities. This kind of freedom would always have to be able to advance production, and it is clear that the ideas and wishes of the headworkers in respect of freedom cannot bring about freedom of this kind.

## On the fascination of difficulty

Difficulty exerts a certain fascination. Headworkers just like mountaineers often love the peak that's hard to climb, which gives them the opportunity to demonstrate their skill, or to develop it. Headworkers almost seem the most useful of all in badly functioning communities, where their skill is needed to declare absurd principles to be the best ones. Even the unclimbable peak isn't completely unclimbable: you can definitely climb to a certain height. It's like this with the completely incomprehensible sentences of some philosophers: a certain number of them somehow make sense. In addition, the headworker knows that in thinking he has to account for as much as possible, so to speak, carrying about with him all sorts of things in as much detail as possible that is not absolutely clear, whose sheer volume is confusing, but whose broad fuzzy accumulation gives a certain stability to his thought. The little man, on the other hand, who gets involved in such general considerations, is not unhappy to discover everything is so very complicated, that thinking does not help that much. The disorder that prevails in his head is also the disorder that prevails in the world. From his point of view in particular it is most difficult of all to order the world. How then can he order his thoughts?

## On the indispensability of economic leaders

Me-ti often made fun of the fairy tale economic leaders circulate about their indispensability. He said: They tell the workers the economy is enormously complicated, which it is, but only as long as they themselves are there and complicate it. They themselves, you see, are the greatest complication. Their economy is completely unplanned, people work against each other, one gains when another loses, and if they say it's so difficult to make such plans, you must reply to them, it's quite unnecessary, even harmful. Their complexity is the complexity of disorder, their work maintains and increases disorder from which they profit. These economic leaders are only indispensable to disorder; their ideas are only valuable to exploitation.

## Time for the overthrow

Mi-en-leh knew there were many prerequisites for the overthrow, but he knew there was no moment not to be working for it.

[Like 'upheaval', overthrow also stands for revolution.]

## Mi-en-leh's needs

Mi-en-leh only needed a small room, a table, a chair, a bowl and a place to sleep. He ate potatoes and drank weak tea. But he needed: all the food in the world for working people, all the houses, all power and all freedoms for working people, in other words, a complete transformation of the world.

## On testing the emotions

We were taught in our youth, said Me-ti, to mistrust reason, and that was good. But we were also taught to trust our feelings, and that was bad. The source of our feelings is just as polluted as that of our judgements; it is namely just as open to attacks by people and is therefore constantly contaminated by ourselves and by others. If we feel pity, we feel it just as much for the robber in tears because he missed his victim as for the tearful victim who escaped him because he went the wrong, longer way. We often get angrier over a breaking pencil than a tax leaflet. Everyone feels anxious about something different; this feeling kills more people than fearlessness. We are told that our feelings are something natural; but they can be so easily manufactured, and how quickly they can be changed! Quite similar events produce quite different feelings at different times and it's like this at one and the same time with different sections of the population. What makes some happy, makes others sad, if not they will regret it. And although all have experienced this time and again and much else as well, the superstitious belief in people's genuine and unchanging feelings still continues.

To assume that there were emotions without reasonable cause would be to misunderstand what is meant by reason.

## On pity

Me-ti said: Mi-en-leh showed no pity. Seeing the misery of the exploited and oppressed engendered a feeling he immediately transformed into anger. Those who are guileless by nature turn the same feeling into pity. It is a sort of vague melancholy, comparable to despair. Pity, said Mi-en-leh, is what you don't refuse those, whom you refuse to help. I don't identify with the sufferers in order to suffer but in order to end their suffering.

## A person said to Mi-en-leh

Outraged over the cruelties of the rulers a person said to Mi-en-leh: For the cause I would do any decent thing.

And what else would you do for the cause? asked Mi-en-leh, who did not appear satisfied.

## Mi-en-leh said: You must be as radical as reality

Mi-en-leh constantly pointed out the radicality and revolutionary boldness of the rulers. Just look, he said, at the risks they take, how they break all conventions und endanger their own holy treasures, how they don't spare themselves when it's a question of gaining advantages through sacrifice or damage limitation. Learn from them, how to rule.

Me-ti taught: Revolutions occur in blind alleys.

## Routine

Routine is dangerous. For example, you must be careful about caution, being routinely cautious is dangerous. A person who always washes cherries before eating them, can easily drink the water by mistake in which they were washed and catch cholera, people say.

## Mi-en-leh's vote

Mi-en-leh's country Su was attacked by the robber state Ga. The predatory state Ga had an enemy in the predatory state I-jeh. I-jeh then offered Mi-en-leh's country weapons and provisions for its defence. The people of Su hesitated to accept this help.

Mi-en-leh said straightaway: Sometimes you must distinguish between what you say and what you do. But you then must also do both. Since he couldn't be present during the discussions he sent a letter saying: I ask that my vote be cast *for* accepting aid and guns from the hands of the I-jeh robbers.

[I-jeh stands for France. Negotiations before the Brest–Litovsk peace involved accepting assistance from 'Anglo-French imperialism' to end the war with Germany.]

## Mi-en-leh described his students

Like this: They have no special qualities other than those gained through the struggle; they will receive their names from their deeds; they live in houses they will conquer.

Before they know what they should be, they know what the association should be.

If they are to travel, they go to the station without knowing where to. Those who know, don't know who's going.

## Mi-en-leh's students

Me-ti recounted: Mi-en-leh's students are wonderfully versatile without make-up or false beards. One of the best works in the poorer part of town. For about a year he has been busy bringing workers into the association. Sometimes he seems to me to achieve his purpose through vehemence, sometimes by means of great patience. A year ago he seemed to me a worker, a few months later an intellectual. The workers trusted him since he was often right and hardly ever failed them. By the way, he constantly has other names, never lives long in one place and always looks different. But he sticks to his views.

I knew that in that part of town four or five of Mi-en-leh's organizers had worked one after another. But Me-ti spoke of them as if they were one person, as if he didn't register that this good student of Mi-en-leh had four or five mothers.

## Mi-en-leh's parable on climbing high mountains

When the ploughsmiths and poor farmers had seized power with the help of Mi-en-leh, they weren't able to realize all their plans straightaway. Their advance seemed to falter and sometimes they even had to retreat a few steps. This sight was intolerable to many watching from afar. Whenever the ploughsmiths, led by Mi-en-leh's Association of the Ownerless, experienced a setback or postponed a plan in order to avoid one, the onlookers began to scream that the ploughsmiths were betraying their principles and the association was leaving things as they always were. They thought of radical change as a one-off affair, like jumping across a rock crevasse that either does or doesn't succeed and if it fails kills the jumper.

Mi-en-leh said: Let's imagine someone wants to climb a very high, steep and hitherto unstudied mountain. Let's assume he succeeds, after overcoming unparalleled difficulties and dangers, in climbing much higher than his predecessors but hadn't yet reached the summit. He faced a situation in which it was not only difficult and dangerous to advance along the chosen route, but simply impossible. He had to turn back, go down again and look for new routes, which, if perhaps less challenging, nevertheless offered the possibility of reaching the summit. To climb down from this height nobody had reached before, where our supposed wanderer found himself, presented more dangers and difficulties than the ascent: it's easier to slip on the way down, when descending it's more difficult to see where you're placing your feet. The descent isn't accompanied by the feeling of elation present on the way up directly towards the goal. You have to rope up, losing a lot of time hacking out places to secure the rope. You have to move, slowly as a tortoise, all the while climbing down, further away from the goal and without seeing whether this dangerous and harrowing descent will end in discovering a promising detour through which you can continue again, more safely, quickly and straight ahead, upwards to the goal, the summit.

Isn't it natural to assume that a person in such a situation, in spite of having climbed to an unparalleled height, will experience moments of despondency? And such moments will certainly occur more frequently and be more difficult if he hears voices below, watching the dangerous descent from a safe distance through a telescope, which can't be called 'braking' since braking assumes an already calculated and tested vehicle, a well prepared road, an already tested mechanism. And here there's no vehicle, no road, absolutely nothing, nothing at all that might have already been tried out.

From below you can hear malicious voices. Some express their delight openly by shouting: He's just about to fall, serve him right! Why is he so crazy? Others try to conceal their delight by following the example of that Judas Golovlyov. They turn up their eyes in sorrow and complain: Unfortunately our fears have been justified. Haven't we spent our whole life devising the right plan for removing this mountain, didn't we call for the ascent to be postponed until our plan was completed? And when we fought so passionately against the route that even this fool has now abandoned (look, look, he's retreating, he's climbing down, he's working for hours just to fall back a few inches. And he cursed us with the worst curses, when we systematically asked for measurements and accuracy), when we condemned this senseless person so vigorously and warned everyone not to help him, we did that exclusively out of love for the great plan to climb the mountain, so that this great plan will not in any way be compromised.

Fortunately, given the conditions of our illustration, the imaginary tourist cannot hear the voice of these 'true friends' of the idea of the ascent, otherwise he would have felt sick. But feeling sick, they say, isn't good for a clear head and for steady feet, especially at great heights.

[The ploughsmiths stand for industrial workers. Brecht said: 'Every realist writer would be happy to have written Lenin's short parable, *On climbing high mountains*, and that piece, a classical short work of Realism, would, for example, only be spoilt by realistic details, and over expanding the material.' Lenin's text is therefore closely followed with minor adaptations and perhaps completed by Margarete Steffin. 'Little Judas' Golovlyov, a character in Mikhail Saltykov's novel *The Golovlyov Family* (1880), became a byword for degradation and hypocrisy.]

## Objective and partisan

Me-ti was asked: How can you demand that somebody should be objective and partisan at the same time?

Me-ti replied: If the party is objectively right, there's no longer any difference between being objective and partisan.

## The art of manoeuvring

Mi-en-leh taught: If you're driving a car on a narrow road, you need to watch the car in front since you would otherwise bump into it. How do you watch the car in front? You watch the car ahead of the car that is in front of you. You watch out for everything that obstructs the car in front of you, since its driving or stopping depends on all these things. It's as if you're also driving the car ahead of you. If something gets in its way, it has to stop. I must therefore also stop if anything gets in the way of the one driving in front of me, since it is not independent. It's extremely important always to ask yourself what the car ahead of you depends on.

## On the association

Mi-en-leh said: Only recognizing your own conscience, only taking your own thoughts into account, after every failed attempt crawling back into your own burrow, always joining whatever is new, always preserving yourself for the most important things, only acting from convictions, only loving dangers, all this you can practise outside the association. In the association you can fight for victory.

Mi-en-leh said: Trusting your own strength mostly means also and above all trusting a suddenly emerging strength of unknown people. Those who do not acknowledge people known to them, mostly acknowledge people they don't know. Without the mass of unknown people nothing can be achieved, but a single person can also achieve nothing with the mass of unknown people. The association – that is people you know, those that can be reached, those who get to know many others and who achieve much in the mass of unknown people.

Mi-en-leh said: Just as you must be able to make good moves in chess, you must also be able to make mistakes. If the cat makes a mistake and falls off the roof, it must be able to fall on its feet. An individual is often destroyed by a single mistake. The association is not so easily destroyed. The association can take more risks because it isn't destroyed by just one mistake.

The leaders of the farmers considered the whole people, with the exception of the exploiters and their servants, a homogeneous unit that could do away with exploitation. Many workers considered the confidants of the large workshops such a unit. But Mi-en-leh only considered the association as the really executive unit, the active agent of the uprising. The councils and the people, he said, need the uprising for their existence, and are not prepared for it. Not all the people and the councils are equally informed and act according to what they know. The association knows so much as could be learned and also acts without knowing everything (according to the instructions of a few).

Mi-en-leh said: The people develop slowly and unevenly, they forget a lot and learn much that is wrong. The individuals grow apart from each other, they are ambitious and vengeful. The association develops consistently. It gathers experience, tests people, lets them try out things and holds everything together.

## The master and the slave

Master Sa taught: Liberation comes about like a volcanic eruption. Master Lan-kü taught: liberation is brought about like an assault. Mi-en-leh taught: Both are necessary. Something that erupts and something that assaults.

In his analyses he anticipated great unrest and hence he formed the association.

Master Sa accused Master Mi-en-leh of pretending that the people rule, but the truth is, he rules the people.

Mi-en-leh told a story: I knew two men. They lived in a house, but in different rooms. The older one slept in a comfortable bed, the younger one on a leather mattress. Early in the morning the older one shook the younger one out of a deep sleep whenever he didn't want to wake up. At mealtimes the older one often took away whatever the younger one most liked to eat. If the younger one wanted a drink, the older one gave him only water or milk, and if he secretly got intoxicating rice wine for himself the older one scolded him sharply in front of everyone. If he answered angrily, he had to apologize in public. In the morning I saw the older one sitting on a horse and driving the younger one ahead of him. One day, I asked the older one about his slave. Shaken, he said he's not my slave at all. He's the champion and I'm training him for his biggest fight. He has hired me to get him into shape. I am the slave.

In order to find out who is the master and who is the slave, said Mi-en-leh, it's a good idea to ask who gains most from this relationship.

When the ploughsmiths with Mi-en-leh's help had chased away the smithmasters, they needed some instructors for their workshops. Trusting in their indispensability, the instructors demanded large concessions. Mi-en-leh who himself, though sick and overworked, ate only little and frugally, usually advised the ploughsmiths: give this scum the best chickens and the freshest milk! And he added softly, looking round cunningly: and your most impatient contempt.

[Meister Sa stands for Rosa Luxemburg (1871–1919), Meister Lan-kü for Karl Liebknecht (1871–1919). Both were founders of the Spartacus League in 1914 and participated in the Spartacus uprising in 1919 against the newly declared German Republic. With the connivance of the government they were captured by officers of the Freikorps, tortured and assassinated. Luxemburg spoke of the volcanic eruption of the revolution in Russia. Commenting on later developments in Russia, she argued that freedom is not just for the government supporters or party members, but always 'the freedom of those who think differently'. She maintained that the Soviet Union was not moving to 'a dictatorship of the proletariat but to a dictatorship of a small group of politicians'. This issue arises in Brecht's discussions with Karl Korsch and later. This text is entitled *On the association 2*, in BBA 133/57.]

## On discipline and alliances

When Mi-en-leh built up his association it was very difficult to get on with him. He insisted on very strict discipline. His teacher Le-peh told him: You can't achieve victory over the ploughsmiths with so few allies who are prepared to submit to you. The ploughsmiths have to join forces with other fighters since they are too weak on their own.

Mi-en-leh answered: It's exactly because the ploughsmiths need allies that we must maintain very strict discipline. If you want to establish alliances, as one of the partners you must be very united otherwise mergers will take place.

The headworkers in particular were strongly opposed to discipline in Mi-en-leh's association. Mi-en-leh said: For you, to be free means to participate in power. By participation in power you mean in ruling. You call your ruling: the rule of thought. In order to rule, you are ready to join up with the hungry, since theirs is a struggle for power. But the hungry want power in order to do away with starvation, hence a particular kind of power that consists in breaking the power of those who bring about hunger. The hungry have nothing against being ruled if it gets rid of hunger by increasing the fighting strength of the hungry. They don't think much of your all too free freedom.

## On compromises or drinking wine and water from two glasses

Mi-en-leh taught about compromises: They are often necessary. For many people that's like pouring water into wine. Which is taken to mean, undiluted wine is supposed to be bad for you. Or, the available wine is not going to satisfy your thirst. I have a different view of compromises. I then drink wine and water out of two glasses. Because it's far too difficult to pour the water out of the wine again.

[Tactical compromise without diluting intentions is possible provided you don't confuse them.]

## Do your own thing and let nature do the same

In the country of Su a violent struggle was taking place between many groups. Mi-en-leh sided with the ploughsmiths, since he believed only they could really help the country. You could expect them to make the greatest effort and their efforts helped the rest of the people most of all.

He said: If just the farmers redoubled their efforts, the harvests would still increase only a little. But if a sufficient number of ploughs are delivered, much will be achieved. In those days there were two kinds of ploughs. Some were traditionally made of wood, the other, newer ones were made of iron in large foundries belonging to powerful masters. But there were relatively few such iron ploughs. They were expensive and could only be properly used in large fields and drawn by horses. The simple wooden ploughs, on the other hand, could be made and drawn by the farmers themselves. They only cut a shallow furrow in the earth. These ploughs were used by the poor farmers. They had so little land and couldn't produce enough food. They often had to hire themselves out to work on the large estates. Many farmers' sons moved to the towns and sought work in the large foundries and other workshops. But only some of those who couldn't live off the land found refuge in the towns. The plough business was strictly limited. For one thing, there was only a small number of large estates and, secondly, the smithmasters had to maintain a high price for their ploughs. They didn't increase their profit by selling more ploughs, but mostly by increasing the pressure on their apprentices. Through the continuous flight of the poor farmers' sons from the land, apprentice smiths were always cheap to employ. They suffered great poverty.

With the help of Mi-en-leh, the ploughsmiths drove away the smithmasters and took power.

The poor farmers assisted the smiths in expelling the smithmasters and now the smiths helped them to expel the estate owners. The poor farmers immediately divided up the land among themselves.

Before Mi-en-leh came to power he had taught that above all the whole country should be supplied with iron ploughs. And many had understood him to mean that he wanted to get rid of the small farms straightaway. But when he took power together with the ploughsmiths, he did the opposite. He left the poor farmers their land and the apprentice smiths their workshops, for each one as much as they could manage on their own. Thus he increased quite considerably the number of small fields, which were too small for the iron ploughs. He took over the management of only a few large estates with his students.

The philosopher Sa vigorously blamed Mi-en-leh. He said: Mi-en-leh is like all the others. Power weakens memory. And: The new arrival forgets a lot.

Mi-en-leh replied: I taught, now they are learning. They listened, now they're finding out for themselves.

Mi-en-leh laughed at all those who believed you could bring an end to a thousand years of deprivation in one day by means of decrees, and continued on his way.

Soon the following situation had arisen. After chasing away their oppressors the ploughsmiths made as many iron ploughs as possible without asking what price they would get for them. The estate owners had also been chased away and now the state or countless small farmers worked their land. Among the farmers, some had almost enough land and also horses to pull the ploughs. It still wasn't worth buying iron ploughs, since their land was too small for them. The really poor farmers had no horses and were hungry. They had to go to the more prosperous ones again and work for wages or do jobs, in order to be allowed to borrow the horses. They soon became very dissatisfied. Their hate was directed at the prosperous farmers.

Mi-en-leh did nothing about this hate, instead he stoked it. The ploughsmiths sent people into the villages in order to promote the iron ploughs. They advised the poor farmers to come together, as many as possible, and join up the fields as much as possible to make it worthwhile to use the iron ploughs. Those who agreed were sent the iron ploughs on credit. They gave the prosperous single farmers no credit and sent them the ploughs after a long delay. They simply said we and the poor farmers belong together; not each of us ploughsmiths owns their own vice; so they couldn't produce ploughs.

Mi-en-leh's message was: You want the land because of the corn; now give up the land because of the corn! In other words: If you give up your own little strips of land, you'll get more corn. That was the truth.

Soon huge farms were formed, bigger than the former estates. After a while, the more prosperous farmers also had to join these farms, since they couldn't get workers any more for wages and their fields delivered little corn, because the old wooden ploughs didn't turn over enough earth. Thus Mi-en-leh realized his programme by doing his own thing and letting nature do the same.

[Sa (Rosa Luxemburg) objected to Lenin's handling of land reform since, by allowing the small farmers to retain their small holdings, their misery increased as they discovered by themselves how they could not compete with larger holdings, which could afford to mechanize on their own. Lenin argued that those who opposed land reform must discover for themselves the disadvantages of not enabling it under the new developing circumstances. The BFA retains the confusing 'Ni-en-leh' for Lenin (otherwise Mi-en-leh), which had been sensibly corrected in all the earlier editions, though substituting 'Su' for the original 'Tsen' or Soviet Union. Should details in this account seem scarcely credible to modern readers in the 'West', in the 1990s one could see wooden ploughs pulled by hand across small fields in backward parts of China.]

## Skill

Me-ti praised Mi-en-leh for being able to throw coals on to the fire without getting his hands dirty.

## On the flow of things

To-tsi observed before the great upheaval that the smithmasters were lost when they couldn't continue exploiting the smiths. When the workshops were closed for lack of iron and because the smithmasters feared the government would give them no more money for war chariots, the smiths, who had often refused to work in order to force better wages out of them, now insisted that their exploitation should continue. For them, life meant being exploited; now they feared for their lives. They rebelled against the smithmasters and chased them away, so to speak because they had refused to exploit them any longer.

[The title – On the flow of things – stands for the contradictory, here comical–dialectical, sequence of expectations and events, which lead to the workers expelling their 'smithmasters' for not exploiting them.]

## Mi-en-leh caught making false arguments

When Mi-en-leh gave land to the peasants after the great upheaval, a great shaking of heads began among the theorists of the *Great Order* in countries outside Su. Everyone agreed that the peasants should be given the land, but Mi-en-leh hadn't intended to give the peasants land. The goal was the whole of the economy, common farming of the land by everyone, not an increase of small owners. Putting aside for the time being the organization of the whole economy, Mi-en-leh only gave in to the wishes of the large mass of peasants in order to win them over. At that time many talked about a deception and accused him of only giving the land in order to take it back again at the first opportunity. He was also taxed with stealing the policy of another association, which had always demanded land for the peasants, in order to steal a march on it. In reality he merely took the next possible step. But it is interesting that when justifying in his own association the need for a policy change, he only made use of political arguments. He too doesn't seem to have seen that the organization of the whole economy would not have succeeded economically at this early stage, since it required not only a political but also an industrial revolution. Without machinery, farming in common was not an advance on individual farming, and machinery had not been built for several years. So it was just as well Mi-en-leh took account of the peasants' wishes and found sufficient arguments for doing so.

## The philosopher Ko's view of constructing order in Su

The philosopher Ko recognized that the class of workers and peasants had never in history achieved such success as in *Su* under the leadership of Mi-en-leh and his association. It was, however, important for him to state that Mi-en-leh's successes for the workers and peasants were due to a course of action that resulted in great disadvantages and possible future failures for the workers and peasants. In order to construct the *Great Order* Mi-en-leh created a powerful state apparatus, which in the foreseeable future was bound to be an obstacle for the *Great Order*. The *Orderer* as an impediment to *Order*, that was what worried Ko. Indeed, this apparatus always functioned very badly and decayed steadily, spreading a penetrating stink. The greatest progress and upheavals, like the introduction of collective farming on a huge scale und the planning of production, occurred together with the simultaneous unmasking of criminal gangs at the head of the state who led as well as hindered these measures. In Ko's opinion, the struggle between the divided students of Mi-en-leh (Ni-en and To-tsi) only showed that Mi-en-leh's principles were exhausted. Neither their real application by Ni-en, nor their proposed application by To-tsi, ensured decisive success. According to Ko, To-tsi proposed all kinds of doubtful reforms of the apparatus, which began to constitute the real impediment. The principles Ko himself proposed showed a definite weakness where Mi-en-leh's principles drew their strength, but he indicated excellently the weakness of Mi-en-leh's principles whom, unlike his students, he always treated with the highest regard.

[In his 1975 *Me-ti* edition, Mittenzwei denied that Korsch's criticism of Lenin's party had an effect on Brecht, let alone any credibility in itself. Brecht admired Lenin's tactical and practical skills but here he acknowledges Korsch's effective critique. Writing to Korsch from Svendborg in March 1934, Brecht posed some questions, including 'What Marxist Leninist methods and constructions seemed to you to have taken on an ideological character, i.e. to have detracted from the solution of certain questions and the launching of certain operations and which methods and constructions have (to the detriment of the revolutionary movement) been mistakenly discontinued?' and 'What would you think of doing a critique of Stalin's *Problems of Leninism*?' (*Letters*, 170)]

## On the absence of freedom under Mi-en-leh and Ni-en

After chasing off the smithmasters, many vigorously attacked Mi-en-leh's association because there wasn't enough freedom in Su. The association did indeed suppress the remnants of the smithmasters everywhere and for a long time as well as certain property owning sections among the farmers, and to do this it needed iron discipline among its members so that a great absence of freedom also seemed to exist in the association. Me-ti turned against all those who regretted this absence of freedom in Su, while themselves living in countries that had not yet chased away their economic masters.

He said: I hear you prefer to live where you're now living, rather than in Su. Your freedom, where you now live, seems greater to you. That's a strange kind of freedom!

The smiths of Su deposed the emperor of Su, because he defended the smithies of the smithmasters. They freed themselves from the emperor in order to be free of the smithmasters. Now they are trying after their own manner, in the manner of smiths, to free themselves from hunger, without hindrance from the smithmasters, by enlarging the smithies and supplying the country with ploughs, and they have also freed the country from all obstructing forces. Naturally they know that, unlike the smithmasters and landowners, they cannot be economically free as individuals, only all together. They have organized their liberation and constraints have thereby arisen; compulsion is used against all movements that threaten the great production of goods for everyone. An outcry now arises against this compulsion from those who as individuals wish to be organizationally free and are mostly economically free, as if this compulsion were like that of the emperor's.

They have not grasped that liberation is an economic task and one that must be organized.

[Marx had argued that freedom had long been associated with the ownership of private property but that in a true community individuals achieve their freedom by virtue of their mutual association. Rousseau held that freedom was not achieved outside but was only conceivable *within* society, and only through *yielding* rights, though not to a sovereign, or to any form of absolutism, but to what he called the *general* will, which meant to a *community*. When forced into subjection or compelled to work for another, man lives in a state of 'alienation', the opposite of freedom. Rousseau's historically specific discourse had special resonance in the eighteenth century. This relationship between 'association' and 'freedom' would remain unbalanced and an enduring problem for Brecht in the German Democratic Republic.]

## More to be done

When Ka-meh, the intervening thinker, died, the power of the robbers he fought was still growing. The greatest time for his enemy was yet to come.

[On the same typescript page (BBA 134/21), there is another text with the same title but quite different reference, whose meaning I do not fully understand: 'When Ka-meh, the intervening thinker, died, the names of slaughterers instead of doctors were still inscribed on the columns of fame; works were named after those who enjoyed them, not after those who made them.']

## Ka-meh's students have an answer for everything

Ka-meh's students irritated many philosophers because, when you listened to them, they seemed to have solved all questions. Their complaint was: With regard to the most difficult questions they declare the matter is very simple. They attribute absolutely every single thing to the economy and expect everything from a change in the way manufacturing takes place. When you hear them, they've solved all the riddles and the world is as simple as baking a cake.

Me-ti defended them and said: If we can assume that many problems would no longer arise if some were solved, then it really is possible that people urgently seeking the solution of fundamental problems grow impatient if they are faced with too many questions that can't be settled individually. The current state of society is so bad that all areas are devastated. Hence something important is said about each one, when something is said about the state of society.

## The cook should be able to govern the state

Mi-en-leh said, every cook ought to be able to govern the state. He was thinking of a change in the state as well as the cook. But you can also conclude from this that it's advantageous to arrange the state like a kitchen, but also the kitchen like a state.

## Realizing the *Great Order*

Many consider the *Great Order*, which Ka-meh, En-fu and Mi-en-leh spoke about, as an order utterly opposed to all existing order or disorder, a completed plan that had to be realized. Now it's certain that what we have is disorder, and what we are planning is order, but the new arises out of the old and is its next stage. We are trying to bring about less, something quite different, to which there is no access, rather than taking the next step, that is to say, drawing the conclusion from what already exists. The new comes about by upheaving, continuing, developing the old. The classical writers recognized the disorder of their time as an order and have shown that it was once introduced with difficulty and in a violent manner as a continuation, upheaval, development of a previous order. That's why you cannot expect the *Great Order* to be introduced in one go, on one day, through a decision. Because its opponents use violence against it, the introduction of the *Great Order* is an act of violence, practised by the great majority of the people, but constructing it is a long process and a production.

## On crude materialism

Me-ti said: A certain bold superficiality is useful to research. It's not afraid of complications. I refer to our doctors, especially where they are very useful and at the same time very superficial. Who would ever think of simply chiselling open a painful skull or, if an arm was amputated, of pulling out the nerves and muscles and attaching them with wire to an artificial hand? For that you need a certain crudity of thought. The fear of complexities paralyses many people. They find everything necessary that happens. But often only some things are really necessary in what happens, the rest can be dispensed with or simply be different. Mi-en-leh had never set up a workshop or had access to much money or enquired how you get milk into the cities, when he changed everything. He wasn't afraid of complexities and didn't find that everything that happened was necessary for workshops to function, for money to circulate and for milk to reach the cities.

## The old new

A student said to Me-ti: What you're teaching isn't new. Ka-meh and Mi-en-leh and countless others have taught this too.

Me-ti replied: I'm teaching it, because it's old, that means because it can be forgotten and only considered suitable for past times. Are there not huge numbers for whom it is completely new?

## Against tyrannical advice

Me-ti said: Even if it's good to defer to good advice, it's dangerous to defer to good advisers. That leads to not examining the advice any more, and making use of unexamined, that is, unamended, unadapted advice is foolish. And the advisers should be told that apart from their suggestions they should always make other ones in case the suggestions are not heeded. And those seeking advice should also demand the sort of advice that they can follow, if they can't or don't wish to heed the first kind.

## The people's right to self-determination

Me-ti said: Part of the *Great Order* is the people's right to self-determination, and he added: provided it benefits the *Great Order*.

## Appeals for the *Great Order*

Are the accomplices of hunger, cold and insecurity. The *Great Order* will be founded in the centres of the great disorder.

## On transience

Due to the *Great Method* taught by the masters He-leh and Ka-meh, there's too much talk about the transience of all things, said Me-ti with a sigh. Many consider that alone very subversive. They threaten the rulers with this transience. But that is a bad use of the *Great Method*. It requires us to speak about how certain things can be made to vanish.

[Marx spoke of the 'flow of movement'. A note in the Brecht Archive encapsulates this problem of the transient flow of things, tracing it from Heraclitus and, as it were, via Lao Tse, to Marx: 'their teaching of the flow of things/ not just that everything flows/ but how it flows/ and can be made to flow.'(BBA 328/10)]

## The *Great Order* and love

Jü said to Me-ti: The supporters of the *Great Order* want to do away with love.

Me-ti said: I've heard nothing about this. I only know that the enemies of the *Great Order* have almost done away with it already. Where it still exists, the great disorder thrusts them into the most terrible difficulties, it ruins them.

## Ka-meh on realizing the *Great Order*

Ka-meh said to the workers: Beware of people who preach to you that you must realize the *Great Order*. They are priests. Once again these stargazers discover something that you should do. Right now you're there for the sake of the great disorder, hence you should be there for the *Great Order*. In reality, for you it's really a question of ordering your own affairs; by doing that, you'll create the *Great Order*. The bad experiences you had with the great disorder may well guide you and, in addition, experiences of a more agreeable kind, which people like you have had during certain uprisings. But it would be well if you didn't plan your house down to the very last nail, which then has to be 'realized'. Leave as much as possible open. It's easier to quarrel over plans than when realizing them and when realizing them more things occur to you than when planning. Beware of becoming the servants of ideals; otherwise you'll soon become the servants of priests.

[Communism, Marx warned, is not a realizable 'ideal' but rather a real movement for change.]

## The robber's servant

The robber who attacked the merchants
May well laugh at the clerics' chatter
When he consumes his booty in the evening.
But what's to be said about the robber's servant
Sitting hungry beside him?

The robber doesn't fear the rope.
A fat man will hang from it.
But beside him
Hangs a thin man.

The robber says: what they don't give me, I'll take from them.
But if his servant says that of him
He gets very angry.

[Who is the robber and who the servant?]

## Liberation and freedom

Ka-osch asked Me-ti: Doesn't the great upheaval come about through the hunger for freedom? Me-ti confirmed this. Ka-osch continued: How can you explain the complaints that after the upheaval those who upheaved it enjoy less freedom than before?

Me-ti replied: Before the upheaval they fought voluntarily. Nobody could force them to fight nor how to fight. Their victory was indeed made more difficult through the lack of power they could use against themselves. After the victory this power was secured and no less necessary, since now the defeated had to be kept down. Ka-osch said: I understand; so their proletarian freedom disappeared when their civic freedom also disappeared.

Me-ti replied: The goal of the great upheaval was liberation from exploitation. The upheaval abolished the freedom to exploit and simultaneously the freedom to be exploited. This last freedom was expressed in many ways, which did not always enable it to be easily seen as simply allowing oneself to be exploited. Ka-osch asked: So you don't see that hunger for freedom has any further role to play? Does it no longer mean to you that liberation is needed?

Me-ti replied: What's needed is freedom from want. That's the goal. It necessitates many liberation campaigns and needs hunger for freedom all the time.

[Ka-osch stands for Korsch.]

## Freedom

Me-ti said: We are then free if we're allowed to begin to tackle what the greatest part of humanity has recognized as the best solution for its difficulties. For this the smallest degree of compulsion is necessary. And to achieve freedom it's also necessary that it is contested as little as possible, that we're compelled as little as possible to apply compulsion.

The discovery of new worlds and the invention of new machines signified a great liberation for humanity. By learning how to make better use of nature, humans freed themselves from many limitations. However, the new freedom soon became a freedom for one person to oppress and exploit another. In our day the ruling classes, who oppress and exploit the other classes, call upon the other classes to liberate the nation, in other words to secure its freedom to oppress and exploit other nations. The more this kind of freedom were to come about, the more slavery there would be.

## Masters Ka-meh and Eh-fu

Masters Ka-meh and Eh-fu, the greatest teachers of the science of behaviour in their time, taught little about individual behaviour. How they should relate to their families, how they should earn their living, treat their fellow human beings, gain a reputation, marry, practise art, in short, how they should live: about such matters their students heard little. The course of the masters' lives was also unexceptional. Their behaviour to their families or close friends did not attract attention. While one was wealthy, the other had money problems. They were not able to convince all the people who spoke with them and they experienced many defeats. A number of their predictions did not come true. They left important works unfinished. They expressed most of their views by attacking the views of others, so that their books can in part only be understood by reading the bad books of their opponents.

## On theory and practice

Me-ti asked: Should Master Ka-meh drink his tea as if he were draining the Bay of Si? Would it not be better to drain the Bay of Si as if he were drinking his tea? Since you are only making drawings on a table while thousands are shovelling? Or should Master Ka-meh show no fear when facing the bailiff, he who didn't fear the rulers of a whole continent?

[Underneath this text Brecht wrote: 'we don't fly to heaven when conducting astronomy' (BBA 134/17). The text has no title, so I have suggested one. Like the previous text, it also reflects on personal dilemmas, on the difference between private and public life: how to behave and preserve equanimity under difficult conditions while planning for what should change them.]

## On the state

Me-ti said: In Mi-en-leh's and Ni-en's day the opposite of the smithmasters' state was not no state at all but a state of the smiths. Instead of oppressing the smiths there was not simply no oppression but rather an oppression of the smithmasters. And since nobody is free where somebody is oppressed, the smiths were also not fully free.

People continuously appeared who were connected with the state and maintained there was no longer any oppression. They were continuously refuted not just by the kind of people who hated the state in any form but also by those who understood the need for a state of the smiths to destroy and replace the state of the smithmasters. People continuously appeared who attacked the state even when it oppressed the smithmasters, but nobody was able to suggest a way of organizing production that did not look like a state.

Me-ti laughed at those who maintained that even at this stage the individual was free or even freer than before. He said: Whether you say, better to be unfree in a good country than free in a bad one or: we were free to do what harmed most people, now we're free to do what helps most people, whatever you say, you can't say that you're free. This is the time when the great producing collectives are acquiring their legal status. So it's the job of the individual to get used to the collective. Only later can it be helpful to keep your distance again. Of course, participating now shouldn't extinguish the individual, just as keeping apart then shouldn't destroy the collective.

Hemmed in on all sides, the individual must surrender, yield, give ground. It's the collectives that have gained freedom and room to manoeuvre.

Me-ti hated bureaucrats. But he admitted he couldn't think of any other way of getting rid of them except by making everyone a bureaucrat.

Once, said Me-ti thoughtfully, there was something precious about individuals, that's to say, they were what they were, at others' expense. If they were so precious, they also had a price. What's precious is pricy, but that also means they were appreciated.

[This succinctly expresses the dilemma that haunts Brecht's texts, and would eventually collapse the system he continuously supported, even though he consistently sought to ameliorate the bureaucratic practices it institutionalized. Facing this unresolved contradiction, his work demonstrates, and recognizes, the failure of this attempt. What his work has recorded, together with the hope that energized the attempt, is its own justification. The failure to reconcile individual 'freedom' and collective interest has grown increasingly dangerous and now threatens to collapse more than a particular socio-economic system.]

## The bad bureaucrat

This is how Me-ti described the bad bureaucrat: He is sent out to alleviate relations, but he gets in their way. He is expensive not on account of what he does but also of what he doesn't do. He costs more than his salary. His ambition is to be indispensable. If he has completed what he was assigned to do, he stays, and if he hasn't completed it, because he is incapable, he also stays. Usually he's lazy, but if he's industrious, he isn't less harmful. Mostly he's corrupt, but if he isn't corruptible, he can't be persuaded to do anything. Even if there's nothing more to be administered, the administrator stays put.

## On personality

Me-ti taught: It is not true that the poor are less different among themselves than the rich. The rich are distinguished by many characteristics, the poor by few. What will it be like in the future when there is no more rich and poor? When there is no rich and poor, there will naturally still be distinctions between people, but they will be different ones. Let's take trees, for example, as a comparison. The differences between such trees as grow under various conditions, where there is light from one side only or from several sides, or on different soil, or exposed or not exposed to the wind, are at first glance greater than the differences between trees under similar conditions. These ones spread out freely as they grow. Whatever is misshapen stands out more among what's normal. Just to mention one case: Progress and head start are not the same thing.

## On the productivity of individuals

Through the way we practise the division of labour, production becomes a system that hinders productivity. People don't keep anything in reserve. They let themselves be homogenized. The time is all used up, there's not a minute for the unforeseen. Much is asked of them. But what isn't asked is resisted. So people no longer have anything that's undefined, fruitful, uncontrollable. They are defined, clearly demarcated, made reliable in order to be controllable.

[Two different ideas of what production and productivity can mean are set against each other. Production stands here for the mechanical activities that result in the maximization of output designated as productivity, not for an intrinsically preferred production as the development of individual personality to the benefit of all. Production measured mechanically by productivity prevents the development of what is 'undefined, fruitful, uncontrollable'. It is thematically connected with the next text. Both appear on one typescript page (BBA 132/38).]

## On the division of labour

Me-ti said: The division of labour is certainly an improvement. But it has become an instrument of oppression. If you tell a worker, he should above all be able to construct motorcars well, you are telling him he should, for example, let his wages be determined by other people who understand such things, good entrepreneurs or good politicians. If you tell a doctor he should above all be a good tuberculosis specialist, you are telling him he shouldn't concern himself with building houses, which cause tuberculosis. The division of labour is so organized that exploitation and oppression can still continue as if it was also a form of labour some people have to provide.

## On physical exercise

The weavers of Sen-se were enthusiastic about physical exercise. Me-ti said to them: I hear that the weaving mill owners have had your looms so constructed that through constant weaving your right arm has grown thick and your left one thin. In order to counteract this abnormality you take physical exercise in your free time. This work that you do in order to get rid of the consequences of working is naturally not paid and is completely unproductive. I suggest you make better sense of it by exercising with guns. Is your eyesight not also weakened and won't it improve by taking aim? Yet again, knotting ropes strengthens the hands. And nothing is more necessary for your backs than knowing how to crawl under a war truck. Through the right kind of sport not only your abnormalities but also the abnormalities of your machines will disappear.

## On equality

Me-ti said: Only when equal conditions have been created can we speak of inequality. Only when all feet are standing on the same level is it possible to decide who is taller than others.

## Causality

Me-ti warned against disputing the determinacy of natural phenomena or letting physicists dispute it. The activity of natural scientists consists, he said, in establishing as many determinants as possible and making them useful for people.

[This and the following passage address the metaphorical predicaments and possibilities of Heisenberg's uncertainty principle. Me-ti, we remember, 'was against constructing too complete images of the world'.]

## The unpredictability of the smallest particles

Me-ti said: Just now physics has established that the smallest particles are unpredictable; their movements cannot be forecast. Like individuals they seem to possess their own free will.

But individuals do not possess their own free will. Their movements are hard or impossible to forecast because for us there are too many determinants and not none at all.

## On individual behaviour

Kin-jeh, who wrote a textbook on behaviour, paid little attention to the behaviour of the individual in his current situation. And those before him who taught behaviour did precisely this. He said: In our times the individual is only one small part and the situation is particularly volatile. There are no longer any simple acts. For example, how much cunning must a woman employ to become a mother or effort not to become one. How is she to know what the man is like with whom she associates or what will happen to him? Just to get milk for her child she must perhaps take part in a revolution.

## Individuals also have a history

We know how useful it is for nations to record their own history. It is also useful for individuals to record their own history.

Me-ti said: Everyone should be their own historian, they will then live more carefully and more critically.

## Proud to be useless

Me-ti said: Taking pride in being useless is more usual than taking pride in being useful. Pride in being part of the few is pride in being part of the useless.

## The duty of the individual

In a well-ordered state there's no need to speak continually about the individual's duty to the state. The individual there is not so burdened, he has a lighter life. Mistakes are corrected without haste yet still in good time; what an individual can't do, another can, if he doesn't show up, enough others will be there.

## Parliament in bourgeois society

Parliamentary representation, said Me-ti, is a great swindle. It has nothing to do with production. As producers, citizens are not represented. Doctors are not represented as healers, architects are not represented as builders, engineers are not represented as inventors, textile workers are not represented as makers of clothes, farmers are not represented as carers for cattle, planters of corn. They all choose their parliament only as classes opposed to each other. Some politicians, stooges of the property owners, have of course proposed such corporations; they wanted to establish them as if there were no classes, thereby making the swindle even greater, since there are classes and such corporations would have been constituted by people with completely contrary interests, producing for different reasons, for different purposes, with different demands. In this way the ruling class would just be more easily able to organize everyone's production so that it only brought advantages for the property owners. As long as production is only supposed to profit a few, representation by occupation is no use to the people, it would just help to secure that very system that creates profit by slowing down production. If, however, classes are abolished, then the producers can vote for parliaments as producers and so arrange production that it brings advantages to all, instead of profits for a few.

## Relations between states

In respect of mutual relations, it's damaging to allow or expect of states more than can be allowed or expected of individual people. Arranging, just for them, a particular legality or lawlessness turns them into something inhuman, something superior to people. Nothing should be superior to people. Governments often say they are not acting on their own account but for the people, thereby representing their crimes and their violations of what is lawful as disinterested and therefore justified. But crimes do not become good deeds because they are committed for others. A state that will disappear, if it does not rob and murder, deserves to disappear.

## The government as dialectical phenomenon

Ken-jeh said: If we want to create a transitory strong state, that means a state that disappears, the more its function disappears, that means a state dispensed with by its success, we must create the government as a dialectical phenomenon, that means bringing about a good conflict. There should be a state apparatus in which orders flow downwards from above, and a trade union apparatus in which they flow upwards from below. The government then consists of a committee in which the most important questions are decided by a two-thirds majority.

## The history of Keh Ming*

Keh Ming is celebrated in Su as the mother of history.

*Ming means fate or destiny; Keh Ming means, abolish fate (order) or Revolution.

[This Romanization of the Chinese term in the conventional Wade-Giles system, which in pinyin would be gémìng, means 'revolution', literally 'change fate'. The appended note is correct.]

## The contradictions in Su

Me-ti said of Su: The decision of the association in Su to realize the *Great Order* has become a nightmare for the people of Su. The progressive tendencies are tripping them up. Bread is hurled at the people with such force that it kills many of them. The most beneficial institutions are created by scoundrels and not a few virtuous people are impeding progress.

## Me-ti said:

Whenever misery spills over everything, few know about the sources of misery. If the inundation diminishes for a while, they make themselves ridiculous by pointing out that it's drying up. Everything seems to be getting better. The administration whose hand is on the tiller as things improve is praised for its competence. Where extreme misery has prevailed, even a little alleviation is felt to be enormous. But the friends of the miserable are pursued as agitators. They are like people talking about the fragility of a boat's keel during a flat calm.

[This and the following text appear on the same typescript page (BBA 134/25).]

## Me-ti said:

If a kingdom is led into an abyss by gangsters who have taken control of the government, those who predict how it will end are not thought credible for the following reasons: great kingdoms have something enduring about them on account of their size. Ordinary life continues just the same, the bakers sell bread, books are printed, newspapers appear, people get married, the dead are buried, houses are built. In all of which reason still seems to prevail. Without thinking more closely, someone observing this will hope that such an accumulation of reasonableness, these tried and trusted activities, must somehow counteract the demented propensities of their rulers. These demented propensities begin to acquire the appearance of feasibility, even of reasonableness.

## Thought in the works of the classics

Naked and unadorned
It steps before you, without shame, certain
Of its usefulness.
It is not worried
That you already know, it is enough
That you have forgotten.
It speaks
With the crudity of greatness. Without circumlocutions
Without introduction
It appears, accustomed
To respect, because it is useful.
Its audience is misery, with no time to waste.
Cold and hunger keep watch over
Their attention. The slightest lapse
Condemns them to further destruction.
Though it appears so commanding
It still shows that it means nothing without an audience
Would neither have come nor know
Where to go or where to stay

If not accepted. Indeed, if not taught
By those ignorant yesterday
It would quickly lose its force and rapidly collapse.

[This poem appears among the other *Me-ti* texts in BBA 134/38 but has so far been excluded, in spite of its appropriateness. It is printed in BFA 14/337f.]

## Me-ti's advice

Even when a friend leaves, you must close the door, said Me-ti, otherwise it gets too cold.

It can't get any colder, said Kin-jeh.

Oh yes it can, said Me-ti.

## Me-ti's strictness

When a student accused him of being too strict, Me-ti answered him with these lines of Ki-en-leh:

If I speak to you
Coldly and impersonal
In the driest words
Without looking at you
(Seemingly I don't recognize you
In your special condition and difficulty)

I'm really only speaking
Like reality itself
(Soberly, impervious to your special condition
Fed up with your difficulty)
Which you do not seem to recognize.

## The lack of freedom in Su

Me-ti said: I hear that in Su, where the *Great Order* is being established, lack of freedom is the rule. The people there are said to be free for one thing only: namely, establishing the *Great Order*. But even concerning how it ought to be established there is no freedom. What's to be said about that? Is the *Great Order* not the foundation of freedom?

As long as it was believed that freedom was independent of the manner in which people produce the necessities of life, and in what form of cooperation they do it, they could also believe that people could be free as a result of certain freedoms or permissions to do this and that as they thought best. But this way they didn't become free.

[The context of these arguments about the lack of freedom in the Soviet Union, and Brecht's defence of Stalin, is that apart from his increasingly frustrated hopes for the development of a truly progressive and democratic socialism, Brecht saw the Soviet Union as the only serious opponent of Hitler, and to say there is no freedom there would then be to encourage war against it.]

## To-tsi's theory

To-tsi said: Su was too backward. We should not judge socialism by what happened to it in Su. When the workers took power, with the help of the mostly peasant army, defeated by the enemy, they found very little industry and miserable farming. Together with the workers and peasants, the middle-class were also oppressed. The best of them led the workers during the overthrow. Mi-en-leh's association won tremendous power and with the help of the workers and the poorest peasants set about building up industry and renewing agriculture, which the middle class had done in other countries. For a while the association waited for the overthrow in neighbouring countries, but this did not happen. For this process of construction a great deal of middleclass work and the knowledge owned by the bourgeoisie, our own and also that of other countries, was needed. The struggle against the prosperous peasants and middleclass headworkers as well as planning the economy steadily increased the power of the association. The workers needed the association's authority over the prosperous peasants and middle-class headworkers in order to keep them in check and over themselves in order to realize the plan. In place of the competition between middle-class employers there emerged competition among workers to build up industry. Differences of income increased accordingly. There was much want and individual lack of freedom and the arts and philosophy stagnated. In particular the position of the head of state was like that of the heads of those bourgeois states where during an increased class struggle planning the economy was attempted for the purpose of warfare. The difference from these states was very great, since they sought to perpetuate classes, to finally limit production and perpetuate the state, while Su sought the opposite of all this. However, the question was whether this goal could be reached in Su. The main question was whether without help from other countries production could really be so increased for class differences to disappear and the state thereby to become superfluous. The basis of the association, which was responsible for everything, was narrow among the people, the cause of its strict rule, and it was questionable whether it could become very much wider. Twenty years after the association took power the prisons were still overcrowded and everywhere there were death sentences and trials that involved even old members of the association. Great wars with bourgeois states were impending.

[This describes Trotsky's critical analysis, neither more nor less.]

## Better to accept shortcomings than to justify them

When Me-ti travelled through Su, the country was expecting a great war. Countless arrests had been made, since the association felt that enemies were internally at work. Me-ti stressed as praiseworthy that almost nobody believed they were guilty just because they had been arrested. On the other hand, many approved that only those who were suspects had also been arrested. That the authorities were not able to identify the guilty was considered a shortcoming; however, it was accepted that, unable to check, they were at least, if crudely, addressing this evil. Good surgeons, it was said, remove the cancer from healthy flesh, bad ones cut out the healthy flesh as well. Me-ti found the attitude of the people admirable and said: they treat their police like lousy, crude, stupid servants, at least that's something.

[This commentary on events in the Soviet Union was written in 1941, when Brecht experienced at first hand what was happening to many of his friends, who had disappeared or been executed. This and the two following texts appear on the same typescript page (BBA 132/63).]

## The Su police

Me-ti said: Don't ask for good people, create good positions! A good position is one that doesn't need a good person. To be a policeman is not a profession. It can be a temporary mission. Some kinds of work can only be done for a short time. Police work is one of them. A policeman doesn't need the experience of being a policeman, but of being a working person.

## Experiences must be socialized

Me-ti said: Nobody should be retained in a public position because they have 'experience' in this particular matter. They should learn to pass on their experience instead of exploiting it like a possession.

## On the police

Me-ti said: The state has no right to make someone a policeman for ever.

## Ni-en's reputation

Me-ti said: Ni-en's reputation is diminished by bad praise. There's so much incense that you can't see the image and people say: they're trying to hide something here. This praise smells of bribery. Of course, if praise is needed then it must be acquired from somewhere. In order to praise a good thing, bad people must be bribed. And at that time praise was much needed; for the way ahead was uncertain and the one who led couldn't prove anything. Hungry people who have never seen crops growing were told to sow the seed. They had to believe that they were being forced to throw away the corn with both hands and to hide the potatoes in the earth.

[Brecht's attitude to Stalin, initially supportive and, later, highly critical, is clearly documented in conversations, especially with Benjamin, and other writings. In *Me-ti*, this doubleness is similarly evident. He supported Stalin in any contest with Hitler, gave him the benefit of the doubt often, as here, with a degree of irony and some verbal juggling, but later saw him as the intolerable tyrant he had become. A later 1950s version, preferred by the BFA over this earlier one (BBA 233/13), though it is used in the other *Me-ti* editions, amends, and slightly softens, this story: 'Some of Ni-en's students said: Ni-en's reputation is diminished by bad praise. There's so much incense, you can't see the image and people say: they're trying to hide something here. – Others answered: the main reason we praise those who praise is because they're praising. Praise is greatly needed. For the way ahead is unclear since it has never been taken before, and the leaders cannot always prove their proposals are the right ones. Hungry people who have never seen crops growing are told to sow the seed. They have to believe they're being forced to throw away the corn with both hands and to hide the potatoes in the earth.' (BBA 233/15)]

## Me-ti's suggestion concerning Ni-en's epithets

Me-ti suggested that Ni-en should not always be called the Great, but rather the Useful. It was still, however, too early for praise of this kind. Useful people had remained for too long without fame of any kind, such that to say now that he is useful would not cause anyone to trust that he was capable of leading. Leaders had always been recognized for being useful to themselves. Me-ti soon realized his suggestion was unworkable. He said himself: What I really wanted was for the useful ones to be recognized as great. But that's exactly what's happening now with Ni-en. The bunch of oppressors who used to be in power always tried to prove to the oppressed that the greatest of the oppressors was really very useful. Now they call the useful one great.

[This first and fuller version, printed in the three separate German editions, appears on the same page as the previous text, *Ni-en's reputation* (BBA 233/13), whereas the BFA uses a later, slightly different and shortened one (BBA 233/14).]

## Destroying as a form of learning

When the smiths in Su had driven out their masters and seized power, the country experienced a huge upswing. The smithies no longer tried to get rich at the expense of those who needed their tools, large numbers of which they sent wherever work was underway. Because they had to learn how to handle these new tools, much was destroyed. Soon voices were raised that it would be better first to teach how to handle them and then to send them. Ni-en, Mi-en-leh's student, stopped that from happening. He said: You learn well if you destroy your own thing. (By well, he meant quickly because the country had little time.)

On one occasion the smiths sent the woodcutters on the border new powerful saws, who till then had only felled trees with axes. The woodcutters didn't believe in the saws. However, they began to saw down smaller soft wood trees. The blade cut through them like butter. They were amazed and selected bigger soft wood trees. When this also went well they turned to small hard wood trees. The blade just went straight through them. The woodcutters then fell into a kind of intoxication. They dragged along the bulbous roots of the hardest trees and applied the saw to them. It didn't go through so easily and became very hot but they managed to cut through the bulbous roots. Carried away, they applied the saw to a huge stone. Then of course it broke.

Worried, some woodcutters travelled to Ni-en to ask for a new saw. They described with shame how the saw had screamed and broken apart.

Did no teachers arrive with the saw? Ni-en asked them smiling.

Of course, they said, now we remember them.

Did they not scream, asked Ni-en.

Not as loud as the saw, said the woodcutters.

Ni-en said: You'll get new saws. We like you. We would never have invented saws that could cut through the bulbous roots of the hardest trees if, just like you, we hadn't always tried to do ever more impossible things.

[*Destroying as a form of learning* is the title for this text in Steffin's typescript, hence in the three separate German editions of *Me-ti*. In the early 1950s Brecht made some small changes and altered the title to *Ni-en on learning* for an envisaged but never used inclusion in a theatre programme, preceded by a short preface in brackets: 'Exiled in a half Fascist country Bertolt Brecht wrote a *Book of Experiences* in which the following story can be found. In order to conceal its authorship it is written as if it derived from an ancient Chinese historian. Su stands for Soviet Union, Ni-en for Stalin.' Minus the preface in BBA 1334/145, another copy of which with a Berliner Ensemble stamp can be found in BBA 233/16, this amended version appears under the second title in BFA 18/66.]

## On possible wars

So as not to stand alone in the impending great wars, Ni-en made use of the disunity among the exploiting states and formed alliances with some of them. But a few philosophers, opposed to exploitation, demanded that also the workers in those states allied with Su should immediately fight their governments and thus hinder their participation in war on the side of Su. They said, these wars too were wars of exploitation.

Me-ti said: These philosophers have understood nothing of the *Great Method* and are misleading the exploited. Three times already war seemed imminent and I noticed that on each occasion they preached against participation of the exploited, although each time the constellations were different. They paid no attention whatever to the circumstances. If war is declared on Su today, the exploited must support Su. They have to do this by hindering war on Su in those states, which fight against Su, and by supporting and demanding war in the states that fight on Su's side. If the states attacking Su are defeated, the exploited there will then be liberated. If this liberation is hindered by the states fighting on the side of Su, the exploited in these states must fight against their government and unite with the exploited of the defeated states to achieve this end. If Su and its allies are defeated, then the exploited in the defeated states must rise up against their governments, which have been weakened in defeat, and continue the struggle for Su. The position of the exploited can anyway be decisive only during the war and not at its start. How should a war, conducted for the liberation of the exploited and in defence of Su be capable of damaging any of the exploited? Such a war has limited aims and contains all possibilities for the exploited.

[This text probably results from reading Fritz Sternberg's, *Der Faschismus an der Macht* ('Fascism in Power') (Amsterdam: Contact Verlag, 1935). Brecht wrote to him from Svendborg in October 1935 that he had read it with great benefit, but regretting Sternberg had argued too 'politically', meaning not dialectically enough, with too inflexible arguments in respect of the question of war, and he continued: 'In a world war the proletariat is really fighting at many quite different points, engaged for quite different purposes, the non-Russian for imperialist ones, but the imperialist states are very different complexes and in certain alliances the aims do not vary but perhaps the points of arrival do! [...] And wars, again, have different phases, at the very least, beginning, middle and end, and the proletariats intervene in these phases with different force. A victory for France on the side of the Soviet Union could well mean a victory for the German proletariat, thereby endangering certain imperialist goals for France, while those of its own proletariat are within a discernible range. If France loses on the side of the Soviet Union, then there will be a separate peace (1000 to 1) and the French proletariat must naturally oppose it, a kind of commune situation then occurs. [...] The fact is that hardly a state today could survive defeat in war! And some won't survive a victory!' (BFA 28/526)]

## On unfruitfulness

The fruit tree bearing no fruit
Is called unfruitful. Who
Investigates the soil?

The branch which breaks
Is called rotten, but
Wasn't it covered in snow?

[A poem about imperfect circumstances, later entitled 'Ni-en's song' and finally recycled as 'Mao's Song'.]

## Creating order in one country

To-tsi declared it impossible to create order in one country. Ni-en set about creating it. To-tsi always found this and that was missing, Ni-en provided it. To-tsi didn't think it possible to create order unless simultaneously in all countries. Ni-en thought it possible to create order in all countries if it was created in one. To-tsi planned for an upheaval in all countries and then for creating order in all countries. Ni-en began to create order in his country and knew it would cause upheaval in all countries. As a student of Ka-meh, Ni-en believed in the importance of the economy, of industry, in the firm organization of the largest number on the basis of a new economic order in one country for an upheaval in all countries.

[Here, Brecht takes Stalin's side vis-à-vis Trotsky.]

## Me-ti for Ni-en

Me-ti stayed on Ni-en's side. On the question whether creating *Order* in one country was possible, he took the view that its creation had to begin in one country and then be perfected in other countries. Creating it in one country was just as much a condition for creating it in other countries as that would be a condition for completing it in one country.

## On the rule of the people

At the time of the great upheaval, said Me-ti, Mi-en-leh and his friends acquired as much power as they convinced people. Mi-en-leh's orders were tersely formulated convictions. Mi-en-leh could not say the superior power of his opponents forced him to give orders. It forced him to convince. Ni-en had fewer opponents and gave orders.

[This and the following text appear on the same typescript page (BBA 132/40).]

## Conviction (new meaning of the word)

In order to talk about the rule of the people, you need a new interpretation of the word conviction. It must mean: convincing people. Rule of the people means winning the argument.

## The weaknesses of fellow workers

Me-ti said: Mi-en-leh knew everybody's weaknesses and could work with everyone. Ni-en could work with very few and didn't know their weaknesses.

## Venerating Ni-en

The veneration of Ni-en often took such forms that it amounted to dishonouring those who honoured him. Me-ti was not particularly concerned about this. He said: Ni-en is creating the great production. That is an extremely daring undertaking, since such a thing has never been attempted anywhere. It deserves great credit from the people. Ni-en knows how to acquire it. How, if not though production, shall the people become wiser and more self-confident? Merely through instructions?

## Venerating Ni-en 2

Me-ti said: Some know that in some respects Ni-en is a useful person. To them that means a lot. Some know that he is a genius, the greatest of all people, a kind of god. Perhaps that doesn't mean so much to them as the other does to the others.

## Development and decline under Ni-en

Under Ni-en's leadership industry in Su was developed without exploiters and farming was collectively managed and supplied with machinery. But the associations outside Su declined. The members did not choose their secretaries, the secretaries chose the members. The slogans were decreed by Su and Su paid for the secretaries. When mistakes were made, those who criticized were punished; but those who made them retained their posts. Soon they were no longer the best, merely the most compliant. Some good ones stayed the whole time because, if they had left, they would not have been able to speak with the members but, staying, they could only tell them what they thought was wrong. As a result they also lost the trust of the members and their own as well. Under these circumstances not a single decent description of the situation appeared that would have enabled planned activities, and those who at least had experience of the situation did nothing that had not already been approved by those who did not understand it. Those in charge in Su heard nothing themselves, because the secretaries reported nothing they might not like to hear. In view of these conditions the best despaired. Me-ti deplored the decline of the *Great Method*. Master Ko turned his back on it. To-tsi denied there was any kind of progress in Su, even the most obvious. Those outside Su who fought against Ni-en's influence on the associations soon found themselves alone, those who fought him within Su found themselves surrounded by criminals and themselves committed crimes against the people. In Su all wisdom was focused on development and driven out of politics. Outside Su, everyone was suspected of corruption who praised Ni-en's achievements, even the undeniable ones, within Su everyone was suspected of treason who revealed his mistakes, even those under which they themselves suffered.

[This and the following texts, also all undated, will have been written in 1937–8, at least fifteen years after the Soviet Union was founded in 1922. Commenting on this text, Mittenzwei finds it an insufficiently discriminating and objective account of Stalin's influence and stresses the positive remarks, while ignoring the political criticisms in Brecht's views.]

## Ni-en's trials

One and a half decades after its foundation Su, the workers and peasants state, also came under the influence of the Tuis. The enormous task of constructing the *Great Order* created a great conflict of opinions that naturally attracted the Tuis.

At this time the country was ruled by two regents, Ni-en and To-tsi. Ni-en lived within the country, To-tsi lived overseas, a long way off. However, they had approximately the same amount of power. Ni-en defended and To-tsi attacked everything that happened in the country. About everything that was done in the country Ni-en said: I did that, and To-tsi: I advised against it. In reality much happened that To-tsi wanted and much that Ni-en didn't want. Whoever could influence the course of events was contented; but the discontented naturally also influenced the course of events. To-tsi continually pointed to Ni-en's huge power and spoke almost about nothing else except this huge power. Some Tuis called Ni-en, others To-tsi, the father of the people and the corrupter of the people. And all the Tuis called themselves Tuis in the worst sense of the word.

[Tui, based on an inverted shorthand anagram of in-tellekt-uell, was Brecht's dismissive term for merely speculating intellectuals. Throughout this period he was gathering material for an unfinished Tui novel. This passage, which says nothing about those scandalous trials and their horrendous consequences, seems to express Brecht's extreme frustration over the course of events in the Communist movement. Since the trials, held in 1936–38, were supposedly directed against an anti-Soviet Trotskyite centre, it is noticeable that Brecht does not here take sides even if this seems to reduce real events to a theoretical squabble. On his own typescript (BBA 132/26) Brecht wrote, presumably referring to the Stalinists and Trotskyites: 'impossible to distinguish between them and also differently concocted' (zweierlei Bäckerei).]

## Ni-en's trials

Me-ti blamed Ni-en for seeking too much trust from the people during his trials against his enemies in the association. He said: If I am asked to believe something provable (without the proof) it's like asking me to believe something unprovable: I won't do it. Ni-en may well have been useful to the people by removing his enemies in the association, but he hasn't proved it. Through this trial without proof he has damaged the people. He ought to have taught them to require proof, and particularly from him, who is generally speaking so useful.

## Thinking and knowing

Unknown to the association and against its advice, Keh Lan negotiated with foreign politicians. Me-ti said: Keh Lan mentions that he deserves to be trusted. He may well deserve to be trusted. We don't think he has betrayed us. But if he demands that we say we know he hasn't betrayed us, then he's asking too much. There's a difference between thinking and knowing and it's dangerous not to notice it. If he wants us to know, he shouldn't call upon our trust. He says we shouldn't rely on outward appearances but on inner feelings. Why doesn't he allow us to rely on outward appearances? Outward appearances can be deceptive but they can also be proven. Inner feelings cannot be proven; they simply have to be believed. Does he want to teach us to believe when he could allow us to know? Keh Lan may have had the best intentions and represented our cause as best he could, but he's saddling us with a bad custom, it he gets us to believe thinking is knowing.

[Keh Lan is unidentified.]

## It is easier to say what's credible than what's true

People often try to make us believe what can't be proved. Doing this, they refer to their love of truth. Unfortunately, what's true isn't always what's probable. The truth often only becomes probable with the help of a little untruthfulness. Hence people begin to lie just when they can only achieve credibility by relying on proven truthfulness. Me-ti said: I would be better advised to make sure that my friend can believe himself rather than me.

## Ni-en's constitution

Me-ti opposed all those who attacked associating Su's constitution with the name of Ni-en and said: It is indeed a constitution whose responsibility belongs to the person who wrote it. The progressive people in the whole world are split into two camps. Some think the *Great Order* is the rule in Su, the others that it doesn't rule there. Both are wrong and right. Some main aspects of the *Great Order* have been set out and are being developed. Individual ownership of the means of production has been abolished and since the earth is also considered such a means of production and individual ownership of the earth is abolished, the distinction between town and country is disappearing, for the earth too can now be cultivated according to a wide-ranging coherent plan. But the new system, the most progressive in world history, still functions very badly and not organically and demands so much effort and use of force that individual freedoms are very limited. Since it is enforced by small groups of people, there is compulsion everywhere and no real democracy. The absence of freedom of speech, of freedom to form coalitions, lip service, acts of violence by town councils prove that all the fundamental elements of the *Great Order* are far from being realized or developed.

[The new 1936 Constitution of the Soviet Union was known as the Stalin Constitution.]

## Ni-en's autocracy

Me-ti spoke with Kin-jeh about Ni-en, who practised autocracy. Me-ti said: Mi-en-leh, whose student we must consider Ni-en to be, thought before the great upheaval that the workers had to help the peasants free themselves from the Emperorship. The workers on their own seemed to him still unable to build up the great machinery in a democracy. Later the workers acquired power under his leadership but his successor Ni-en already behaved just like an emperor. Su's backwardness, which Mi-en-leh had always spoken about, still showed itself here as well. The great machinery was not built up by the citizens in a democracy but rather by the workers under an Emperor. Kin-jeh asked: How do you explain that?

Me-ti said: The workers fought with the peasants. In the beginning they had democracy at least among themselves, but as the struggle got worse the state apparatus separated itself from the working people and took on an antiquated form. For the peasants Ni-en became an Emperor, when he was still a secretary for the workers. Then he also became an Emperor for the workers, when class struggles developed among them. Kin-jeh asked: Could we name a mistake by Ni-en? Me-ti said: Turning the organization of planning into an economical instead of a political matter was a mistake.

[Walter Benjamin records what Brecht was saying about Stalin. In one conversation, he says that the Moscow line was 'a catastrophe for everything we've committed ourselves to for 20 years'. The Soviet Union was 'thrown back to long-superseded stages of historical development. Monarchy, among others. In Russia personal authority reigns supreme. Obviously, only idiots could deny this'. His later descriptions of Stalin in writing, 'honoured murderer of the people' and 'criminal dictator' were also unequivocal. Had Brecht's vision of the role of the party and of the individual within it been realized, it would have precluded what happened, but that is not how things turned out. It is hard to imagine that, had he really known what occurred in China, or lived long enough to experience the Cultural Revolution, his residual faith in the progress of a Communist system, without real public accountability and self-serving as all bureaucracies, could hardly have survived.]

## Living according to the *Great Method*

Me-ti said: It's advantageous not just to think according to the *Great Method* but also to live according to the *Great Method*. Not being at one with yourself, forcing yourself into crisis, turning small changes into large ones and so forth, you cannot only observe all of this, you can also do it. You can live with more or fewer interventions in more or fewer contexts. You can achieve or aim for a lasting change of consciousness by changing your social existence. You can help to make the state institutions contradictory and capable of development.

[This and the following text appear on the same typescript page (BBA 131/44). According to the BFA, the paper quality indicates they were probably written after Brecht's return to Berlin in 1949. This suggests a more immediate critical intention and that the following text, instead, as it may first appear, of praising Stalin's perspicacity, in reality amounts to criticism of the dominant conservative Stalinists in Berlin.]

## Living and dying

Ni-en said: In life, something is always withering away. What's withering doesn't simply want to die, but rather fights for its existence, for something whose time has passed. In life, something new is always being born. What's awakening to life isn't simply coming into the world; it hurts and screams and insists on its right to life.

## On exhausting trust

Me-ti said: The trust of nations is exhausted by being called on.

[This and the following text appear on the same typescript page (BBA 132/42).]

## On terror

Me-ti said: Terror increases cowardice and courage, two characteristics that are highly dangerous for dictators.

## Conversations about Su

Kin-jeh told Ko about a court case that he had seen in Su. A farmer had come to town in order to work in the smithies. A family had taken him in since the son was away and so there was room. He promised to leave if the son returned. But when the son returned he didn't leave because it was difficult to find accommodation. The house administration took him to court. The court didn't reach a proper judgement. It demanded that the house administration should find accommodation for the man and promised to look for some itself. Kin-jeh praised the court for recognizing that moving out of a flat necessarily meant moving into another one. Ko said: it would be nice if that was the case. We would then be dealing with a state such as the master teachers had demanded. But I know that in Su a great deal can't be done as they would have liked, so I don't believe this story. Just think what the conditions would be like if matters were conducted so casually!

Kin-jeh replied: It seems that they are so casually conducted. Perhaps the conditions you mention will also come about. What happens then?

Ko had said: I don't believe this story. Kin-jeh said: I saw it. Then they put on a performance for you, Ko insisted. Kin-jeh said: Even if it only happened once and only for my sake, it would still have been a great achievement to reach so reasonable a judgement. If you heard there was a man somewhere who could run faster than anyone else but would only do it if you were present – wouldn't that still be a great achievement?

[Kin-jeh (Brecht) argues with Ko (Korsch) about what he says he personally witnessed in the Soviet Union. Could he have been in this particular court during his 1935 visit to Moscow? We don't know.]

## Improving those in need of it

Someone said to Me-ti: There will always be some who need improvement.

Me-ti replied: The asocial people I've seen tried to improve society all on their own, by making such improvements as benefitted themselves. Those who found it exceptionally difficult to carry out such stratagems often became ill and behaved nonsensically, but all this says is that it wasn't possible to see the meaning of their actions clearly. They, too, wanted to improve things all on their own.

In the land of Tsen, inequality has been eliminated, the oppression of man by man has been made as difficult as possible. Yet asocial people still exist. Their treatment is very distinctive. So that they cannot continue causing damage all on their own, they are isolated for a while. Previously, they were locked up in special buildings, now they are isolated simply through the reserve shown them by all socially conscious people. They are sentenced to improve social institutions. The ones who had to be tried are changing themselves into attorneys. They must figure out the reasons for their misdemeanours and if they find guilty people, they must publicly accuse them. They put both their teachers on trial as well as those responsible for particular social institutions. If they have achieved changes or their suggestions are shown to be unrealizable, their forced labour is deemed to have ended. In the second case, they are usually assigned to the activities they criticized.

The bad ones are improved, said Me-ti, by having them make improvements.

[Tsen presumably refers to the Soviet Union. The source of the story has not been identified.]

## On unwelcome foreigners

Me-ti said: At great expense the Emperor Ming admitted thousands of foreigners into the country, who mastered hitherto unknown arts. Everyone was glad about these guests. The administration was so organized that the arts not only enriched their practitioners but everyone else as well.

In our time foreigners are expelled, and everyone whose predecessors lived outside the country at some time or other is considered a foreigner, as if they wanted to drive away as many, not as few, as possible. In my opinion these expellees cannot complain.

They completely accepted a system of unequal competition, since they profited from competition because they were more proficient than the locals. Expelling them according to the colour of their hair is also only a form of competition with unequal means.

Naturally, I deplore the country. Should the foreigners have been more harmful than useful, then all those with such ability were more harmful than useful to the country. It simply is a country where reason uses dirty tricks and dirty tricks create advantages. If reason created advantages without harming others, if prizes were not awarded for dirty tricks and excellence was not punished, then reasonable people would not have to be expelled – instead, you would try to hold on to them.

[The 1930s brought economic and political migrants in large numbers to the Soviet Union, who suffered various fates, mostly bad. Many foreigners also left, as did Russian artists and intellectuals, often of Jewish origin. There were waves of repression and paranoid fears of foreign influence. This text seems conflicted as was the situation, while implying a preference for tolerance.]

## The great masters

Many people thought the great masters of music and painting must have been proud that they could do what no one else could. But I imagine, said Me-ti, the great masters were proud that humanity could do such things.

[This text is spatially separated from and not connected with another on BBA 131/10, with which it is combined in the German editions. It has no title on the typescript. I have suggested this one.]

## Beautiful is what's useful

The Tuis of Mu-sin were great master builders. They had a huge store of knowledge and experience and no student received the title of master who had not studied with them for at least fifteen years. They were also attuned to everything new and progressive as was to be expected. Thus they were the first to discover the beauty of the machine. Why, they asked in their books, is the machine so beautiful, why is it the most beautiful thing and the most pleasing to the eye that can be seen today? Because it is so thoroughly useful. Because there isn't even the smallest part of it that has no purpose. Because it is the embodiment of harmony.

Overwhelmed by this perception they began to build their houses and even their furniture with the machine as model, plain, simple and practical.

It helped them that owners at that time were also in favour of everything new and progressive, and the reason was as follows: Chima produced, using its machines and its mass of have-nots, a huge amount of commodities that couldn't be sold within the country itself due to the poverty of the people. The great war the Emperor had conducted with seven states in order to conquer those countries in which Chimese commodities, textiles, machines, oil and so forth could be sold, had been lost. Heavy duties everywhere hindered the import of commodities and hence the Chimese manufacturers had to set extremely low prices in order to sell anything. In order to lower the expense of manufacturing they established prizes for new machines that needed fewer workers, and the whole country clamoured for what was new and progressive, for saving money and improvements, for practical methods and useful standpoints.

This was very advantageous for the master builders of Mu-sin and their idea of constructing houses, apartments and furniture like machines, in the cheapest and most useful way possible, pleased everyone.

[The Tuis of Mu-sin stands for members of the influential Bauhaus movement, which established a characteristic sparse modernist design and art style. It began in Weimar in1919 with Walter Gropius and, moving to Dessau and Berlin, lasted until 1933. Displeasing the new political dispensation, it was then dissolved. Its last director was Mies van der Rohe. Chima was Brecht's term for Germany, another Middle Kingdom. On the typescript Brecht wrote 'the rented apartments' and 'elevated taste' (BBA 133/15).]

## What is beautiful?

The great architect Len-ti proposed a new ideal of beauty. He declared the useful to be beautiful. When the city of Ko-ha built apartments for workers, they turned to him and he built houses without embellishments of any kind in which all the needs of the inhabitants were taken care of. The workers moved in and Len-ti soon discovered that they were very dissatisfied with his apartments. They were not beautiful enough for them. But they are beautiful, Len-ti exclaimed in irritation. They are modelled on your machines, which I find the most beautiful things I've ever seen. And they are useful and my idea was: the most useful apartments for the most useful people. The workers said: in the factories where we work, everything is practical, nothing there is not useful. We ourselves are only used in so far as we are useful. We detest whatever is only useful. The machine that consumes our life is built out of metal and glass and now you are building even our furniture out of metal and glass. You might just as well offer a coolie, whipped with leather whips when pulling barges, chairs whose seats are weaved with leather straps. Perhaps useful things really are beautiful. But then our machines are not beautiful because they are not useful to us. But, exclaimed Len-ti in anguish, they could be useful, couldn't they? Yes, said the workers, your apartments could also be beautiful, but they aren't.

[Len-ti probably stands for one of the Bauhaus architects. The BFA suggests Mies van der Rohe, but there seems no evidence for this identification. They designed functional apartments for workers in Berlin and other cities. The coolie barge pullers, a symbol of human degradation, also appear in the 'Song of the Rice Barge Pullers' in *The Measures Taken*. A graphic photograph (in J. J. Firbank, E. O. Reischauer and A.M. Craig, *East Asia: The Modern Transformation* [Boston: Houghton Mifflin, 1965], plate 41, p. 384) shows why this phenomenon caught Brecht's imagination.]

## You must build your lives

You must not only build towns, machines, bridges, and cultivate wheat, said Me-ti. Towns emerged chaotically, house alongside house, one street leading to another, but then early on there were town planners. Of course there are also dreadful towns built according to plans that were also dreadful. (If towns, built according to plan, are dreadful, that's not because they are built according to plan, but according to dreadful plans.)

## Can artists fight?

During the greatest oppression by Hi-jeh a sculptor asked Me-ti which motifs he could choose in order to stick with the truth and yet not fall into the hands of the police? Take a pregnant working woman, Me-ti advised him. Let her look with worry at her body. Then you've said a lot.

## On pure art

Me-ti said: Recently the poet Kin-jeh asked me if he was allowed in these times to write poems about nature's changing moods. I replied: Yes. When I met him again I asked him whether he had written poems about nature's changing moods. He answered: No. I asked, why? He said: I set myself the task to make the sound of falling raindrops a pleasurable experience for the reader. Thinking about this and sketching an outline, I realized it was necessary to make this sound of falling raindrops a pleasurable experience for all people, also for those who had no shelter and for whom the raindrops fall between their collar and their neck, as they try to sleep. I couldn't face that task.

Art is not concerned with the present day, I said, tempting him. Since there will always be raindrops, such a poem could last for a long time. Yes, he said sadly, when there are no longer such people for whom they fall between collar and neck, it can be written.

## On painting and painters

A young painter came to Me-ti whose father and brothers were barge pullers. The following conversation took place: I don't see your father, the barge puller, in your pictures.

Should I only paint my father?

No, it could be other barge pullers, but I don't see any in your pictures.

Why does it have to be barge pullers? Isn't there much else?

Of course, but I don't see any other people who work a lot and are paid little in your pictures.

Aren't I allowed to paint what I want?

Of course, but what do you want to? The barge pullers' situation is terrible, people want to help them or ought to want to help them, you know the situation, you can draw and you're drawing sunflowers! Can that be excused?

I'm not drawing sunflowers, I'm drawing lines and spots of colour and the feelings I sometimes have.

Are those at least feelings about the terrible situation of the barge pullers?

Perhaps.

So you've forgotten them and only remember your feelings?

I participate in the development of painting.

Not in the development of the barge pullers?

As a human being I'm in Mi-en-leh's association, which wants to do away with exploitation and suppression, but as a painter I develop the forms of painting.

That's as if someone said: as a cook I poison the food but as a human being I buy medicines. The situation of the barge pullers is so terrible because they cannot wait. By the time your painting is developed they'll have died of starvation. You are their messenger and you're taking too long learning how to speak. You have feelings in general but the barge pullers who sent you out to look for help, feel something particular, namely hunger. You know what we don't know and you're telling us what we know. What's the point of you learning how to handle ink and paint brush, if you haven't anything particular in mind? They are really only difficult to handle if they have to express something particular. The exploiters talk about thousands of things, but the exploited talk about exploitation. Go and paint barge pullers!

[This preference for art of social intervention rather than abstract or the expression of private emotions characterized Brecht's position during the 1930s, when he argued that abstract art makes material things unrecognizable. Under different circumstances, he later excoriated what he called the petit-bourgeois quality of Soviet realist art.]

## The importunate artist

In a Community Centre in the northern provinces Me-ti discovered a beautiful picture representing eight very poor people of both sexes and various ages who were being taught by one of their own out of a book. Beside them the artist had placed a wooden blackboard on which Kien-leh's poem 'In praise of learning' was written.

Where did you get that? he asked the workers.

Ah, they said laughing, one of these artists forced it on us. All the other pictures here – and they pointed to the other pictures, which were all very bad – we chose ourselves because we liked them. But that one you're looking at we were forced to accept by the artist. He spent a whole day talking to us about it, he read us the poem three times, he said he had planned every line in the picture exactly, he kept on at us whether we didn't see this kind of beauty and that kind of freedom. Finally he really persuaded a couple of us of the quality of his picture, and some that he was at least an artist, and the rest of us just wanted to get rid of him. So we bought his picture and the blackboard, mainly out of pity for him, not to completely disappoint him, we know what it's like to be hungry.

I understand, said Me-ti, that person must have had a thick skin! But why did you leave it hanging when he'd gone away happy, if most of you didn't like it?

They seemed embarrassed.

Well, they said, what then happened was strange. This picture really does reflect something of its painter's importunate character. It's hanging there, talking to us. It's not insulted if we look at it disparagingly, but it would scream blue murder, if we took it down. You could say: it's fighting. It has formed a party that likes it. It's even impatient and talks down the other pictures here; it wants to get rid of them.

Me-ti smiled with pleasure.

I almost think, he said, that buying this picture you didn't so much take pity on the artist as on yourselves and were more generous to yourselves than to him.

[One of the more or less datable texts, supposedly written 1940 in Stockholm, which he left for Finland in April. It refers to a particular painting, since lost, by the German artist Hans Tombrock that represented what is here described. The poem 'In praise of learning', from Brecht's play *The Mother*, set to wonderful music by Hanns Eisler, encourages the untaught to study, starting with the ABC, for 'you will have to take command'. Tombrock, a one-time tramp, autodidact and self-taught painter, escaped Germany for Sweden, and later became a professor in the German Democratic Republic (which he subsequently abandoned in disappointment). He had difficulty getting his eccentric style accepted, and was encouraged by Brecht, for whom he did several illustrations. This picture illustrated that learning process. Brecht particularly admired Tombrock's persistence, a quality they both needed, as this story ironically suggests.]

## On bad art

Kin-jeh said: Inveighing against bad art and demanding something better or vilifying popular taste, what's the point of doing this?

Instead, we ought to ask: Why do people need drugs?

## On state pensions for poets

Me-ti said: I'm fairly dubious about pensions, which the state pays as an honour to certain poets. That may be all right if the poet has done the state a special service, I mean here the state not the nation. For fine writing in general pensions are not justified. The state should not give presents without getting something in return, and it should refrain from wanting to represent the nation in cultural matters. But poets too should not take anything from the state if they don't do something in return. That makes them dangerously dependent on the state – that is to say on the government department in question. What the state can do is support poets by paying them for undertaking translations from foreign languages. That is a job that simply needs the skill of a craftsman. It is easy to check and checking it increases an understanding of literature. Poets can then introduce innovations in their own writings, as much as they think necessary, and nobody can condemn them to starve for that reason – just because they love the old works of art! Whatever innovations may find their way into the translations will always be limited and above all easily determined. The poets themselves will then be able to measure their own creations against those of other poets from other times or other languages. And they get paid for useful services to the nation, since good translations are of the highest importance for every literature. In addition, they must learn foreign languages, which is also very useful, because it leads to a better understanding of their own. In this way, by paying for translations, the state does enough – and not too much – for the creation of new works.

[Poetry rhymes with penury at the best of times, but in wartime it's worse. A shorter version of the thoughts in this passage occurs in Brecht's *Journals* on 10 December 1940 in connection with the significant Finnish poet with left-wing sympathies, Elmer Diktonius, who wrote primarily in Swedish, and helped Brecht and his family when they first arrived in Finland. Brecht called him 'the Finnish Horace'. Diktonius lost his state pension, and Brecht looks for a way of justifying one while keeping the poet free from subservience to the state.]

## Kin-jeh's dream about art examinations

Kin-jeh recounted he once dreamt that because the practice of writing was getting out of hand a government close to the people introduced strict examinations for the profession. The candidates were led across the market place into a room and told to write down everything they had observed on a large sheet of paper. The papers were collected by officials and then new sheets were distributed on which further observations were to be written.

That was repeated many times and finally only those who were able to fill a certain number of sheets with observations were permitted to practise publicly the art of writing. As a result things improved but were still not that satisfactory. Therefore the government introduced new examinations, but only for those who had already passed the first ones. Their work was given back to them again together with a single large sheet of paper and they were then required to summarize their observations on this sheet. Then these sheets were collected and ones half their size distributed for the same purpose. And this was repeated as ever smaller sheets were distributed. And finally only those were permitted to practise the art of writing who were able to write down the most observations in the shortest form. Kin-jeh recounted that in his dream only he and four others passed the examination, three of these four had been unknown.

## On gestural language in literature

Me-ti said: The poet Kin-jeh may take credit for renewing the language of literature. He encountered two ways of speaking: one was stylized and sounded pompous and like writing and was never spoken by the people when taking care of their business or on other occasions, and one that was spoken everywhere, which was just an imitation of daily speech and was not stylized. He employed a way of speaking that was both stylized and natural. He achieved this by paying attention to attitudes, which underlay the sentences: he introduced attitudes into sentences and always let the attitudes show through the sentences. He called such language gestural, because it simply expressed people's gestures. It's best to read his sentences if you carry out certain physical movements that suit them, movements that signify courtesy or anger or the wish to persuade or make fun of or memorize or take someone by surprise or warn or show fear or frighten. Often a particular gesture (like sorrow) includes many other gestures (like calling everyone to witness, restraining oneself, being unjust and so forth). The poet Kin saw language as a tool for taking action and knew that you also speak to others when you speak to yourself.

['Both stylized and natural', perhaps the best summary of Brecht's aesthetic practice, intended to encourage 'taking action', even when, in exile, you seem to be talking only to yourself. It explains why he admired the work of the Tang Dynasty poet, Po Chu-yi, of whom it is said that he first showed his poems to an old peasant woman to ensure they could be understood.]

## Comparisons

The celebrated author Lu said: My pen is made of gold, my orders are carried out, my wife is faithful, my friends are geniuses, the arts works in my house are genuine.

Me-ti said: My pen is made of iron, my requests are hardly even considered, my wife is not faithful, my students and friends are as little infallible as I am, the only picture I own is a cheap copy of a doubtful work. So what?

[The BFA supposes the comparison is with the successful writer, Emil Ludwig, who boasted about all he could buy with the money he had earned. The picture possibly alludes to the much-copied Confucius portrait or perhaps even to the one Brecht finally hung above his bed in Berlin, the source of his poem 'The Doubter'.]

## Frugality and luxury

Frugality is something that presupposes luxury. It must be voluntary, otherwise it signifies subjection to those in power.

[This is documented in the Brecht Archive Catalogue (Bestandsverzeichnis), vol. 3, which registers 515 texts with some doubling, here, p. 244. 'Me ti' is handwritten above it. Presumed date 1947/48.]

# The Third Thing

## The third thing

Me-ti said that the relationship between two people will be a good one if a third thing is present in which both are interested. Mi-en-leh added, this is also true of the relationship between any large number of people. When they are all dedicated to something beyond themselves, everything can be more easily arranged between them according to the needs of this thing. The good effect Me-ti expected when two hands, perhaps of a man and a woman, touch each other when working together, when carrying a bucket, Mi-en-leh expected of whole peoples when their hands touch while moving the wheel of history.

[The title for this text, I suggest, should stand for all the texts connected with Ruth Berlau. Here, Me-ti and Mi-en-leh look with different emphasis at the 'third thing'. For Me-ti, an erotic charge is heightened when two individuals share a goal beyond themselves. Mi-en-leh anticipated the pleasure of cooperation when producing new ways of social living.]

## Kin-jeh on love

I'm not speaking about pleasures of the flesh, although there's much to be said about them, nor about falling in love, where there's less to say. The world would get by with these two phenomena, but love must be considered separately, since it is a production. It changes the lover and the beloved whether for better or for worse. Even from their appearance, lovers look like producers and of a high order. They show their passion, they are uninhibitable, they are soft without being weak, always looking for friendly acts they could perform (not just, in their perfection, for the beloved). They shape their love and give it a legendary quality as if they were expecting a historical description. For them, the difference between no mistake and making just one mistake is enormous – a distinction the world can happily ignore. If they turn their love into something extraordinary, they have only themselves to thank, if they fail, they can just as little excuse themselves with the mistakes of the beloved as can leaders of the people with mistakes of the people. The obligations they accept are obligations to themselves; nobody could be so severe over breaching the obligations they undertake. It's the nature of love as of other great productions that the lovers take many things seriously that others treat casually, the slightest touches, the smallest shifts of emphasis. The best succeed in harmonizing completely their love with other productions; then their friendliness becomes something general, their inventiveness useful to many others, and they support everything that is productive.

[Love is accounted a production because of its power to transform the person. Love as a production also changes how the lover sees everything else. Not to be confused with productivity as a quantitative measure, production as qualitative change affects the world in which everyone lives. Culture, in language once employed, as a humanizing process, a higher development or self-improvement, relates, of course, to what Marx meant by Communism as achievable only when the 'free development of each' is possible and the condition for 'the free development of all'. The centralization of production in the hands of the state, instead of Marx's bourgeoisie, created arguably more intractable antagonisms than those addressed by but not solved through the *Communist Manifesto*.]

## Lai-tu's mistakes

Lai-tu had a husband she didn't get on with because she didn't like sleeping with him, and apart from a degree of sympathy nothing bound her to him. She profited from Me-ti's advice about the third thing, by suggesting her husband should work for the oppressed, for whom she was also working. Her husband agreed and Lai-tu slept with him again. Me-ti reprimanded her for this and said: What's the point of finding a third thing that unites you and of retaining another third thing that unifies you? That means: getting a piece of bread and washing it down with poison.

[The Lai-tu stories are often directly autobiographical. This one, for example, alludes to her still sleeping with her husband, which Brecht apparently considered illogical.]

## Justified suspicion

When a woman told Kin-jeh she couldn't live without him, she loved him so much, he was immediately afraid she was deceiving him with anybody else.

[Some Lai-tu texts reflect the strain of exceptional private and political circumstances. The difference in their personalities, something close to polar opposites, produced more than an understandable fascination with each other, as well as the inevitable lovers' quarrels. 'Your love', Brecht once wrote, 'could make five continents happy'. The propensity of this vibrant and beautiful woman to sleep with other men disturbed Brecht, anyway unsettled by her emotional intensity. A poem about Berlau, probably connected with *Justified suspicion*, and suggesting a degree of independence that irritated Brecht, reads in literal translation: 'If she drinks, she falls into every bed / If she doesn't drink, she lets nobody close / For she says: she only needs one man / And that man is me. That's very nice / Pity she can't help it: / If she drinks, she falls into every bed. // She really is a pain. / For the whole town knows about it. / Even though whoever has had her / Is not at all in her good books / Just the reverse: she's fed up with him / If she drinks, she falls into every bed. // Look, she says, I'm not just a mattress. / Thank God she's still healthy … / Just one thing will soon be too much for me: / If she sees one she'd like to have / She starts unfortunately to drink and / If she drinks, she falls into every bed' (BFA 14/351f.).]

## How Lai-tu lights the fire

Me-ti said to Lai-tu: I watched you lighting the fire. If I didn't know you, I would surely have been offended. You looked like someone who was forced to light the fire, and since I was the only one there, I had to assume that I was this exploiter. She said: I wanted to get the room warm as quickly as possible. Me-ti said, smiling: I know what you wanted. But do you know? You wanted to make it comfortable for me, your guest; it should happen quickly so the conversation could begin; I should enjoy seeing you; the wood should start to burn; the water for the tea should boil. But of all these things, only the fire happened. The moment was lost. It happened quickly but the conversations had to wait; the water boiled but the tea wasn't ready; one thing happened for another but nothing for itself. And imagine what could have been expressed in lighting the fire! There's a whole custom in this, hospitality is a beautiful thing. The movements that cause the beautiful wood to burn can be beautiful and awaken love; you can take advantage of the moment, it won't return again. A painter wanting to paint how you lit the fire for your teacher would hardly have found anything to paint. There was no fun in the way you lit the fire, only slavery.

[Berlau says this was the first Lai-tu story. She was understandably ambivalent about it. The pupil–teacher relationship is taken for granted, and she was not so content with this particular lesson.]

## Lai-tu's house for Kin-jeh

Lai-tu furnished a small house for Kin-jeh. She whitened the walls, put in a good stove and made sure there was a comfortable chair. But Kin-jeh only sent his pipe and some tobacco in a pouch and didn't come for a whole year. Lai-tu was a little sad about this and often thought that he had forgotten the house. When they were together once again somewhere else, he said casually: the stove is good, isn't it? Somewhat surprised, she reassured him about the stove. Then another six months passed. Kin-jeh and Lai-tu were together as much as their work permitted, yet they never got round to visiting the little house. Lai-tu was however no longer sad about the house, because in the meantime she once heard Kin-jeh say to someone: I tell the truth about the oppressors as best I can in my poems. But I have a place of refuge. The reason Lai-tu was no longer sad was because she knew that she had given Kin-jeh, whom she loved, a great present and that he made use of it.

[Of this text, Berlau said: 'It would have suited Brecht if I had adopted this attitude. But I didn't feel inclined to, nor to accept his interpretation.' She was, in other words, more interested in the first rather than the third thing.]

## Kin-jeh recounted

Kin-jeh recounted: Before I knew that Lai-tu loved me, she frightened me by describing unpleasant states that afflicted her when she was alone. As she told it, she sat often for hours lost in inconsequential dreaming, unable to do any work. The table and chair in her room stood, so to speak, in a never ending shadow. When I myself was overcome by similar states, I knew that she loved me.

## Telling the truth

Me-ti said to Tu Fu: Do you want to give your teacher a stinking fish? Do you want to leave the room and say: What a stupid person? Do you want him to love you or an imaginary figure? How shall he give you advice if he doesn't know who you are? What use is it to you if he tells you how to cook lentils, but you're supposed to cook apples? Right now times are peaceful, but what happens when they are not?

[Tu Fu, otherwise the name of a celebrated Chinese poet, stands for Berlau.]

## The truth

Tu Fu did something that was bound to irritate Kien-leh deeply yet told him the whole truth. Kien-leh was very affected, but gathered together carefully all the truth she told him, a lot of truth; Kien-leh had quite a job gathering it, it was something like a harvest. Finally Kien-leh said: I have learnt something about Tu Fu that hurt me, but I also learnt something that did me good: she dares to tell the truth.

## Me-ti was asked whether it went against good manners

Me-ti was asked whether it went against good manners if a wife was unfaithful to her husband. He said: In a country where you have to buy everything, a cup of tea and a bed and a book and a woman's sexual organs, you can't prevent him from claiming his purchase for himself. If I have rented an apartment in a house, is the landlord allowed to house others in the apartment? It is immoral if a woman, who takes money for renting her sexual organs, then rents them elsewhere, unless it's been agreed. Though in such countries a woman will get nothing to eat nor anywhere to sleep, if she doesn't rent her sexual organs, so that her deception really only breaks an immoral contract. She simply hasn't anything with which to cover her nakedness if she doesn't sell it! I think: In a country like ours everything is immoral, both adultery as well as marriage.

## Shen Te said to someone who didn't want to hear it, so she could just as well have kept her mouth shut

The torn rope can be knotted again
It holds again, but
It was severed.

Perhaps we will meet again, but
Where you left me
You won't find me again.

[Perhaps we can understand this as a female response, attributed here to Shen Te, alias Ruth Berlau, to the man who once said in *Of Poor BB*: 'Here you have someone on whom you can't rely.']

## Tu wants to learn how to fight and learns to stay seated

Tu came to Me-ti and said: I want to take part in the war of the classes. Teach me. Me-ti said: Sit down.

Tu sat down and asked: How shall I fight? Me-ti laughed and said: Are you sitting comfortably? I don't know, said Tu, astonished, how should I sit differently?

Me-ti explained it to him. But, said Tu impatiently, I didn't come to learn how to sit. I know, you want to fight, said Me-ti patiently, but for that you must be sitting comfortably, since we're sitting right now and want to learn sitting down.

Tu said: If you're always looking to find the most comfortable position and to make the best of current circumstances, in short, if you're striving for pleasure, then how can you fight? Me-ti said: If you're not striving for pleasure and don't want to make the best of current circumstances and aren't looking to adopt the best position, what's the point of fighting?

[Tu otherwise stands for Berlau. This one is male, and maybe so disguised. The advice about sitting comfortably recalls the story that opens the Keuner collection, where the philosophy professor is told his views cannot be taken seriously because his whole deportment lacks credibility. This text tells Tu to clear the mind before considering what action to take.]

## Equanimity and love

Ken-jeh tried to preserve his equanimity; Lai-tu tried to upset it.

Are equanimity and love compatible? asked Lai-tu. Ken-jeh replied: Yes.

## Avoiding too grand words

Me-ti said to Tu-fu: Rather than 'for ever' say 'for a while', rather than 'I know' say 'I hope', rather than 'I can't live without this or that', say 'it's harder to live without this or that'. Then you'll be on the safe side and cause others to be more on the safe side.

## Kien-leh's way of speaking

Lai-tu complained to Me-ti about Kien-leh's reserved letters. Me-ti looked at her sympathetically and said: When I asked Kien-leh why he built a country house particularly in U-ting, he replied, the countryside there was not disagreeable. Hui-jeh took away his house and he said: What a shame. After some study (fifteen years) he called Mi-en-leh a useful man and my classical studies on the superfluousness of virtues he praised as 'quite well done'. Lai-tu pulled out the last of Kien-leh's letters, had a look at it and went away satisfied.

[Brecht bought and for a short time owned a house in Utting on Lake Ammersee, southwest of Munich, until Hitler put an end to it.]

## Lai-tu's love

Me-ti said: Lai-tu loves me. She comes to me, when she's happy and when she's sad. She writes that she loves me and about the cost of meat. She laughs with me at her silliness and is proud with me over her cleverness. And that's how we react to my silliness and my cleverness.

On another occasion Me-ti said: My work is coming on well; Lai-tu has written to me how her wall is painted.

## Anger over injustice

Me-ti said to Lai-tu: You show no sign of anger over injustice. Without anger over injustice you can't be a real supporter of the *Great Order*. Anger over injustice is more than simply condemning injustice or fear of participating in injustice. Whoever isn't capable of getting angry over injustice done to others won't be able to fight for the *Great Order*. And anger mustn't flare up quickly without consequences, but must last a long time, and know how to choose the right means. Mi-en-leh and Ka-meh didn't exactly act in anger, but without anger they would never have acted against injustice as they did.

## Lai-tu's way of learning

There are different ways of learning, said Me-ti. Today Lai-tu is cheerful, in good heart, honest, tenacious and a good fighter. She wasn't like that before. She became so when she was cheerful over her brother, Ken-jeh, was attached to him with all her heart, was honest with him, showed tenacity, when he was tired and when she fought for him. Ken-jeh, however, was cheerful over the successes of the oppressed, was for them with all his heart, honest with them, tenacious in their service and a good fighter. So we can perhaps say that without him, she wouldn't so easily have become like that, but now she's like that without him.

## Lai-tu's beauty and happiness

Me-ti and Kin-jeh talked about Lai-tu's beauty. I think happy people always seem beautiful to us, said Me-ti, smiling, and you make her happy.

That's wrong, said Kin-jeh, it's not me who makes her happy – she makes herself happy for me.

## Lai-tu flirts

Earlier on Lai Tu made use of her effect on men in order to advance Me-ti's plans or when Ken-jeh was in danger. Me-ti disapproved of this. When Ken-jeh just laughed, since he was sure Lai Tu was faithful, Me-ti said seriously: If Lai Tu was flirting in order to be unfaithful to you I would say nothing. But that she only flirts in order to be true to our cause will destroy her. Yesterday she even gazed lovingly at me as if I were a stockbroker.

## On behaviour after failure

If you suffer an injustice, Me-ti said to Lai-tu, fight to the death, but if you achieve justice, stop fighting. Compare your voice, if you apologize for your mistakes, with the mistakes of others. Isn't it quite hard? One of the greatest sentences is 'I am ashamed.' Speaking this sentence, almost every voice sounds good.

## On behaviour after failure 2

You can always say, Me-ti continued to Lai-tu, that under ordinary circumstances you ought to be declared innocent of an accusation. But what's really bad about this is that you will be judged under ordinary circumstances. You won't like it.

## Kien-leh loses Lai-tu

Kien-leh came to Me-ti and said: Excuse my bad mood. I prepared everything for a big journey and now I hear that all the ships have departed. I don't know what to do. Me-ti asked him, without success, not to control himself. Some time later Me-ti was told that Kien-leh had been seen walking around his garden at night. Now I understand, said Me-ti, Lai-tu has left him.

[This refers to Berlau's extended absence in Spain from July to October 1937, when she went to the front after attending a conference in Madrid, without telling Brecht what she was doing or when she would return.]

## Kien-leh on partners

The businessman B travelled to a distant town. Very busy and believing his partner trusted him, he forgot to write to him. The latter was so offended or so distanced himself from B that he broke off the business relationship and even threw B's goods onto the street and let them go to rot. He never got a reply from B to his letter about this. The silence was the same but the reason had changed.

[Brecht was very upset that Berlau stayed away. He feared for her life. Several texts are in all likelihood connected with these events, the 'businessman B' here standing for Berlau.]

## A recommendation

Those who receive a blow, easily become bitter. Ken-jeh said to Lai-tu: I want to make sure you don't receive a blow, so you take care that you don't become bitter.

## Kien-leh on the polite soldiers

In a certain province the soldiers in alliance with the peasants rose up in rebellion and murdered their officers, except for one, a peasant's son, who had joined them. In the subsequent fight the soldiers heaped a great deal of responsibility on this officer, until he mistreated one of them on account of a mistake. From then on he was suddenly treated quite differently, namely much more politely. He got his own food and was not, as before, put any longer in harm's way without consultation. Half a year after the event he committed suicide.

[This story was supposedly written after Berlau returned from Spain. It probably embodies something she told him about the complex positions among combatants she encountered. In its terseness it reads like one of Kleist's celebrated anecdotes.]

## Kien-leh and the student who left

It is well known that when times were difficult Kien-leh was abandoned by his student Tu. Tu returned and was accepted again, but the relationship was never again the same, not because Tu had left but because he did not make known and discuss his decision to leave. Tu, Kien-leh said gloomily, cannot be reached and is therefore unpredictable.

## Me-ti on the death of Tu

When Me-ti's favourite student Tu was killed in the civil war because, though furnished with a particular commission and with other commissions in view, he had taken up arms, Me-ti refused to call him a good revolutionary. He gave no satisfactory reason why he had changed one commission for another. He thought war was only where there was shooting; he didn't see any further than twenty metres and actually died like a hoodlum.

[Fearing the worst as a result of her silence, Brecht reckons with Berlau's death.]

## Kin-jeh said of his sister

We made love between battles.
During marches
We waved to each other. There were letters
In the defeated cities
Waiting for my friends
Hiding in a hut, I heard
Her light step, she
Brought food and news. Quickly, at the station
We discussed the course of our operations.
The dust from the road still on my lips

I kissed her. Around us
Everything changed. Our affection
Did not change.

## Second song of Kin-jeh for his sister

I sent you away to take part
In foreign battles, to eat
Foreign food with foreign forks, to tempt
Foreign men, to think
Foreign thoughts.

I made you curious
And I warned you.
I hung on to you
And I sent you off.

If you stay away
Where will I stay?
And if you come back
Who will be coming back?

## Kin-jeh's song about his sister in the civil war

Kin-jeh's sister went to the front to write a report about the civil war. For a long time he got no news and he could not write to her. He wrote the following song.

Our endless conversation, like
A conversation of two poplars, our year long conversation
Has ceased, I can't hear any longer
What you say or write, nor can you hear
What I say.
I held you on my lap and combed your hair
I taught you the rules of warfare
I showed you how to treat a man
How to read books and faces
How to fight and how to rest
But now I see
How much I didn't say to you.
Often I get up at night, and my throat
Chokes with meaningless advice.

## Kin-jeh and his sister 2

After his sister had been far away from him in the civil war, Kin-jeh always counted himself, because he worried about her, among the cowardly people.

[These numbered texts were written shortly after Berlau had returned from Spain in October 1937.]

## Kin-jeh and his sister 3

Kin-jeh was afraid for his sister in the civil war. In order to limit the extent of his fear, he asked her to come back with a particular ship after such and such a length of time. When she didn't come, he wrote to her: I often urged you not to say to me: I love you, but rather: I like being together with you; not: trust me, but rather: count on me to a certain extent; not: for me you're the only thing, but rather: it's a pleasure that you're there. That I once believed by mistake that you had completely betrayed me, was bad, because afterwards I believed I could completely rely on you.

## Kin-jeh and his sister 4

Kin-jeh finally received a letter from his sister in which she wrote that she wanted to come on a certain day. He drove across the islands to fetch her. When she didn't come and there was some indication that when she wrote, she didn't intend to come, he wrote a poem.

If the stone says it wants to fall to the ground
If you fling it into the air
Then believe it.
If the water says you'll get wet
If you enter it
Believe it.
If your friend writes that she wants to come
Don't believe her. Here
There is no natural force at work.

## Kin-jeh's second poem about his sister

In all those years, when after long absences I
Entered her house, it looked as if I was expected, as if
The chair was waiting for me, the teapot over the stove.
Laughing she told me all the silly things

That had happened. Hers too and
Even mine. And I always waited
For her light step in front of the door, ready
To put everything aside if she were to enter. Our experiences
We counted like historical events, we spoke
Of the eight nights and of the return from Spain.
And of the journey in the Ford and of
Collecting the carpet.

## Me-ti's advice

Lai-tu, a student of Me-ti, once said to him she wanted to go on a long journey. Me-ti said: How can you go away when the three kingdoms Deh, Sueh and Noh are still not unified although they face such a powerful common enemy? Lai-tu was a young woman without influence and it didn't seem to her that unifying the three kingdoms lay within her power. When she said that, Me-ti replied: Unifying the three kingdoms is a far off goal. But still further than a far off goal is no goal. Your journey has no goal.

[Finding what Brecht called 'the little islands' too small, Berlau said she wanted to go to America, whereupon Brecht wrote this poem. Deh, Sueh and Noh stand for Denmark, Sweden and Norway. She decided against it and went instead to England. Brecht was then visiting London in the hope of working on a project.]

## Kin-jeh's shadow

Lai-tu recounted: When Kin-jeh left for the eastern war, I was afraid, he could distance himself from me completely. Therefore he left me his shadow to be with me always.

The shadow always followed me and I was very contented, since I knew that Kin-jeh was thinking of me. The shadow, however, behaved strangely.

Namely, it didn't follow me across every threshold and into every house. At certain doors it stopped and waited for me. It never sat down as long as I was inside. This fact, and that it kept an eye on the clouds while waiting, often made me uneasy, since it seemed as if it could also go away.

When I came out of the door again, it followed me once more. But sometimes it seemed to have trouble recognizing me, it was uncertain and didn't know for sure, if it really was me.

I didn't always lead the way, sometimes it did too. But then it always stopped if I didn't follow or didn't want to, and waited for me. It took some time till I learnt that for *closeness* you need two. When I moved away from Kin-jeh, didn't need him or was no use to him, then I was distant and not close.

## Lai-tu is importunate

In the besieged and hungry town, Hel-sing, Lai-tu was handed two pounds of meat on the side because of her friendly appearance. She took it straightaway to people with children. But her gift was refused and she had to go away like an importunate person. She complained to Me-ti when she met him a few days later on the street. But in the middle of her story, she stopped, interrupted herself and exclaimed eagerly: I would almost have forgotten it, I was supposed to get eggs for you today in this shop! At this moment she wanted to go into the shop, but saw Me-ti's smiling face and began to laugh at herself, only a little of course, because she then said seriously: I really will go in, hunger has got worse since the day before yesterday and I can't allow myself to be infected by foolishness.

[This refers to an incident in Helsinki when they stayed there after fleeing Sweden. Brecht wrote his *Conversations of Refugees* as a result of eating in Helsinki railway station. Everybody was worried about the effects of the spreading war, though Finland remained relatively unscathed, and Brecht wrote poems praising the quality of their food.]

## Lai-tu's value

Lai-tu had a poor opinion of herself because she hadn't produced a great work. She had no special achievements to show either as actor or poet. That literature had been written with her in mind and good people behaved better than normal she considered negligible. Me-ti said to her: It's true, you haven't supplied any product. But that doesn't mean that you still haven't supplied any achievement. Your excellence is acknowledged and appreciated because it is called upon. That's why the apple is famous for being eaten.

## Lai-tu's production

The poet Kin-jeh said: It's hard to tell what Lai-tu produced. Perhaps it's the twenty-two lines I added to my play about the countryside, lines that would never have been written without her. Naturally, we never talked about the countryside. What she called enjoyable has also influenced me. It's not what others call enjoyable. Of course I probably also used the way she moves in constructing my poems. She does a lot of other things, but even if she only produced what made me produce and enabled me to produce she would have been well worthwhile. (Kin-jeh did not suffer from modesty.)

[The play referred to here is *Mr Puntila and his Man Matti*, written in Finland.]

## Kin-jeh has trouble writing

How can I still write to Lai-tu, asked Kin-jeh? She writes with chewing gum in her mouth; I write with trembling hands. I know I'm wrong, but she writes that she's right. I am sad that something valuable is broken, she explains why it's broken. Always when I wrote to her, I could write coolly, now it ought to be fiery. I was used to writing to her as to a lover. Lovers are generous people.

## Kin-jeh on Lai-tu's love

Me-ti said about Lai-tu's love for Kin-jeh: Lai-tu's love for Kin-jeh was enough to make a whole nation happy. The more she took that course, the happier she could make Kin-jeh.

## Kin-jeh said to Me-ti

Kin-jeh said to Me-ti: Lai-tu, the selfless one, came with a basket and took away her presents. She tells my enemies, I'm stealing from my collaborators. She's gone mad, what shall I do?

Me-ti said: She must be mad if she's doing that, since she loves you. She's asking too much, because she has given too much; she's insulting you too much, because she praised you too highly. Take care no harm comes to her and that she has enough to eat. Since she loves you, she will permit it.

[Dated by Brecht, February 1950.]

## Lai Tu insulted Ken-jeh

Lai-tu insulted Ken-jeh but then bought him a flower pot so that he could give it to her. Ken-jeh gave it to her, since he recognized the friendliness of what she'd done.

[Brecht sent this text to Berlau with a bunch of white hyacinths. She dated it February 1951.]

## Lai Tu said to Kin-jeh

Lai-tu said to Kin-jeh: I love you so much, what will become of me?

Kin-jeh replied to Lai-tu: What you do with love cannot disgrace you.

[This last Lai-tu text was written in 1955.]

## One of Me-ti's mistakes

Me-ti said: I'm a sorry case. Everywhere rumours are spread about me that I've said the silliest things. And between ourselves, the trouble is I really did say most of them.

It happens like this: if somebody maintains, 2 times 2 is 4, because 8 minus 5 is 7, I then say straightaway, then 2 times 2 is not four. That then gets repeated. So I've been heard to say that there are no classes, that the superiors sacrifice themselves for their inferiors, that you can be free in chains, that literature is ruined by intelligence and similar nonsense.

I can't stand it when the truth is believed like this or told like a lie, without proof or on purpose. Coming from these irresponsible mugs it sounds like superstition.

But my behaviour really is mistaken.

[When declaring that man, born free, is everywhere in chains, Rousseau did not mean, as is often assumed, free in nature, but that he could only become 'free' in a truly communal society, the utopian antithesis of the hierarchical system of his day.

Brecht translated, via Arthur Waley, a poem by Su Shi, also known as Su Tung-p'o (1037–1101), 'On the Birth of his Son', included in the *Svendborg Poems*, which Berlau published in 1939, in which he hopes his son will be born stupid and lazy, and thus rise to a post in the Cabinet, since he has ruined his own life through intelligence. Like Bai Quyi (or Po Chu-yi, 772–846), whom Brecht also translated, Su Shi, a government official and a governor, was also exiled for disobedience.

Brecht once said to Benjamin: 'I know that when people talk about me they'll say: "He was a maniac." If accounts of these times are handed down, an understanding of my mania will be handed down as well. The times will be the backdrop for my mania. But what I actually want is for them to say: "He was a *middling* maniac."'

Me-ti's reflection on the difficulties distinguishing between when truth makes no sense and nonsense makes sense may conclude his book of interventions in the flow of things.]

# Bibliography

## Bertolt Brecht's works

*Me-ti. Buch der Wendungen. Fragment*, ed. Uwe Johnson, in *Prosa V* (Frankfurt: Suhrkamp, 1965).

*Me-ti/Buch der Wendungen*, ed. Klaus Völker, *Gesammelte Werke* (Frankfurt: Suhrkamp, 1967), pp. 417–585.

*Me-ti. Buch der Wendungen*, ed. Werner Mittenzwei, *Prosa IV* (Berlin & Weimar: Aufbau-Verlag, 1975).

*Werke. Große kommentierte Berliner und Frankfurter Ausgabe* (Berlin and Frankfurt: Aufbau/Suhrkamp, 1989–) (referred to in the text as BFA).

*Collected Plays*, 8 vols, various translators, ed. John Willett, Ralph Manheim and Tom Kuhn (London: Methuen and Bloomsbury: Methuen Drama, 1970–).

*Letters 1913–1956*, translated Ralph Manheim and ed. John Willett (London: Methuen, 1990).

*Journals 1934–1955*, translated Hugh Rorrison and ed. John Willett (London: Methuen, 1993).

*Brecht on Art and Politics*, translated and ed. Tom Kuhn and Steve Giles (London: Bloomsbury, 2003).

*Brecht on Theatre*, various translators, ed. Marc Silberman, Steve Giles and Tom Kuhn (London: Bloomsbury, 2015).

*Brecht on Performance*, various translators, ed. Tom Kuhn, Steve Giles and Marc Silberman (London: Bloomsbury, 2015).

## Other works cited

Berlau, Ruth, *Brechts Lai-tu, Erinnerungen und Notate von Ruth Berlau*. Herausgegeben und mit einem Nachwort von Hans Bunge (Darmstadt: Luchterhand, 1985).

Bormans, Peter, 'Brecht und der Stalinismus', *Brecht Jahrbuch* (1974): 53–76.

Brenner, Hildegard and Hermann Haarman, 'Brecht/Korsch-Diskussion. Positionen der Literaturwissenschaft', *Alternative* 105 (December 1975).

*Dschuang Dsi, Das wahre Buch vom südlichen Blütenland* (Jena: Eugen Dietrichs Verlag, 1912).

Korsch, Karl, *Marxism and Philosophy*, translated and introduced by Fred Halliday (London: Verso, 2012).

Lenin, V. I., 'Materialism and Empirio-criticism', in *Collected Works*, vol. 14 (Moscow: Progress Publishers, 1968), p. 326.

*Liä Dsi. Die Lehren der Philosophen Liä Yu Kou und Yang Dschu* (Jena: Eugen Dietrichs Verlag, 1911).

Lucretius, *De Rerum Natura* (London: Dent, 1916).

Marx, Karl and Friedrich Engels, *Collected Works* (London: Lawrence & Wishart, 1975).

Marx, Karl, *Capital*, vol. 1, translated by Ben Fowkes (New York: Random House, 1977).

Marx, Karl, see https://www.marxists.org/archive/marx/works/1847/wage-labour/ch02.htm

*Mê Ti, des Sozialethikers und seiner Schüler philosophische Werke* zum ersten Mal vollständig übersetzt, mit ausführlicher Einleitung, erläuternden und textkritischen Erklärungen versehen von Professor Alfred Forke (Berlin: Kommissionsverlag der Vereinigung wissenschaftlicher Verleger, 1922), in the series *Mitteilungen des Seminars für orientalische Sprachen an der Friedrich-Wilhlems-Universität zu Berlin*.

Müller, Klaus-Detlef, 'Brecht und Stalin', *Von Poesie und Politik. Zur Geschichte einer dubiösen Beziehung*, ed. Jürgen Wertheimer (Tübingen: Attempto Verlag, 1994), pp. 106–22.

Needham, Joseph, *Moulds of Understanding* (London: George Allen & Unwin, 1976).

Needham, Joseph, *Science and Civilization in China*, vol. 2 (Cambridge: Cambridge University Press, 1956).

Rasch, Wolfdietrich, 'Brechts marxistischer Lehrer. Zu einem ungedruckten Briefwechsel zwischen Brecht und Korsch', *Merkur* 88 (1963): 988–1003.

Stalin, Joseph, 'Marxism and Linguistics', in *The Essential Stalin. Major Theoretical Writings* 1905–1952, ed. Bruce Franklin (London: Croom Helm, 1973), p. 426.

Sternberg, Fritz, *Der Faschismus an der Macht* (Amsterdam: Contact Verlag, 1935).

Tatlow, Antony, 'Brecht's East Asia: A Conspectus', *Brecht in/and Asia, The Brecht Yearbook 36* (2011): 353–68.

Tatlow, *The Mask of Evil: Brecht's response to the Poetry, Theatre and Thought of China and Japan. A Comparative and Critical Evaluation* (Bern: Peter Lang, 1977).

Wilde, Oscar: 'The Soul of Man under Socialism', *De Profundis. The Ballad of Reading Gaol and Other Writings* (London: Wordsworth Classics, 1999), pp. 247–80.

Wizisla, Erdmut: '"Aus jenem Fach bin ich weggelaufen": Uwe Johnson im Bertolt-Brecht-Archiv – die Edition von *Me-ti, Buch der Wendungen*', in '*Wo ich her bin ...' Uwe Johnson in der DDR*, ed. Roland Berbig and Erdmut Wizisla (Berlin: Kontext Verlag, 1993), pp. 301–19, 406–11.

# Appendix A: Sequential listing of texts

# Appendix B: Alphabetical listing of texts

The following index of titles and concordance of texts permits the reader, not only to find a particular text in the present volume, but also to find the German original in the *Berliner und Frankfurter Ausgabe*, where *Me-ti* occupies pages 47 to 194 in volume 18. In four instances, where the text in question is not included or is not included in this form in that volume of the BFA, there is a reference to another volume or to the relevant archive sheet in the Bertolt Brecht-Archiv, Berlin (BBA).

www.ingramcontent.com/pod-product-compliance
Lightning Source LLC
Chambersburg PA
CBHW070540100726
47907CB00004B/1198
* 9 7 8 1 4 7 2 5 7 9 1 6 4 *